D0952354

The DARK LORD CLEMENTINE

ALSO BY SARAH JEAN HORWITZ

Carmer and Grit, Book One:
The Wingsnatchers

Carmer and Grit, Book Two:
The Crooked Castle

The DARK LORD CLEMENTINE

Sarah Jean Horwitz

ALGONQUIN YOUNG READERS 2019

For Alice, the girls, and the real Clementine,
none of whom are Dark Lords

Published by
Algonquin Young Readers
an imprint of Algonquin Books of Chapel Hill
Post Office Box 2225
Chapel Hill, North Carolina 27515-2225

a division of
Workman Publishing
225 Varick Street
New York, New York 10014

Printed in the United States of America.
Published simultaneously in Canada by Thomas Allen & Son Limited.
Design by Carla Weise.

LIBRARY OF CONGRESS CATALOGING-IN-PUBLICATION DATA

Names: Horwitz, Sarah Jean, author.
Title: The Dark Lord Clementine / Sarah Jean Horwitz.
Description: Chapel Hill, North Carolina : Algonquin Young Readers, [2019] |
Summary: When her father is cursed by a rival witch, twelve-year-old
Clementine Morcerous assumes his duties as Dark Lord of the realm,
but soon questions her father's code of good and evil.
Identifiers: LCCN 2019006072 | ISBN 9781616208943 (hardcover : alk. paper)
Subjects: | CYAC: Witches—Fiction. | Magic—Fiction. | Fathers and daughters—
Fiction. | Good and evil—Fiction. | Blessing and cursing—Fiction. | Fantasy.
Classification: LCC PZ7.1.H665 Dar 2019 | DDC [Fic]—dc23
LC record available at https://lccn.loc.gov/2019006072

10 9 8 7 6 5 4 3 2 1
First Edition

NOT. CHIPPING.

Clementine Morcerous awoke one morning to discover that her father had no nose.

This was not exactly unexpected. Several mornings previously, the Dark Lord Elithor Morcerous had greeted her with slightly less nose than usual, and a bit of a weaker chin. The difference was so small that Clementine, who was quite small herself, barely noticed it. She did notice something different about him—he was her father, after all—but she thought perhaps he had gotten a rather unflattering haircut.

An unflattering haircut could not explain the next few days, however, as the Dark Lord Elithor's nose became skinnier and skinnier, and his chin weaker and weaker. It could also not explain why his skin took on the raw-looking texture of freshly chopped wood, or why the ends of his fingers sharpened first into long points, and then shorter and shorter ones. It was as if every day, something were eating away at him—*chipping* away at him, Clementine's mind helpfully suggested—but the Dark Lord carried on as if nothing were the matter, even when the tip of his finger snapped off as he was ladling out the pea soup at dinner.

It was so light it barely made a *plop* as it landed in the tureen. They ate the soup anyway.

Clementine Morcerous knew that if the Dark Lord Elithor had three gifts in this world, they were:

1. The invention and implementation of magical Dastardly Deeds
2. Math
3. Not Talking About Anything

But the day she sat down to breakfast, rubbed the last bits of sleep from her eyes, and looked up to see her father sitting across the table from her, quite alarmingly noseless . . . well. Clementine decided that was the day they were going to Talk About Something.

"Father," Clementine said as she watched him spear a piece of melon on the tip of his pointy wooden finger. "I do believe you have been cursed."

The melon cube paused on its journey to his poor thin lips.

"Ah," said her father, his thick eyebrows rising. "Do you?"

He then returned his focus to his plate, as if she'd merely made a comment on the weather. His finger had sliced through the melon cube. He picked it up again with some difficulty.

"Well, it's obvious, isn't it?" demanded Clementine. "*Something* is . . . well . . . chipping away at you!"

Clementine regretted using the word "chipping" as soon as it was out of her mouth. Yet a consequence of Finally Talking About Anything is that words, once set free into the world, aren't in the habit of going back where they came from.

The only sound in the room was the Dark Lord's labored breathing, a thin whistling from the two tiny slits left in his face where his nostrils should've been. His eyebrows threatened to meet in the middle. He looked down at his plate again, and even the melon seemed to turn a paler green under the force of his glare.

"No . . ." he said softly. "Not. Chipping." He spat out the words like they were curses themselves and finally looked up at a very concerned Clementine.

"Whittling."

CHAPTER 1

VOLUME M–Z

or

The Criminal Audacity of Witches: A History

Clementine said nothing more about the matter at breakfast, due in no small part to the fact that she had no idea what "whittling" was. She was wise enough not to ask. After the Dark Lord Morcerous had shut himself up in his laboratory in the tallest tower of Castle Brack—as he did with increasing frequency these days—and Clementine had completed most of her morning chores, she slipped quietly into the Dark Lord's cavernous library and considered her options, of which there were many.

There were many options because there were many *books*. Books of every kind covered the walls from floor to ceiling: spellbooks and cookbooks, encyclopedias and fairy tales, encyclopedias *of* fairy tales, books about botany and chemistry and sailing and gravedigging and reading the stars, and books about *other* books. There were even a few slim volumes of poetry her father pulled out to scowl over once in a while, presumably to brush up on his brooding skills when nothing else in life was going appropriately pear-shaped. Clementine admired his commitment to his work.

The library was built deep into the mountain that surrounded Castle Brack, and Clementine could barely see from one end of it to the other in the dim light that came from the enchanted moonstone set into the rocky ceiling. The crystals very courteously brightened up wherever a reader happened to prop open his or her volume of choice. But otherwise, her father kept the library as he liked most things: dark, neat, and—most importantly—*quiet*. Rather embarrassingly, the moonstones on the ceiling decided to twinkle wherever Clementine walked under them, creating a far too cheery path of light all around the library as they followed the lady of the house's every step. She'd given them several stern warnings about such displays of whimsy, but she hadn't the energy to scold them today. It was only early afternoon, but confronting her father seemed to have used up what small stores of gumption she had at the ready. Finally Talking About Things was exhausting work. It was no wonder her father usually avoided it.

Clementine climbed up the ladder to the shelf she needed, and winced as one of the rungs creaked sharply under her foot. The furry chimaera's head mounted on the closest wall looked at her reprovingly. Clementine shushed him with her finger.

She had decided to start simply, which was, in Clementine's opinion, the best way to start most things. She slid the large leather-bound dictionary (volume M–Z) off the shelf with some difficulty. It was so unwieldy she had to carry it with both arms, leaving her teetering on the edge of the ladder, and it was so very *dusty* from being untouched for so long—

"*Achoo!*" Clementine sneezed. Actually *sneezed*. In the *library*. In the second that followed, she reflected on several important points: that it was arguably the loudest sneeze that had ever been sneezed in all of human history and she was therefore doomed (and very surprised at herself), and also that she was so off-balance she had no choice but to let go of the dictionary, which she did. As she clung to the ladder, the book clattered to the ground, bouncing off the rungs and the nearby shelves with downright joyful abandon.

Volume M–Z hit the floor with a *thud* that seemed to shake the entire castle.

Clementine froze, contorting her face to hold back another dreadful sneeze. But after a few tense moments, she found she was still alone, and the only reprimand came from the disapproving stares of the mounted beasts' heads. The chimaera looked positively offended.

Perhaps it was for the best the Dark Lord Elithor was locked up in his study at the moment. Such a disturbance would have annoyed him *greatly*.

Clementine carefully climbed down the ladder and picked up the dictionary. She removed the rest of the dust with her handkerchief and settled down on the comfiest of the ornate straight-backed thrones scattered throughout the library. Like the dead beasts on the walls, they, too, were trophies—thrones of the kings and queens toppled by the Dark Lords Morcerous of old. Clementine's favorite had a dusky-pink velvet seat that was only a *little* bit ruined in one corner by ancient bloodstains. She flipped to "W" and read:

> **whittle** | noun
> - a large knife

That hardly seemed appropriate. But just below . . .

> **whittle** | verb
> whittled; whittling
> - to carve an object from wood by cutting or chipping away small pieces
> - to reduce, wear away, or destroy bit by bit

It seemed that "chipping" hadn't been far off the mark. Clementine had seen some of her father's more adventurous spellwork go wrong before, but she was fairly confident in his ability (and his own sense of self-preservation) not to put himself in the way of magic that would literally cut off parts of his body. No. Clementine had been right about the chipping, and she was almost certain her father had been cursed. But by whom?

Clementine had an idea, but just to confirm, she needed another kind of dictionary altogether. She supposed it was more of an encyclopedia, but she couldn't fault the Dark Lord Morcerous of generations past who had named the book for a bit of harmless portmanteau. Clementine carefully placed the dictionary back up on its shelf—making sure to skip the creaky rung this time—and perused the reference section for her second source of information: the Witchionary.

The Witchionary was one of the longest-kept records of House Morcerous's generations of Dark Lords, perhaps because it catalogued and chronicled one of their longest-running enemies: witches. From the rare but deadly Good Witches to the pesky, amateur hedgewitches who cropped up like daisies in seemingly every village in the land, witches and Dark Lords had been enemies for as long as there had *been* witches and Dark Lords. Clementine's father detested witches—especially hedgewitches. Oh, the peasants might call them "wise women" or "healers" or the slightly less flattering (but equally mysterious-sounding) "cunning folk," but there was nothing wise or cunning about them at all, he'd assured Clementine.

Some of these so-called witches didn't even have *magic*, but made their living duping silly peasants into buying their "love potions" and "protective amulets," which amounted to little more than watered-down herbal teas and bags of rocks. These pretenders did everything they could to undermine the Dark Lord and his authority, from upsetting his careful supervision of the magical artifacts trade to even trying to *intervene* when he occasionally menaced the local populace—as if the villagers weren't his rightful subjects to torment however he saw fit! Clementine shook her head at the thought of such audacity.

The Dark Lord had many enemies—he wouldn't be much of a Dark Lord if he didn't—but few would sink to such cowardly methods as *whittling* to take him down. And Lord Elithor didn't have any serious rivalries with other lords at the moment, of that Clementine was fairly certain. She knew he'd made a go at manipulating mandrake root prices once, when she was small, and it had worked well enough to tick off a Dark Lord on the other side of the mountains who had a supposed monopoly on the market. Clementine knew this because she'd spent much of the sixth year of her life under a sleeping curse cast by that very lord in retaliation. Her father, after eventually abandoning the mandrake scheme, explained it all to her when she awoke, along with a stern lecture about touching pointy objects she didn't know the origin of, no matter *how* shiny they were.

No, a proper Dark Lord would strike at Clementine—who was, after all, Lord Elithor's only heir—or have brigands intercept her father's crops on the trade routes, or if he was very powerful indeed, send armies of black-hearted men and beasts over the mountains to lay waste to Lord Elithor's entire estate. The attack would be swift. It would be brutal. Most importantly, it would send a clear message: *Stay clear of my wrath!* or *Your castle is mine, weakling swine!* or *For evilness' sake, Elithor, stop trying to start a trade war, it's bad for business.*

As far as Clementine knew, her father had steered clear of trying to pad his Dastardly Deeds quota with such ambitious plans since the mandrake incident, and had focused on inflicting misery at the local level. And this curse . . . this curse was different. It had been eating at her father for quite some time, and no other Dark Lord had stepped forward to claim responsibility. No army had come charging over the Seven Sisters Mountains and stuck Clementine's head on a spike. Whoever it was seemed content to strike from the shadows and simply . . . wait.

None of the villagers in the valley had magic, and if they did, they wouldn't have lived long enough to use it—not under Lord Elithor's watch. And though the traders and peddlers her father worked with spat into the earth and muttered prayers of forgiveness when they thought he wasn't looking, they were also willing enough to take their cut of the profits. No, the answer was plain and simple: this curse had to have come from a witch, and a powerful one at that.

"Whittling" even started with a "W," after all.

Clementine paged through the Witchionary, skimming entries about witches with green scaly skin, witches who turned into cats and rats, witches who *commanded* cats and rats, witches who flew on broomsticks or plague-ridden winds, and witches who ate children or disguised themselves as beautiful maidens to lure unsuspecting knights to their doom. It was all very pedestrian, and the cannibalism was just in poor taste—no pun intended. (Dark Lords *hated* puns.) But then, on one of the very last pages, in her father's own handwriting, she saw it:

THE WHITTLE WITCH

REAL NAME: Unknown

ALIASES: The Whittle Witch,
the Witch of the Woods

How original, Lord Elithor had scrawled sarcastically next to the second name. Clementine agreed with him.

ORIGIN: Unknown
TRANSFORMATIVE ABILITIES:
Unknown (eternal youth?)
FAMILIARS: Unknown
SPECIALTIES: Simulacra, arbomancy
LAST KNOWN WHEREABOUTS: Unknown

NOTES:
TO BE WATCHED

Clementine stared at the last line of the entry, wondering how her father had come to cross paths with such an elusive enemy. Arbomancy, she knew, was tree-based magic—an unsurprising skill for someone who called herself the Witch of the Woods. "Simulacra," on the other hand, would require another trip up the ladder for volume M–Z. And the "Unknowns"—so many of them!—stared right back at her, taunting. Who was the Whittle Witch? Why was she whittling away at Lord Elithor? How did her curse even work?

And how much longer could her father go on pretending that nothing was the matter at all?

* * *

The Dark Lord Elithor did not summon Clementine for her magic lessons that day, nor did he come down from his tower for lunch.

* * *

* * *

Or dinner.

* * *

* * *

simulacrum | noun

plural **simulacra**

- an image or representation of a person or thing
- a poor copy or imitation

* * *

CHAPTER 2

THE SILENT FARM

or

The Unexpected Disadvantages of Nonsentient Servants

The changes to the farm were small, at first.

One afternoon, Clementine visited her favorite nightmare in the stables—a young foal, barely a few weeks old, with a skinny, bony frame that still just looked pathetic and not at all haunting, like it would fully grown. She pet it between its twitchy ears for a few moments (but not for too long—it was dangerous to show nightmares *too* much affection) before she began grooming the rest of the mares, brushing the silky black coats that covered their skeletal bodies until they shone like polished ebony. Her hands were trembling with fear by the time she was halfway done, which was an encouraging sign that they were all in good health.

But a sudden quiet settled over the stables, stopping Clementine midbrushstroke. It was . . . an absence, rather than a presence. The stables were always quiet. Everything in Lord Elithor's domain was always quiet.

Once, a few years ago, Clementine had wandered away from her father's side on one of his rare trips into the village. She'd walked all the way to the edge of town, all by herself, where the shops and houses began to give way to fields and pastures. She came across a young mother sitting on a stool in a kitchen garden, bouncing a child of about one or two years old on her knee. Clementine watched them from behind a tree on the other side of the lane, too shy (and too aware of what the townspeople thought of her, even then) to approach.

They were playing a game. The young woman would point to a sheep munching on a patch of grass, turn to the child, and say something like, "Look, it's a *sheep*! What sound does a sheep make, darling?" She snuggled closer to the child, smiling. "Does the sheep say *baah*?" The baby giggled and gurgled at her imitation, trying to make the sound. Next, she'd gesture to the piglet drinking from the trough, or the chickens pecking around the yard for their supper.

"What sound does the pig make?"

"*Ernk*," said the baby, flapping its chubby arms.

"What about the chicken? Do chickens go *cluck*

cluck cluck?" And she'd tickle the child underneath the arms, clucking all the while, until the baby shrieked with laughter.

When the woman finished her game and took the child inside, Clementine shrank back into the shadows. She could hear the woman singing an out-of-tune folk song at the top of her voice. Clementine shook her head and walked quickly back toward town, hoping her father hadn't noticed her absence.

That had been a waste of time. Besides the fact that it was clearly a questionable educational method—how would the child ever learn while so distracted by laughter and affection?—those sounds had been simply *ridiculous*. Clementine knew that proper animals would never dare make such a ruckus. The animals under her father's command knew their place. They did not *cluck*, or *moo*, or *baah*, or make any such unflattering noises.

Every animal on the Dark Lord Elithor's estate was entirely silent.

It's not that there weren't *any* sounds on their farm. Muffling every footstep or tail swish or closing door would have taken up far too much magical energy, even if Elithor had wished it. It was a safety issue as well—better to be able to hear any approaching invaders. But as far as was within his power, Lord Elithor Morcerous liked things *quiet*, and so quiet they remained. The nightmares could not neigh. The mandrakes could not cry (though that was for the best, considering their cries were deadly). There was no music and no singing and very, very little laughter, with the exception of occasional maniacal cackling practice. (A Dark Lord must always be prepared to deliver a decent maniacal cackle.)

So on the day the stable became even more quiet than usual, Clementine noticed. She put down her brush and edged out of the nightmare's stall, conscious of the sound of her skirt rustling against the hay, the nightmares shifting from hoof to hoof. A black sheep dozing in front of one of the stalls peered at her blearily, blinked, and stood up to follow her. She walked to the back of the barn, expecting to see one of the farmhands pitching hay, as it had been doing when she'd entered.

But the farmhand had stopped pitching hay. It had stopped doing anything at all. The scarecrow—one of many that did most of the manual labor on the farm—was frozen midshovel, its grip on the pitchfork gone slack. The pitchfork slid free of the scarecrow's skinny iron fingers and fell to the ground, landing in the hay with a *thump.* The black sheep skittered back at the sound; no doubt it would have *baah*ed had it been able.

Clementine stared at the scarecrow. Not once, in all the years she'd spent watching the animated scarecrows at work, had one *ever* stopped in the middle of a task. In fact, sometimes they were a little *too* enthusiastic in their work. They had to be given specific instructions, like exactly when to start and stop, or they were liable to turn the same pile of hay over and over again for days on end, or trim the grass in the castle courtyard until there was nothing left but dirt.

Like many things on the farm, the scarecrows were animated by her father's magic—a complex combination of spells and wards and willpower that kept their estate secure, productive, and most importantly, operating according to the Dark Lord's express rules and wishes. Nonhuman farmhands would never show up late, or demand vacation time or dental insurance, or even tire. The Dark Lord's estate hadn't employed any actual people—with the exception of their castle cook and Clementine's ever-rotating cast of ill-fated governesses—for decades, at least since her father had inherited the title. Why bother with human workers when the alternative was so much simpler and efficient?

But Clementine had never seen Ethel the cook *or* any of her governesses simply stop like this, every limb frozen in place. This scarecrow wouldn't have looked out of place in an actual cornfield—and what use would the Morcerouses have for it then?

Clementine carefully smoothed her expression, hiding her shock as best she could—it wouldn't do to look too vulnerable in front of the nightmares *or* the overly inquisitive black sheep—and picked up the pitchfork. She held it out to the scarecrow, looked him right in his black beaded eyes, and pointedly cleared her throat.

"Ahem."

The scarecrow remained stubbornly still. The sheep shuffled behind her. Clementine glared at it.

Clementine took a deep breath, standing as tall as her four-foot frame would allow, and stared down her nose at the scarecrow with her most commanding air.

"Don't you have *work* to be doing?" she demanded with a sneer, returning the pitchfork to the scarecrow's hands with a shove. The scarecrow teetered on its feet, but to Clementine's relief, it grasped the pitchfork and gave the tool a mighty swing. Clementine dashed out of the way. It continued spearing hay as if it hadn't been interrupted at all.

Clementine put her hands on her hips with satisfaction. The scarecrow had just been a temporary hiccup—nothing more—and she had been more than up to the task of setting things right. It shouldn't have surprised her that things on the farm might get a bit . . . out of sorts . . . while her father worked on lifting the Whittle Witch's curse.

She would just have to make sure things ran as smoothly as possible in the meantime.

* * *

The next morning, Clementine was surprised to find that her hair had turned blue. It had remained a subdued mousy brown for several days in a row—due in no small part to Clementine's anxiety over her father, she was sure—and she'd been a little worried it would simply stay that color forever. Clementine's ever-changing hair was a great source of irritation for her father, who was always trying to spell it back to a more dignified black, befitting a future Dark Lord, but Clementine didn't really mind. Besides, since almost all of her clothes were black, too . . . well, a *little* color never hurt anyone, did it?

Clementine took a few extra minutes to brush out her newly cobalt locks until they fell in shining waves to her waist. Though Clementine would have preferred to braid her hair, she left it hanging long and loose, as her father preferred. He ought to see her looking well when she checked in on him.

Perhaps her hair was a sign that all of this . . . unpleasantness would soon fade away, as well. The Dark Lord Elithor was hard at work on a cure to reverse the Whittle Witch's curse, and it was only a matter of time before he perfected it.

The fluttering of wings outside her window made her start as she secured the finishing touch—a black velvet bow—to the top of her head. A raven hovered just outside, flapping its shiny black wings close enough to clip the edge of the window.

"You've got the wrong room," Clementine said patiently, pointing out the window and to the right, careful of the raven's beak. It wasn't a real raven, but Clementine still paid heed to her father's lesson about pointy objects.

The raven cawed.

"Shh!" scolded Clementine. She snatched back her hand. "There's no need to be rude," she told the bird in a whisper. "He's in his laboratory, in the far tower. Shoo!"

The bird ignored her, hopping onto the stone windowsill and poking its head into Clementine's room, no doubt looking for a spare bit of parchment on which to imprint itself. Clementine scampered over to volume M–Z, which lay open on her bed, and snapped it shut, lest the bird get any ideas. When presented with a clean writing surface by its intended recipient, the bird would dive right into the parchment, the inky black of its feathers splintering and reforming into the decoded words of the letter it contained. Only sorcerers sent messenger birds, most often to other sorcerers. They were common but tricky bits of magic; Clementine hadn't mastered them yet herself.

Lord Elithor had been receiving a steady stream of ravens, crows, and sooty owls the last week or so, and more letters flew in every day. Clementine only had to look at the birds' red, gleaming eyes to know where most of them were from: the Council of Evil Overlords.

Clementine held up volume M–Z threateningly. "You aren't for me," she told the raven. Clementine had never received a messenger bird in her life—she was far too young and unimportant (for now) to be involved in official Evil Overlord business. No, this messenger surely wanted her father . . . though Clementine didn't care to dwell on why. If the Council had found out about Lord Elithor's curse . . . if they declared him unfit for evildoing . . .

Clementine hefted the dictionary again and gave the bird her best evil eye. It screeched and finally turned tail with a great flap of its dark wings, the draft strong enough to blow Clementine's carefully brushed hair out of place. She huffed.

So it was going to be *that* kind of day.

Clementine couldn't remember precisely when she started getting up earlier to feed the chickens (both the fire-breathing and the normal ones) or rotate the mandrake pots in the greenhouse so they faced the shade, or milk the demonic cows. Suddenly, there were just more things that needed doing every day, like brushing her teeth or practicing her threatening posturing, than there had been before.

She took her father's meals up to his study. She unearthed past years' ledgers from the library and made a few to-do lists—just to keep things running smoothly. Just for a little while. She kept track of when the snake pit needed cleaning and when the magic beans needed watering and when Stan, the first trader of the season, would come across the mountains.

It wasn't . . . bad, exactly. But it was a little bit harder. Everything was a little bit harder.

One morning, Clementine discovered that the fence between the fire-breathing chickens and the regular chickens had been burned to a crisp (shouldn't her father's fireproofing charms have stopped that from happening?), and she spent over an hour corralling terrified hens back into their coop. Afterward, a slightly singed Clementine trudged into the dining hall for breakfast, only to find there was no breakfast to be had. She tiptoed into the kitchen and was greeted by nothing but a cold hearth and a smug note from Ethel the cook, a sullen kitchen witch who'd owed Lord Elithor a debt. Ethel had cheerfully absconded with her freedom, a handful of magic beans, and two weeks' grocery money. That was what one got for keeping witches around, Clementine couldn't help but think, even if they *were* servants who'd signed a contract in their own blood to make you supper for the next forty years.

Clementine made herself some peanut butter toast—it took her two tries not to burn the bread—and took one of the last mealy bananas.

It occurred to her that she did not even know where the bananas came from. They certainly weren't for sale in the village. She would have to ask Lord Elithor—and that meant telling him that one of his prisoners had escaped.

She found him in one of the smaller studies in Castle Brack, sitting at the Decimaker—a machine of his own invention that was part abacus, part printing press, and part pipe organ. It was a genius thing, really; into the pipes went a few samples of their exports, a few facts and figures, and a smattering of hair and teeth or a dead mouse or two for the blood price—and a few (silent) keystrokes and foot pedals later, out came a neatly printed, detailed financial report on whatever matter her father required.

Lord Elithor struggled to pick up the papers shooting out of the Decimaker with his feeble wooden fingers. Clementine helped him pick them up and politely looked away as he scowled at them, muttering to himself.

A shiny black disk the size of a serving platter skittered across the floor with a whirring sound—her father's mechanical assistant, a slightly *too* intelligent creation that Lord Elithor did not have a name for but that Clementine privately called the Brack Butler. (Castle Brack had no real butler, as far as she knew, though a few of the castle ghosts occasionally insisted they'd been stewards long ago.) The Brack Butler zoomed over to Lord Elithor, another report clenched in one of its extended metal appendages, and placed the paper on his desk. The metal arm shrank back into the disk with a soft click.

"Father," said Clementine. She was loath to interrupt him at work at the Decimaker, but a missing kitchen witch was surely to affect their finances, as well. "I do believe Ethel has run away."

Clementine took a step back, preparing for her father to jump to his feet in an explosion of rage at the idea that any of his prisoners might *dare* to escape. His wrath would be a sight to behold. Fire and shadow would shoot from his fingertips. His thunderous voice would shake the whole mountain. He would scour every inch of the Seven Sisters for any trace of the traitorous kitchen witch, and when he found her . . . Clementine shuddered at the thought. What a foolish woman.

But the Dark Lord Elithor did not destroy the room in his wrath, or lock Clementine in their dungeons for being the bearer of ill news, or even seem very upset at all. He simply looked down at the Decimaker's reports, frowned, and muttered, "Yes, well, feeding *her* was an expense, as well," and turned his back on Clementine completely.

If the Dark Lord Elithor noticed the sharp decline in the quality of Castle Brack's cuisine, he did not mention it to his daughter.

* * *

More ravens came, by day and by night. Clementine took to closing her window to keep out the noise of their fast, fluttering wings.

If only they could be silent, too.

* * *

Of all the Seven Sisters Mountains, the Fourth Sister was Clementine's favorite.

The villagers might suppose it was because the Fourth Sister was the Morcerouses' ancestral home. Castle Brack was built right into the side of the mountain, overlooking the entire valley and reachable only by a long, narrow winding staircase carved into the cliffside. Located at the very center of the mountain range, it was a formidable fortress, and a good reason why the rule of the Dark Lords Morcerous had gone unchallenged for hundreds of years. How could such an advantageous position not be prized?

But Clementine had another reason—a secret reason—for loving the Fourth Sister (as much as a future Dark Lord was capable of loving anything): it was also home to the Lady in White.

Castle Brack, though higher than the surrounding farm and the village in the valley, was only a third of the way up the mountain. Few except the wild mountain goats trekked much higher than that—not even the Dark Lord Morcerous, though there were plenty of ledges that looked perfect for standing on while looking lordly and impressive. Near the top, the Lady in White—a patch of snow shaped like a woman in a beautiful white dress—watched over the whole valley. The Lady in White never melted, even on the hottest days of summer. She was taller than the castle at her feet, and she had been there as long as anyone could remember. The people of the village couldn't help but look up at her shining form and feel a sense of hope, no matter what sorrows the Dark Lord Morcerous inflicted upon them. He could never squash them down forever—not when the Lady was watching.

The villagers were not the only ones who looked to the Lady in White, who wished upon her and whispered to her out of their windows on starry nights. In a small, forgotten courtyard on the eastern side of the castle, a few crumbling doorways from the snake pit and down a set of rough, narrow stone stairs, there was a garden. It had not always been a garden. It had not always even been a courtyard. Clementine suspected it was a subfloor of some sort—the start of some addition to the castle that was never finished. Clementine had been eight when she'd discovered it, clambering about the hidden parts of the castle to avoid her latest (and ultimately last) governess, a chatty young woman from over the mountains who hadn't even believed in magic. (She was quickly disabused of this notion—and then of all notions, when she quite literally lost her head in an unfortunate encounter with some strangling vines.)

Clementine had mentioned the courtyard to her father shortly after finding it, but he hadn't seemed aware of or concerned with its existence. He merely told her to be careful of old booby traps if she was going to go exploring the older parts of the castle, and to alert him to the presence of any interesting plant life that might prove useful in his potions.

The courtyard *had* contained plant life, but not the kind that the Dark Lord Elithor would have approved of. It was full of flowers. Plucky clusters of white and light purple primroses had sprung up between the stones, and even more surprisingly, they bloomed brightest in the moonlight. A few sessions in the library researching night-blooming plants, and Clementine was able to call up even more flowers from the damp earth. The flowers came more easily to her than any of the other plants she helped her father conjure or cultivate, and it was rather nice, after a long and stressful day of *very carefully* picking hemlock or trimming stinging trees, to sneak down to her secret garden and tend to something that was much less likely to kill her.

But the flowers weren't the only reason Clementine loved her secret garden. The ledge the garden was perched on jutted out just enough so that if Clementine looked—if she *really* looked, up and up and up—she could catch a glimpse of the Lady in White on a clear night. She might see only the corner of her white, flowing skirt, but it was enough. She'd tell the Lady her troubles, and suddenly, life wouldn't seem quite so hard.

But Clementine's list of troubles was getting longer and longer.

Dear Lady, she thought, *the chicken fence has burned to a crisp, and I can't find any books in the library that will tell me how to mend it.*

I found another scarecrow today, frozen as still as . . . well, a scarecrow. I worry the time will come when they won't listen to a good talking-to at all.

We ran out of bananas, and I still don't know where they come from. I asked the Brack Butler, but all it did was vibrate threateningly. I don't think it likes me.

The mandrakes will be ready for pickling soon, but I've never harvested them without an extra soundproofing spell of Father's before.

I've never done any of this without Father before.

Father is eating less and less. I wonder if it's because of my cooking, or because—

But Clementine would not let herself think it, not even in her secret garden, not even if only the Lady and her moonlit blossoms would ever bear witness.

CHAPTER 3

A STRANGER COMES TO TOWN

or

Why All Hair Ribbons Should Just Be Black and No One Should Talk to Anyone Else, Ever

As terrible and powerful as the Dark Lord Morcerous was, and as ideal as the silent farm was for raising nightmares and mandrakes and poisonous herbs, there were some more mundane necessities that Clementine and her father had neither the time, the resources, nor the inclination to produce or conjure themselves. Unless Clementine wanted to spend all of her days squinting at a needle and thread or sweating over a hot stove, items like soap, bread, and bolts of cloth were best purchased (or threateningly demanded) from outside the estate—and that meant the occasional trip into the local village. Clementine had been putting off such an excursion for too long.

Clementine ran her fingers over the ends of her hair as she walked down into the valley of the Seven Sisters, coaxing that day's purple strands into a more natural dark auburn. It was a mostly superficial gesture—there was no way she would ever blend in with the locals—but as her father had taught her, it was important to exude authority with one's appearance, and she doubted her bright violet locks would do much to instill fear in the hearts of men. She smoothed her black taffeta skirt and tugged at the high collar of her blouse, wincing as her shiny black boots pinched her toes. It had been a while since she'd put on anything nicer than a day dress and her worn leather work boots around the farm. (With mild horror, she realized she couldn't even remember the last time she'd changed for dinner.) But for a trip into the village, she needed to be sleek and refined and just dainty enough to still look deadly, as perfect as one of the poison apples in her orchard.

From the first step Clementine took onto the main road, news of her arrival spread from villager to villager, a worried whisper on the wind. Mothers hurried their young children inside or tried to hide them behind their skirts. A few shopkeepers closed their shutters when they thought Clementine wasn't looking. Another group thatching a roof paused in their work until Clementine was at least a full block away, their hammers poised midstrike. They would not dare continue with their noisy activity until she was out of sight—just in case Lord Elithor should follow.

As Clementine filled her basket with bread, candles, hoof polish, and the special licorice-scented soap the apothecary ordered just for Lord Elithor, she kept her head held high, speaking to the locals as little as possible. She could feel the eyes *avoiding* her just as keenly as the piercing, resentful gazes that followed her as she walked away. It shouldn't have bothered her, and under normal circumstances, it wouldn't have—especially if Elithor were with her. In fact, she sometimes felt a little thrill striding into town at his side, turning heads with each step. There was something satisfying about knowing people disapproved of you, that they thought you were strange or frightening, and that there was nothing they could do about it. Only Clementine could spot the smile tugging at the corner of Lord Elithor's mouth as the townspeople bowed or cowered or stammered respectful greetings as they passed, and it made her happy to know that *he* was happy, and that all things were as they should be.

As Father had explained when she was younger and upset that the village children wouldn't play with her, why should she care if the villagers didn't like her? Their hatred, in fact, was a sign of her success. They weren't supposed to like her at all.

They were supposed to fear her.

But as Clementine hurriedly made her way through her shopping routine, reminding herself to snap at the baker's wife for not making change fast enough and threaten the blacksmith's apprentice for staring at her too long, it occurred to her that for the first time, *she* was the one who was afraid. The same question circled round and round in her head until she was seeing suspicious glances (well, more suspicious than usual) around every corner: *What if they know?* What if the townspeople had found out about Lord Elithor's curse? What if they knew that the man who had overtaxed their grain and serviced them with predatory loans and once turned the whole soprano section of the church choir into cats was holed up in his tower like a recluse, slowly being whittled away? What would they do if they figured out that the Dark Lord Elithor couldn't threaten them with more than a baleful glare and a pointy wooden finger?

They would overthrow you, a little voice inside Clementine said. *They would raze your farm and castle to dust and run you out of town forever—or worse. And what would you do then?*

Clementine forced herself to walk with confident, measured steps—back straight and head up. She was being silly. There was no reason the townspeople should know of her father's condition—at least not yet. They all avoided the silent farm like the plague, and the Whittle Witch—if she was indeed the one who had cursed him—seemed content to wait in the shadows for the moment. Lord Elithor had plenty of time to find a cure. The whole incident was likely to go entirely unnoticed by their clueless subjects.

As Clementine walked, the doors to the white-painted schoolhouse at the edge of the town square suddenly burst open. A gaggle of schoolchildren spilled out onto the lawn to play and eat their lunch in the sun. Clementine hung back, suddenly much less confident. A group of girls settled themselves under the biggest oak tree on the school's lawn, chatting and giggling as they set out their lunch baskets. Clementine eyed the pale pink, blue, and green bows at the ends of their braids and self-consciously straightened her own black velvet one. She hefted her basket and left the main road, edging around the backs of the simple stone and wooden buildings so she could approach the schoolyard from the rear.

Clementine stopped just inside the tree line of the forest that bordered the back of the school. There were a few moss-covered boulders from ancient landslides and avalanches, which offered excellent cover for snooping young Dark Lords in training. Not that Clementine needed to snoop, of course. But sometimes . . . sometimes it was, well, *interesting* to see how they acted when she and Lord

Elithor weren't around. It was good practice to get to know her subjects, wasn't it?

From behind her chosen rock, Clementine watched the village boys toss a ball back and forth, running and laughing and clapping one another on the back. (No matter how many years Clementine had watched them from afar, she could never quite make out exactly what the *point* of their game was, or how they even decided who won. She had a suspicion they just made the rules up as they went along.) And as Clementine watched them, she started to wonder . . .

The scarecrow farmhands were getting less and less dependable by the day, and the chicken fence was *still* broken. (How the massive Morcerous library didn't have a single book on carpentry was a mystery and a major failing.) She'd had to hide the regular chickens in the small, overgrown kitchen garden near the currently unoccupied gatehouse, far away from their fire-breathing counterparts, creating an entirely separate errand for herself to feed them every morning. If she could fix the fence and learn the fireproofing spell, it would save her a good deal of trouble. Surely, the villagers' farms couldn't be that different from her own—ferocious animals and poisonous plants aside. Some of those boys and girls must know something about building a fence. Perhaps . . . perhaps she could ask for their assistance with her task.

Clementine cringed at the thought. Father would *never* allow outsiders onto the farm—especially the villagers. They were sluggish and stupid and resentful, and could never be trusted to do a good job unless threatened with death, and constant threats were just an exhausting business for everyone involved. They could never be trusted with the farm's magical secrets. And yet, with her father unable to leave Castle Brack, and the needs of the estate growing ever more urgent . . . compromises might have to be made.

The ball suddenly bounced off a nearby rock, and Clementine shrank farther into her hiding place. A boy with tanned, freckled skin and untidy brown hair ran after it. He picked up the ball, bounced it on his knee, and paused, staring into the forest with a pensive look. She ducked fully behind the boulder. Had the boy spotted her spying on them?

"Come on, Sebastien!" one of the other boys shouted from the schoolyard.

"Yeah, Frawley, give it here!" called another.

Clementine peeked around her rock to see the boy—Sebastien Frawley, she presumed—shake his head and bound back to his fellows, throwing the ball in a long pass. Clementine sank to the ground with a sigh of relief—and immediately flushed with shame. How could she, Clementine Morcerous, future Dark Lord of the Seven

Sisters Valley, be afraid to face a handful of commoners? A handful of *children*? It was preposterous. But somehow, it was easier to be lordly and dismissive of the baker and the candlestick maker, alone in their shops, than it was to just *walk past* the schoolyard during recess. What was wrong with her?

She didn't have time to dwell on it for long. The sounds of the children's game had changed from breathless laughter and shouts to the kind of whispering and snickering that Clementine knew never preceded any pleasant sort of interaction. She looked around, once again fearing she'd been spotted, but the boys' attention was fixed on someone else entirely.

A woman was walking by the school—or trying to—but the village boys were blocking her way. She wore men's trousers, a fur vest over a fitted blouse, and a gray traveling cloak with the hood up, which was odd, as it was rather warm. The stranger tugged her hood down low as she hefted her satchel.

"Oy, miss!" called one of the boys. "Who are you, then?"

The woman replied, too low for Clementine to hear so far away. The boys stepped closer.

"Why're you hiding such a pretty face under that hood?" asked a black-haired boy perched on the schoolyard fence.

"Oh, Roderick, just leave her alone!" scolded one of the girls from under their tree, but none of them made a move to stand.

A thin-faced boy grabbed a long twig from the ground and lunged forward, trying to dislodge the stranger's hood, but in a move so fast it was almost a blur, the woman swatted the stick aside, wrenching it from his hand and sending it spinning into the road. The boy snatched back his hand in surprise, and the woman pulled back her hood. All of the onlookers gasped.

"I kindly request that you let me on my way," she said, loud enough for Clementine to hear this time.

But no one was listening to what she was saying. They were all staring at her face. The woman wasn't old, perhaps in her early twenties, with thick chestnut hair held back in a bun at the nape of her neck. Even from a distance, Clementine could tell she was beautiful—but Clementine could also see what had made the boys gasp. A large puckered scar inches wide ran from the corner of the woman's lip, over her cheekbone and almost to her hairline, twisting down the right side of her mouth in a permanent frown.

The boys took a step back, but their hesitation didn't last long.

"She's a witch!" the boy with the stick exclaimed, pointing an accusing finger. The other boys murmured their agreement. Clementine's heart beat faster. Could they be right? Could this be the Whittle Witch, making an appearance at last, finally ready to move in for the kill?

But the woman only sighed. "I assure you, I am only a traveler passing through. Now if you would kindly—"

"Get out of here, ugly witch!" called the boy named Roderick. He spat into the dirt. The few adults milling around on the main street looked away or hurriedly walked on, and one of the shopkeepers who hadn't closed his doors to Clementine did so now—and that, it seemed, was all the encouragement the boys needed.

"You heard him—leave!"

"Scram, witch!"

"We don't want your kind here!"

They circled the woman—though Clementine noticed they didn't actually step any closer—taunting her and throwing more sticks. While Clementine wouldn't have been sad to see a witch forced out of the valley—especially the Whittle Witch—she doubted that this traveler, while mysterious, was actually a witch at all. You could never be too careful, it was true, but if the woman really was a witch, why hadn't she defended herself? Why hadn't she turned all of those boys to slugs where they stood? It was what the Dark Lord Morcerous would have done.

Clementine didn't care to see any more. She knew how this would end—with the woman run out of the village, or worse. And the stranger probably wasn't evil *or* magical at all. She was just different—and that, in the villagers' minds, was enough of an excuse to chase her away.

Clementine picked up her basket and hurried back the way she had come, occasionally checking that the ends of her hair were still resolutely one natural color. *This* was why her father always told her not to stand out too much on trips to the village, future Dark Lord or not. If the people's fearful respect slipped, even for one moment, she could end up on the receiving end of more than a few threatening twigs.

What had she been thinking, considering employing those boys on the farm? They would sooner burn her at the stake than help her with anything.

Clementine skipped her last few errands—she didn't really *need* those new bootlaces, she decided—and hurried back to the silent farm. Back to the place where sheep did not *baah* and pigs did not *oink* and *all* hair ribbons were black, so there was no point wishing otherwise. Where no one dared look at her cross-eyed except the heads mounted on the walls, if only because there *was* no one else to look at her—and that was all just fine.

On the walk back, Clementine looked up at the Lady in White and her cascading snowy gown. And for the first time ever, though she could not say why she did it, Clementine made a wish for someone else.

Please help the traveling stranger, she thought.

***

Sebastien Frawley hung back from the rest of his classmates, hands clasped behind his head and elbows sticking out like chicken wings, idly kicking at patches of dirt. He didn't stand *so* far back as to be deemed a fraidy-cat, but he hoped the few paces he'd put between himself and that bully Roderick would strike just the right note of casual disinterest.

"Hey, guys, what about the game?" he called to his friends. "Bell's gonna ring soon."

A few of the boys looked back at him at that, leaving an opening for the woman to shoulder her way around them. They scowled and kicked up dirt in her wake, and Gregor and Curly Cab pretended to give chase for a few steps, but they backed off soon enough. The woman put up her hood again as she walked away—hopefully for good. Sebastien *was* right—the school bell would be ringing soon, and no one really wanted to risk the schoolmaster's wrath by being late for afternoon class. "Chasing witches" was not likely to be a well-received excuse for tardiness.

Knowing it could be seconds before those stormy expressions turned on him, Sebastien picked up the ball and tossed it at Curly Cab's mop of curls; it bounced off him with a satisfying *thud*. Gregor caught the ball and snickered.

"What was that for?" Curly Cab complained, massaging his head.

"Just making sure your head's still on straight," said Sebastien. "You got awfully close to that witch. She could've gotten you in her thrall." Sebastien waggled his fingers in an exaggerated spell-casting motion—or at least what they all figured a spell-casting motion must look like. The other boys laughed, Sebastien accepted a half-hearted shove in the shoulder from Cab, the girls rolled their eyes in unison, and they all went back to their game for the last few minutes of recess.

But even as he laughed with Gregor and Simon and scored a few points against Roderick, Sebastien couldn't stop thinking about the scarred woman, and he couldn't stop the guilty feeling squirming around his insides. His behavior, while successful at getting the boys' attention away from the woman, hadn't been very chivalrous, and Sebastien Frawley was extremely concerned with chivalry. He wasn't entirely sure what chivalry *was* exactly, but the brave knights in his favorite stories his mother read to him were always very chivalrous. They were usually doing things like defending ladies' honor, rescuing ladies from towers, putting their cloaks over puddles for ladies to step on, and just, you know, being nice to ladies and people in general, and also slaying dragons. The slaying and the fighting in battles seemed to be a separate skill set, though.

Sebastien Frawley wanted to be a knight more than anything in the world. As the son of a poor farmer in a town whose only castle was occupied by an evil Dark Lord, he knew his chances were pretty slim, but there were always options. When he was old enough, he could leave the valley and seek knightly employment beyond the woods, or even on the other side of the mountains—surely, there were good lords as well as evil ones, and it would be Sebastien's highest honor to serve them. And if that didn't pan out, he could always just walk through the forest until he found a maiden to save, or maybe a mystical object. Forests in his mother's books seemed to be chock-full of ancient magical cups and cursed swords, and maidens that needed saving.

But in the meantime, Sebastien still had a few years to work on his knightly skills, and that meant not only practicing his swordsmanship by hacking away at the tree in his backyard with his mother's longest kitchen knife when she wasn't looking, but also cultivating his knightly virtues, chief among them chivalry. And today, he'd been presented with a perfect opportunity to spring to the defense of a lady in need, and he just . . . hadn't. He hadn't yelled at his friends and challenged them to a duel over her honor. He'd made a half-hearted attempt to redirect their attention without sacrificing his own reputation. He'd been cowardly.

In his own defense, Sebastien thought, the lady in question was not at all like the ladies he'd read about in books. For starters, she was not beautiful at all. Though the others were convinced her scar was a witch's mark, Sebastien wasn't so sure. They'd all *seen* a few hedgewitches in their time, and those witches mostly looked like normal people, just with scragglier hair. And Sebastien's father had a scar on his leg, from an unfortunate encounter with a bull, that was just as ugly as the woman's. So it seemed logical to Sebastien that "scar" did not necessarily equal "witch." But she'd also been dressed funny, much like the hedgewitches he'd seen in the past, and worn trousers, like a man. And she hadn't run away or shouted for help when Gregor came at her with the stick, which is what a storybook sort of lady almost certainly would have done.

So if she probably wasn't a witch but she didn't behave like a lady, what was a knight in training to do? Perhaps striking for the middle ground had been the wise decision. There would be plenty more opportunities to practice chivalry in the future.

The school bell rang, and the children began to file inside. Sebastien waited until he was at the back of the line, as he always did. Any way he could prolong the time before he had to cram his too-long limbs behind a tiny desk and stare at numbers and letters that didn't make much sense to him was time well spent, in his opinion.

Still pondering chivalry, he glanced up at the Seven Sisters. If only *all* ladies were as obviously ladies as the Lady in White.

Movement at the foot of the mountain caught his eye, and Sebastien watched a small, distant figure cross the drawbridge, walk under the enormous gatehouse, and start the steep climb up the path to Castle Brack, basket in hand: Clementine Morcerous. He thought he'd spotted her spying on them today, as he had a few times before. The others never seemed to see her watching them—it would surely be the talk of the school if they did—but maybe his classmates, like he did, simply pretended they didn't see her. Perhaps they didn't want to attract her attention—and the possible attention of her father.

Oddly, though, Sebastien didn't feel afraid the few times he'd seen Clementine watching the schoolyard. He'd felt curious, and almost . . . sorry for her. She looked like she wanted nothing more in the world than to join in on their games and sit at the same cramped school desks. He wondered if she had anyone to talk to besides the Dark Lord, up there in that gloomy castle on the mountain.

Sebastien shook his head and followed his friends inside, laughing at something Roderick said and shrugging off a playful shove from Gregor, though he was barely listening to them. He was being ridiculous, of course. There was no reason in the world to feel sorry for Clementine

Morcerous. She had everything the townspeople could only dream of: money, power, a storybook-worthy position guaranteed since birth. What could she possibly have to be sad about? And even if she did, why should Sebastien care?

Clementine Morcerous was going to be their next Dark Lord. She'd grow up to be just as heartless and petty and cruel as her father.

Besides, Dark Lords almost *certainly* did not count as ladies.

CHAPTER 4

AN INTERESTING CHANGE IN DYNAMIC

or

The World Falls Apart

Dear Elithor,

I am, quite frankly, surprised that you have resisted me this long. The rumors of your spinelessness have been overstated.

But now is not the time for digging in one's heels—or what remains of them. We both know I am the only one capable of lifting your curse. (With one rare rumored exception, of course. I find myself even more surprised that this . . . exception . . . is an option you don't seem to have explored. How very noble of you. It seems even Dark Lords have their limits.)

As I've said before, I would prefer to take Castle Brack without unnecessary violence. Why should the innocent people of the Seven Sisters—or your lovely daughter, for that matter—be bothered by an ultimately unavoidable transition of power? If you come quietly, I may even let most of them live—until my rule as the new Dark Lord begins in earnest, of course.

It is time for the Morcerous reign of the Seven Sisters to meet its end, as it is time for you to meet yours. Both are inevitable. But the choice of which happens first is still yours.

I await your response.

—The Witch of the Woods

The Dark Lord Elithor Morcerous read the letter before him and would have snorted, had getting air in and out of his nostril slits not been so difficult. The Whittle Witch was crafty, he had to give her that. Her patience to hide in the shadows all these years, amassing her power and evading his detection, was a commendable trait that most of her fellow witches lacked. They were always shrieking about something—people cutting down trees, the undemocratic nature of the Evil Overlord system—and getting themselves noticed and burned at the stake or smote by a Dark Lord before they could get anything accomplished. Even the licensed Bad Witches were overly preoccupied with instant gratification, capturing small fry like children and young, impressionable knights. They lacked the resources, the authority, and the business sense to actually *rule* as the Dark Lords did.

But the Whittle Witch was not like other witches. Oh, she could say whatever pretty words she wanted about not causing undue violence, but they both knew the real reasons she wouldn't attack him outright, or even kill him quickly. First of all, even a witch knew better than to attack a sorcerer in his own tower. Elithor's power was strongest here, in his home, under the protection of the Fourth Sister. His wards around the farm itself could repel an army. (Well, he was fairly certain they could repel an army. A small one. It had never come to that in Elithor's lifetime.)

As to why she didn't just lop off his simulacrum's head and be done with him, Elithor suspected it was a limitation of the spell itself. The Whittle Witch's initial specialty had been arbomancy. And while most trees could be manipulated to serve a sorceress's needs in a pinch, her control over them was usually temporary, and they would revert to their natural state once her spell ended or she traveled far enough away. Causing *lasting*, significant change—changing the overall energy of a forest from tranquil to sinister, for example—took almost as much time and effort as it took the tree to grow in the first place. It was possible that the task of permanently reshaping something as complex as a person (especially one as far away as Lord Elithor) through her beloved wood required similar subtlety.

But Elithor suspected there was another reason for her uncommon willingness to wait for his surrender. Her letters made it clear enough that the Whittle Witch did not just want to kill Elithor; she wanted to replace him as Dark Lord herself. She expressed none of the usual witchy grievances against him, but had specifically mentioned her desire for his land and titles, and seemed perfectly cheerful at the prospect of leaving his undemocratic system of governance in place. And that meant she had to play by the rules.

If the Whittle Witch simply killed Elithor now, she'd be treated as just another rebellious witch trying to overthrow the system, and the Council of Evil Overlords would come down in force before she got the chance to fly a single victory lap on her broomstick. But if she pretended that everything was aboveboard—that she simply wanted to be the next Dark Lord of the Seven Sisters Valley—there was nothing to keep her from officially challenging Lord Elithor's position.

Anyone could, in theory, challenge a Dark Lord's rule; the odds of success, however, were so low that very few ever tried. Lord Elithor could find no instance of a single significant coup attempt at Castle Brack in the hundreds of years of Morcerous records. He supposed there was a first time for everything.

Lord Elithor tossed aside the witch's letter, but even as he moved on to read the rest of the awaiting messenger birds, he could not shake his suspicion that there was another reason—the *real* reason—the Witch of the Woods wanted to be the next Dark Lord, to lay claim to his side of the Seven Sisters.

She wanted to capture the mountains' unicorn.

* * *

"Please," said Clementine. "For the sake of all that is evil in the world, I need you to *lay an egg*."

The Gricken perched in the branches of the poison apple tree bobbed its head from side to side, ignoring Clementine completely. It flapped its papery wings, each feather dappled with the faded blacks, grays, and reds of the spells once transcribed on its pages, and hurled itself onto an even higher branch, quite out of Clementine's reach. It was times like these that having a grimoire in the form of a chicken—and a moody bird, at that—was very inconvenient.

Of course, it was entirely Clementine's fault that the spellbook was a chicken in the first place. As a younger child, eager to soak up as much magic as she could, she had the unfortunate habit of stealing the family grimoire when her father wasn't looking. No matter how many charms Lord Elithor cast upon it to make it too heavy for her to carry, or to sting her palms when she touched it without permission, or to hide it in some far-flung corner of the library behind a locked door guarded by a fearsome mounted chimaera head, he would inevitably find little Clementine curled up somewhere with the book on her lap, cheerfully flipping through pages she could barely read and babbling the broad strokes of some spell that could bring the castle down around their ears. Sometimes, the Dark Lord had told her, he was worried she was going to be *too* good of a Dark Lord. Clementine smiled at the memory.

One day, Clementine had been trying a new spell to turn toads into chickens. (Well, *anything* into chickens—she just happened to have a toad on hand, and he looked like he wouldn't mind being a chicken for a bit.) But one misinterpreted symbol later, and suddenly the grimoire *itself* exploded into a giant fireball. When the smoke settled and Clementine's hair had finished turning bright red in shock, well . . . the toad was still a toad. The grimoire, however, had been transformed into an oversized hen. Its many pages were now unreadable speckled feathers, and the impressive red wax seal on its front had turned into a sharp, shiny red beak. Lord Elithor's wrath at this unfortunate transformation had been . . . immense.

After he'd finished threatening to string her up in the dungeon by her ankles, Clementine had done extra chores on the farm and kept herself as quiet as a mouse for *months* as penance. Even so, after examining the Gricken,

Lord Elithor had refused to change it back to book form. Clementine would just have to learn from her mistakes.

The grimoire took its new mother hen role a little too seriously, and now only divulged new spells to Clementine in the form of eggs, which it laid if and only if it deemed Clementine was ready, though Clementine could never begin to guess what "ready" for any particular spell meant. The grimoire was *hers*—well, her family's, and mostly her father's, but hers by birthright. What authority did an accidental chicken have to determine if Clementine could handle a bit of new magic or not? Lord Elithor, however, seemed as pleased as punch to have finally discovered a way to censor the grimoire's deepest, darkest secrets until Clementine was old enough.

But surely—*surely*—the Gricken could sense that times were not what they once were. Gone were the days of innocent, carefree Clementine, who could afford to practice every carefully doled-out new spell to perfection. Clementine had real duties to attend to now—duties that required no small amount of spellwork. It was the *Gricken's* duty to ensure that she succeeded.

Her pleas, however, fell on deaf ears. The only acknowledgment came from the black sheep, who had taken to following Clementine around the farm while she completed her chores. Perhaps he was wary of being near any scarecrows, should the farmhands' behavior get any more unpredictable. Resting under the shade of one of the apple trees, hooves politely tucked under his woolly belly, the sheep looked at her with the kind of skeptical expression that said exactly what *he* thought about the Morcerous heir lowering herself to bargain with uppity chickens.

Clementine surveyed the orchard around her and sighed. It should have been about a month before the poison apples were ripe enough for picking, but unless it was Clementine's imagination, they weren't getting any riper. In fact, they were looking decidedly . . . spotty. She grabbed one small apple and inspected it; sure enough, some of the skin had patches of green showing through, and there was even a small bruise on one side. Clementine dropped the apple in disgust.

Poison apples were supposed to be *perfect*. They had skin as red and unblemished as polished rubies. Their juicy flesh was as white as snow. They even repelled dirt. They were supposed to look like the most delicious apple their victims had ever seen—that was the whole *point*. These apples, however, did not look like polished rubies. They looked . . . ordinary. Dull and imperfect and—this was what terrified her most—not the least bit magical. Clementine took a sample for the Decimaker, not looking forward to what predictions it might make about the fate of the crop this year, and then returned her attention to the Gricken.

"If you lay me a spell to help with the trees," said Clementine, "I shall . . . I shall let you play with the fire-breathing chickens as much as you like." Now *that* was an offer the Gricken wouldn't be able to refuse. The grimoire was always trying to hop the fence into the yard with its fire-breathing cousins, but Clementine and Elithor—fearing the entire Morcerous magical legacy going up in smoke—forbade it. (Well, Elithor forbade it. Clementine may have allowed a few carefully controlled sessions of frolicking.)

The Gricken merely picked at one of the apples with its sharp red beak.

"Hey, stop that!" Clementine ordered, stomping her foot. She had no idea what the effect of half-ripened poison apples would be on the insides of a magical grimoire chicken, and she was not in the mood to find out.

"Well, this isn't working very well, is it?" asked a voice.

Clementine jumped, knocking the top of her head against a low-hanging branch and falling down on her backside with an *oof.* She rubbed her head and looked up at the Gricken—had the bird somehow chosen this moment to reveal new powers of speech?—but it looked the same as ever, still busy pecking at the apple. Clementine leapt to her feet.

"Who said that?" she demanded, whirling around to look for the intruder. But there was no one in sight.

"Oh, you can hear me now, can you?" asked the voice. It was a boy's voice, but tremulous and reedy-sounding, like whomever it belonged to had a terrible head cold.

Clementine's gaze fell on the black sheep.

"That's going to be an, er, interesting change of dynamic," the sheep observed.

"You can talk," said Clementine flatly, sinking to her knees, not caring about soiling her pretty dress or even getting sap from the apple trees on her skirts. (She should probably have cared a little bit, as the sap was highly acidic and would soon burn through the fabric if left untreated.)

"Believe me," said the sheep, blinking his heavily lidded eyes at her, "I'm as surprised as you are."

"I doubt that," whispered Clementine breathlessly, staring at the creature in front of her.

It didn't surprise her that the sheep was *capable* of speech. Well, not much, anyway; she'd sensed he was a little too intelligent from the start, and it wasn't hard to believe that he'd been granted greater powers of intelligence in one of Lord Elithor's experiments, or even that he wasn't a sheep at all, but a transfigured human. How the sheep came to be a sheep was his own business, but a *talking* sheep? That should have been impossible. *All* animals on the Morcerous farm—whether they'd always been animals or not—were supposed to be quiet.

If the sheep could talk, it meant that all of the signs Clementine had been determinedly ignoring—the kitchen witch breaking her bonds, the stalling scarecrows, the failing fireproof charms—could not be ignored any longer. If the silent farm was silent no more, it could only mean one thing: the Dark Lord Elithor's magic was fading.

His time was running out.

CHAPTER 5

THE DARK LORD IN HIS TOWER

or

How to Lie through Your Teeth

Clementine pounded on the door. She did not lightly tap, or rap, or even knock with conviction. She balled her hand into a fist and *went at it*.

"Father!" she yelled to the other side of the tower door—not "whispered," and not even "spoke in measured tones." Sheep were talking, the world had stopped making sense, and it seemed only right that she should be loud, because she needed to be heard—and Lord Elithor needed to listen. "Father, please open the door. I must speak with you!"

She heard shuffling inside the laboratory, but the lock didn't budge.

"Father, please!" She pounded some more. And pounded and pounded and pounded until—*swish*. The great wooden door swung open on its iron hinges, and Clementine's hand met air. But no one stood in the doorway.

Clementine realized with a start that *she'd* blasted the door open—not with her fists, but with her magic. She'd just dismantled one of her father's spells, and she hadn't even done it on purpose.

Clementine entered the laboratory, suddenly conscious of how loud she'd been. She'd made a spectacle of herself with all that pounding and shouting. If anyone else ever saw her like that—panicked and afraid and not thinking clearly—why, they'd take the first opportunity they got to use her distraction against her.

Those were the lessons she'd learned in this tower laboratory, where her father taught her the secrets of magic and the ways of Evil Overlordship—where his reprimands cut through the air like whips if she missed a single step in a spell, rattling her more than the original mistake ever could. She'd nearly always foul up again, and Elithor's temper would flare, and they'd repeat the miserable cycle for hours until he eventually stormed off, the Brack Butler zooming at his heels and making judgmental clicking noises at Clementine. This was the room where Lord Elithor had once caught her singing—and it had only ever been the one time—and with a wave of his hand, made Clementine's throat burn if she ever tried to raise her voice in song again. This was the room where he'd made Clementine mash fish eyes for his potions and chop freshly picked mandrakes, their faces contorting as they screamed.

Her heart thudded in her chest. It was not her favorite room.

Clementine took a step forward and squinted into the dimly lit laboratory. Her father had put long, dark curtains over the single window in the gray stone walls. Only a few rays of light streaked through the gaps in the fabric, glinting off the bubbling potions, the glass beakers and vials, and a few brass cages, which may or may not have been actually empty. She looked at the window, and the curtains slid aside at her magic's unconscious demand, flooding the room with late afternoon sunlight.

Lord Elithor winced at the sudden brightness and threw an arm up in front of his face—but not before Clementine caught a glimpse of him. He sat slumped over his black marble desk, his back to Clementine, a lamp burning low beside him. His now too-big shoes kept sliding off his feet, which didn't quite touch the ground. The Butler sat under him, looking like a curled black cat in the shadows, except for the fact that it would occasionally reach up and replace the shoes on its master's feet.

But his face was nearly unrecognizable. The hair of his eyebrows and mustache had turned into black paint on his rough, scraped skin. His cheeks were sunken, the bones protruding like those of a starving man. Even though he was turned away from her, she could see what remained of his fists clenched at his sides.

How much she wanted to run to him, to unclench those poor brittle fingers before they broke even more from the stress, to kiss them and press them to her cheek, rough edges or not. For the first time in a long time, she wanted nothing more than to put her head in her father's lap and just *cry*. The tears welled up in her eyes. But she did not dare—especially not in this room. Not in Lord Elithor's tower.

"Clementine," her father said, still bent over his notes, "I thought I told you not to disturb me in my work."

"I-I know, Father, but . . ."

"Fix that door on your way out."

"I'll try, Father, but . . ."

"And do something about those chickens. I can smell the smoke from here."

"Yes, Father, but I came here to—"

"I WILL NOT ASK AGAIN." Elithor's fist slammed down on the desk with a terrible *crack*. He cried out, clutching his arm to his chest.

"Father!" Clementine ran to his side, all fears of the tower forgotten, and knelt beside him. If this was what the witch's curse was doing to him on the outside, she could only imagine what it was doing to him on the *inside*. She reached up and placed her hands on his arms, ever so gently. The Butler skittered around them, buzzing with alarm.

"It doesn't hurt," Lord Elithor muttered, trying to wave her away. He nudged the Butler with the tip of his toe, and it immediately quieted. "At least . . . not in the way you'd expect." He sighed.

Splinters from his damaged hand littered the desk. A breeze from the window scattered the pieces before Clementine could gather them up. Lord Elithor made no attempt to retrieve them.

"Father," said Clementine. "Please, please tell me you're close to finding a cure. Please tell me how to help you."

Lord Elithor said nothing. The only sounds in the room were the strained whistling of his breath and the low hum of the Butler. Clementine looked away.

"The farm is changing, Father," she said softly. *The farm is dying.* "The magic is . . . I'm not sure how much longer I—we—can keep going like this." Clementine looked down, as if the folds in her sap-stained dress were the most fascinating thing in the world, and tried to fight the hitch in her own breath. After a few moments, she felt something touch the top of her head. Her father's other hand, hard and stunted as it was, tentatively caressed her hair. She leaned into the touch.

"Have you so little confidence in my abilities?" her father finally asked with a huff. But the fight was all but gone from his voice.

"I have all the confidence in you, Father," said Clementine. "But I also know that . . . that you're dying."

His hand paused in its stroking. As horrible as it was to admit, Clementine felt . . . almost relieved, to finally say those words out loud. Now there was no putting them back where they'd come from, festering in the back of her mind.

She brushed a handful of splinters off her skirt.

"I *will* counter this curse, Clementine," said her father, resuming his stroking of her hair. "The Morcerouses have not ruled the Seven Sisters for generations to be defeated by a . . ."

"A witch?" guessed Clementine, this time barely in a whisper.

Lord Elithor sighed. "You must promise me something, Clementine," he said. "I will do everything in my power to undo this spell. And until that happens, you are not to come to this tower anymore."

"But what about—"

"That is not a request. My assistant will see to it that I am taken care of." The Brack Butler buzzed in assent, lights flashing on its shiny black surface.

Clementine almost protested, but then she understood. Her father did not want another incident like today's. He did not want Clementine to see him in this condition—especially if things got worse before they got better.

"Do not leave the farm, if you can manage it—though I suppose you must go to town occasionally, lest the villagers begin to suspect something. Trust no one, and tell no one. Do you understand?"

Clementine swallowed the lump in her throat and nodded.

"Y-yes, Father."

"And promise me, above all else, that you will not go looking for her."

Clementine looked up at her father, and even with the sharp corners of his bones and the effort it clearly took him to speak, it was what she saw in his eyes that scared her most of all: fear. Lord Elithor Morcerous, dread Dark Lord of the Seven Sisters Mountains, professional oppressor and perpetrator of Dastardly Deeds, was afraid.

"Promise me," he said, "that you will not go looking for the Whittle Witch."

* * *

The Witch of the Woods sang as she walked through the trees. Birdsong and the chattering of the other small forest creatures fell silent as the eerie, discordant melody washed over them. Squirrels abandoned prized acorns where they lay and skittered away from the sound. A young doe froze in her tracks, as spooked as if she'd been cornered by a hunter's bow, and did not bound away until the Witch was out of sight. Only the trees leaned in to hear the woman sing, their boughs twisting toward her outstretched hands.

A faint buzzing, followed by a soft *pop*, caught the Witch's attention. She paused in her song long enough to watch the small woven charm hanging in an oak limb above her head snap down the middle, threads bursting and scattering to the winds like a broken spiderweb, and fall to the ground. The local hedgewitches' defenses were powerless against her. She knew it, and they knew it. That was why they fled from her, hopscotching around to the parts of the forest still free from her influence. But it would not be long before the whole wood was hers. It was her specialty, after all.

The Witch rolled her neck, sighing at the resulting crackles and pops. She ran a hand along her neck and was displeased to find her skin looser and more wrinkled than it had been when she'd set out that morning. She'd been putting herself through her paces lately, pushing the limits of her magic. Her old bones tired more easily than they used to, when she was a few hundred years younger. Older bones needed stronger magic to keep them going, to keep her skin supple and her hair blond and thick and glossy. What they needed was powdered unicorn horn, and the Whittle Witch's supply had been dwindling for a very long time.

The effort would be worth it, she assured herself, and she resumed her song. The wood was not the only thing that would be hers before long. Soon, when the Dark Lord Elithor was desperate enough, or when his wards grew weak enough, she would rule supreme over the Seven Sisters Mountains. And as the new Dark Lord, the lands where the unicorn roamed would be hers. The unicorn would be hers, and she'd need not worry about rationing its power ever again.

Well, at least not for another hundred and fifty years or so. Eternal youth had a voracious appetite.

* * *

Clementine closed the door to her father's laboratory with much more care than she had opened it. She rubbed her tired, puffy eyes, pushed her hair out of her face, and nearly tripped right over a fluffy black sheep. *The* fluffy black sheep. He had somehow made his way into the corridor—could sheep even climb stairs?—and was watching her with a somber expression.

"You're going to break his rules, aren't you?" the sheep asked in his nasal, shaky voice.

"Shh! Shoo!" Clementine anxiously looked back toward the tower room, the door firmly shut and locked again. Her father might have been ill, but he wasn't deaf, and he didn't need to know things had sunk *so* low on his own farm that cursed talking sheep were now freely wandering the hallways. Clementine led the sheep away from the door.

"I suppose you heard everything then," Clementine said testily. "And what makes you think I would disobey him, exactly?"

"You've got that look in your eye," said the sheep as they made their way down the stone steps. (He could, in fact, navigate the stairs with surprising ease.) "The I'm-going-to-disobey-my-parents look. It's one I'm quite familiar with."

Clementine stopped at the foot of the stairs and glared at the sheep.

"I'm not going to break my promise," said Clementine. "I'm just going to . . . bend it." She strode down the hall and out onto one of the castle's balconies to survey the valley below. "Looking for information *about* the Whittle Witch isn't the same as looking *for* the Whittle Witch."

Clementine rested her hands on the stone railing. Here she was, not two minutes after her tearful promise to her father, confessing the intimate details of their struggles to someone who had apparently irritated Lord Elithor enough to get himself permanently transfigured into a sheep.

Even though Clementine knew that a talking sheep probably couldn't be much help *or* hindrance in fighting a foe as powerful as the Whittle Witch, and that she was making the offer just to have someone—*anyone*—to talk to while her father stayed sequestered in his tower, and that Lord Elithor had instructed her to *trust no one* . . . she couldn't shake the idea.

"And you're going to help me," Clementine declared.

The sheep bleated in surprise.

"I can't keep the farm running *and* research this witch all on my own," Clementine said. "If you help me, I promise . . ." She took a deep breath and turned to face the sheep. "I promise to find a way to turn you human again."

The black sheep shuffled on his hooves but said nothing.

"Well," said Clementine with a huff. "That's honestly an offer that would be good enough for most people."

The sheep chewed on his top lip, evidently considering her proposal.

"Can I have free run of the library, too?" the sheep asked.

Clementine was immediately struck by the mental image of the sheep's woolly bottom sitting on her father's thrones.

Compromises, she reminded herself.

"Done," she said.

* * *

The huntress retreated into the woods. She would have preferred to stay in the village—how long had it been since she'd slept in a real bed?—but her unfortunate encounter with those schoolboys in the town square had put an end to *that* foolish flight of fancy. As soon as she was out of sight of the townspeople and their suspicious glares, she had balled up her cloak and shoved it in her pack for the rest of her journey, half-grateful she no longer needed to bother with wearing it in the late summer heat. The trees and the mountains were unlikely to be as offended by her presence as so many of her fellow humans seemed to be. And it was better to be closer to her prey, wasn't it?—the better to watch and wait, to observe what extraordinary abilities it might put to use against her.

As she walked, the huntress did not see any signs of her quarry—not that she really expected to, this close to the village. But she did start to see other clues that she was not the only one seeking shelter in the woods. It did not take her long to notice the white scratches on the trees that started to form a pattern—trail markers, she guessed—or the rabbit and deer traps, or the small clusters of stone, fur, and wood that others might take for bundles of forest debris but that she immediately recognized as charms. There were hedgewitches in these woods, and they would almost certainly not approve of the huntress's business in their domain. She veered off their marked paths and into less traveled parts of the forest.

It was rougher going, but the huntress was used to rough going by now. And as soon as she'd made the decision to keep near the mountains instead of the heart of the woods, she'd known it was the right one. She'd followed the trail all the way over the mountains, after all. She'd been listening to the villagers for longer than she'd allowed herself to be seen among them, and their rumors all pointed her in the same direction. And the tingling in her bones and the warm breeze's kiss on the back of her neck as she skirted the Third and Fourth Sisters told her that her prey was nearby, close to its rumored center of power.

She had no real evidence to suggest this, of course. Tracking this type of monster was not like hunting deer, or bears, or dragons. There would be no telltale tracks or scorched earth or disturbed brush. But the tingling sensation that prickled from deep in her bones and seemed to skitter across her old wound, making her mouth twitch at the memory of pain, was all she needed to confirm her suspicions. She felt it like a thin but taut string, a thrumming connection between her and the creature she sought, pulling up and up and up into the mountains until it disappeared into the mist.

There was a unicorn in these parts. And Darka Wesk-Starzec was determined to kill it.

CHAPTER 6

THE BLACK SHEEP OF THE FAMILY

or

The Early Bird Is Mightier Than the Sword

There was one small problem with Clementine Morcerous's offer to turn the black sheep back into a human: the black sheep in question wasn't so sure he wanted to be human again at all. With the exception of not being able to talk or read—Seven Sisters, how he *missed* books!—it really wasn't a terrible existence. It was actually rather peaceful, if you asked the black sheep. And now, with those two major inconveniences done away with, life was looking up. He figured he had about a decade of reading material in the utterly fascinating Morcerous library to go through before he even started to get bored.

The black sheep's real name was David Turnacliff. At some point in his youth, in an effort to make his son sound a bit tougher and no-nonsense, David's father had shortened his name to Dave. However, it wasn't long before everyone realized that Dave Turnacliff possessed a mild and nervous temperament uniquely resistant to toughening up by *any* means, but by then, the nickname had stuck, so Dave he remained.

Dave was the eldest and only son of Houston Turnacliff, mayor of the village of the Seven Sisters Valley. The office of mayor was more of a ceremonial position than anything else—and not a terribly sought-after one, as the mayor was sometimes called upon to be the liaison between the villagers and the Dark Lord, and nobody in their right mind wanted *that* job. Houston, while technically an elected official, had been mayor for nearly two decades and run for office entirely unopposed every time.

But Dave had been raised to see his father's position as the highest office in the land, bar the Dark Lordship itself. Naturally, Dave was expected to follow in his father's footsteps, but it did not take him long to figure out that he was not very good at most of the duties associated with being the village mayor: public speaking (or speaking to anyone in general), remembering people's names, smoothing over disputes between neighbors or village elders, kissing babies during election season (not that the babies seemed overly enthused to be kissed by the rough whiskers of his father, either). Dave's father, mother, and older sister, Henrietta, could not understand that Dave was happiest immersing himself in every book he could get his hands on, or weeding the garden by himself, or even just gazing up at the stars and the Lady in White for hours at a time. They were an Important Family who did Important Things.

So Dave, well . . . Dave went and did a rather Cowardly Thing, as opposed to an important one. On the eve of his twelfth birthday, with his father's pressure to take on more responsibility in the village mounting, Dave paid a secret visit to the one person who might have the power to reverse his fortune: the Dark Lord Morcerous. But Dave found Lord Elithor an unsympathetic listener, and he quickly learned his lesson about complaining about being "the black sheep of the family" to an evil wizard. It had been nearly two years of woolly existence since then.

Being a sheep had its drawbacks, sure, but in the end . . . he'd sort of gotten what he wanted, hadn't he? It was true, he sometimes missed his mother and Henrietta, and even his father—and also having opposable thumbs—but there were worse things to be in the world than a reasonably well-cared-for sheep on a beautiful mountain. There were no expectations, no cumbersome family legacies to live up to. Dave had gone from being the black sheep of the family to just another sheep in the flock, ignored and overlooked by everyone, and that mostly suited him just fine.

But Dave the black sheep was far too embarrassed to admit this to Clementine. He knew that humans, traditionally, were not supposed to prefer being sheep. People were *supposed* to want to stay people. Stories were always full of grateful frogs turning back into princes and swans into fair maidens.

Dave felt bad for Clementine. She seemed like a nice enough girl, and he didn't like to see her so sad. He was concerned about the Dark Lord's possible death, too, though for different reasons: he suspected that if Lord Elithor died, the curse keeping him a sheep might break, too. Clementine's proposed "reward" for Dave's help was supposed to be the perfect happy ending, and yet . . . why didn't it feel that way?

* * *

The sun was high and bright in the afternoon sky, and the walk to the lake was a long one—mostly because the lake in question didn't like to stay in one place too long, so you could never be sure exactly where between the Fourth and Fifth Sisters, or even beyond, it might turn up. Dave suggested that Clementine summon a broomstick to ride for the journey, as he'd seen her do a handful of times.

She nearly tripped over her own two feet in surprise. "How do you know about that?" she demanded.

"What?" asked the sheep. "I've seen you do it at least a

few times! Though, come to think of it, it's usually when your father's away or holed up in his tower—" He broke off at the sight of Clementine's hair turning a storm-cloud gray, her expression dark enough to match.

"You will not suggest I do such a thing again," Clementine said, quickening her pace. The sheep scampered after her.

"Why?" asked the sheep. "If *I* could fly like that, I'd—"

"I think I preferred it when you couldn't talk!" snapped Clementine.

They walked for a few moments in silence until Clementine started to gather her gray waves into a braid—her one concession to the heat of the day.

"You don't understand," she said quietly, slowing a little as she combed out her hair with her fingers. "I'm not supposed to be flying broomsticks at all. Father would be so disappointed if he knew I'd even tried it."

The black sheep wasn't sure if his powers of speech had gone back to being appreciated or not, so he did not ask why. And frankly, the Dark Lord Elithor seemed like the kind of person who was disappointed by lots of things for no reason at all.

"Only witches ride broomsticks," Clementine explained with a sigh, tying off the end of her braid. "Not Dark Lords. It would be quite . . . unbefitting."

For people who supposedly made a living causing

death and destruction, Dave thought, the Morcerouses were awfully concerned with propriety.

The first sign that Dave and Clementine were close to their destination was a three-foot sword sticking up out of the ground. It looked to have been there for quite some time; it was rusty from exposure to the elements, and the jewels encrusted in its handle were cloudy from pollen and dirt. Clementine pulled it out of the ground easily and used it as a walking stick the rest of the way.

Dave and Clementine walked down the sloping bank of the lake, picking their way among the increasing number of swords—with special care near the ones pointing up blade-first. The black sheep hung back when the space between them grew too small for him to navigate.

"I'll just . . . wait here, then," said the sheep, not entirely sad to be left out of the impending meeting. The Lady of the Lake was one of the oldest creatures in the valley. If anyone might know something about the Whittle Witch, it would be her. Unfortunately, she was also . . .

"AAAAAAAAAAAAAAHHHHHHHH."

She was also that.

"AAAAAAAAAHHHHHHHHH AHHHHHHHH." The Lady of the Lake's loud and flat singing voice echoed out over the lake, making Clementine and the sheep wince.

Dave *thought* she was trying to sound enticing and mysterious, but unfortunately, she could sing about as well as Dave could. And Dave was a boy turned into a sheep.

The blue-green water swelled and swirled toward the center of the lake in a giant whirlpool. A few surprised fish flopped about on the newly exposed lake bottom.

"AHHHHH AAAAAAHHHHH AAAAAAAAAH HHHHHH."

"Yes, yes, I know," said Clementine, standing with her hands on her hips at the edge of the shore.

The water swirled faster and faster, creating a great foaming column in the middle of the lake. A woman began to emerge from the center, a gleaming sword held aloft in one hand.

"What brave traveler comes this way?" the woman asked, her eyes closed and her face lifted toward the sun. "Who dares to seek what the future may bring? What hero of ages will wield this mighty sword?"

She opened her eyes and thrust her sword upward with a flourish, a great spout of water shooting from its tip. She had eyes as light blue as winter's first frost, and hair as green as the darkest part of the forest. She was the most beautiful woman either Clementine or Dave had ever seen. She was Vivienne, the Lady of the Lake.

And she was also about as unimpressed to see *them* as they were to see her.

"Oh, it's just you," the Lady of the Lake said, rolling her eyes. "Why didn't you say?"

She chucked the sword over her shoulder. It struck another one with a *clang* and barely missed spearing one of the stranded fish. "What can I do you for, Clem?"

"My lady, we've been over this," said Clementine. "You're to call me *Lady Clementine.* I know Father's told you a hundred times."

"Oh, pishposh," said Vivienne with a flick of her wrist. The Lady spun away from Clementine, and the column of water holding her up shrank slightly, returning some of the water to the lake. It lapped against the toes of Clementine's boots. "No Morcerous has ever told me anything a hundred times, because you lot never come to visit me anymore. I remember when the first Dark Lords reigned—they were *always* running to me, begging, 'Lady, lend me a sword so that I might slay that giant coming down the beanstalk,' or 'Lady, how do I woo that princess from the next kingdom over?' But now, who wants to visit poor old Viv anymore? No, no, don't bother protesting, *Lady* Clementine. Though, really, if we're both ladies, and we're both calling each other 'lady,' not to mention the one made out of snow up there, isn't that going to get confusing awfully fast—"

"But that's just it, my lady," said Clementine.

Vivienne spouted a shower of water at the girl through pursed lips.

"All right—*Viv*," corrected Clementine. "That's why I came here today." Her voice carried across the lake, louder and grander than before, as if she'd suddenly stepped into a stage play. "I seek the wise counsel of the Lady of the Lake."

Dave fought to keep himself from snorting, but he knew Vivienne would hardly be able to resist such a dramatic appeal.

The Lady clapped her hands together with a wet *smack*. "Oh, do you *really*?" she asked excitedly, smoothing her hair and pacing over the surface of the lake. "Ooh, what timeless piece of advice shall I bequeath to you? It's been a long time since I've been put on the spot like this. Usually, I've got a decent prophecy all ready to go, but you'll want something special. Let's see . . . What do we have in the vault here?"

"Um, Viv—" tried Clementine.

The Lady waved her off. "Hush, hush, I'm thinking," said Vivienne. "Ah, I've got just the thing! *Ahem.*" Vivienne cleared her throat and hawked up a bit of lake water in a decidedly ungraceful fashion. She spread her pale arms wide, shook out her green hair, and declared, "Do not put all of your eggs in one fire!"

Clementine sighed.

The sheep asked tentatively, "Doesn't she mean—"

"Basket," Clementine said at the same time as Dave. "She means 'basket.'"

"*Basket!*" cried the Lady of the Lake. "That was it! It's been so long, one forgets the details, you know. 'Don't put too many irons in the fire'—that's the other one. Although now that I'm thinking on it, perhaps 'Don't put off until tomorrow what you could've done last week, you lazy schlep, you' would've been better—"

"Lady Vivienne," Clementine said as the Lady prattled on, "I'm afraid you misunderstand me. It's *information* I need." Clementine fiddled with one of the swords at her side, twisting it back and forth in the muddy sand. "I need to know everything you've ever heard about . . . a person who calls herself the Whittle Witch."

"Oooooh," said the Lady, sitting back on a large rock in the center of the lake with a huff. "Well, if it's witches you're dealing with, proverbs aren't going to help much at all, are they? Different realms entirely. Now, you'll want to start by knocking on some brick—or is it wood? It probably doesn't matter. Just get knocking. Then turn your pajamas inside out . . ."

If the early Dark Lords Morcerous really had come to Vivienne for advice as often as she claimed, Dave was surprised they'd gotten any conquering done at all.

"Thank you, Lady Vivienne." Clementine cut

her off with a sweeping bow. "Your wisdom is much appreciated."

Vivienne stopped chattering and blinked at Clementine, looking as if she'd forgotten the girl and the sheep were standing there.

"Oh!" said Vivienne, looking a tad put out at being cut off so early. "Well, all right then. Sorry it took me a few tries to really get going. I'd be less rusty if *someone* didn't scare travelers away from my mountains." Vivienne narrowed her eyes and tossed her green hair over one shoulder. "I've half a mind to give your father a good talking-to about that. You be sure and tell him."

"I will, my lady," said Clementine, backing away from the shore with one last curtsy. She jerked her head for Dave to follow and muttered, "Quick, before she gets going again."

Dave watched the lake water return to its proper levels, the Lady of the Lake sinking below the water feet-first, before scrambling after Clementine.

"Oh, and Clementine?" called Vivienne.

"Yes, my lady?" Clementine said with a small sigh.

"One last piece of advice for you, dear: think happy thoughts."

Clementine and the sheep looked back in surprise, just in time to see Vivienne's head dip below the water. Yet the Lady of the Lake's voice was as clear as day when she added, "You're going to need them."

* * *

As she trudged back to the castle, hot and footsore and strangely uneasy about the Lady of the Lake's final words, Clementine did decide on one thing.

"I should've just flown the blasted broom," she admitted to the sheep.

* * *

It was not long after Clementine left when the Lady of the Lake's usual afternoon musings on the meaning of life—like whether or not the teapot (or was it the glass?) was really half-empty or half-full—were interrupted by the sensation of a cool, pleasant breeze. Vivienne took a deep breath in and out and smiled, letting the sudden feeling of calm contentment wash over her. It had been a stressful afternoon, what with her unexpected visitors, and it had ruffled her more than she'd realized. She knew this sense of peace wouldn't last very long, but she was glad of the gift, anyway. It was always a treat when the unicorn came to visit.

Vivienne looked up from the murky depths of the lake toward a shining pinprick of light from above. The water around her grew clearer and clearer until she could nearly see straight through to the surface. She rose quickly, urging the water to propel her upward, though she knew it was mostly a foolish endeavor. She had hardly ever seen more than a glimpse of the unicorn, even when the unicorn deigned to dip her horn into Vivienne's lake, purifying the water and energizing Vivienne's magic.

But to her surprise, the unicorn had chosen to linger. Vivienne watched her withdraw her horn from the lake and shake her brilliant mane free of water droplets. They flew here and there like flecks of liquid rainbow.

Vivienne waited for the creature to settle before she spoke. She did not want to startle her.

"Thank you, my lady," Vivienne said softly. She knew the unicorn could hear her, and yet Vivienne wondered if she understood. Perhaps Vivienne's earlier mention of the Lady in White had attracted her to the lake. Perhaps she still remembered, after all this time, the part of herself that was forever encased in snow and ice and memory. The villagers prayed to the Lady in White, she knew, but they did not know why it brought them peace. They could not remember that hundreds of years ago, that curious patch of snow had not existed at all.

But the Lady of the Lake remembered. She remembered when the first Dark Lord Morcerous had come over the Seven Sisters, a fearsome young sorcerer eager to prove himself. He had come to her for help—or rather, demanded it of her, after he'd uprooted her lake from her favorite spot so he could call forth his castle from the mountain itself. She had to admit, she'd been impressed. She knew that he was destined for great things—terrible, perhaps, but great. And so when he'd asked for a prophecy that might aid him in his quest, his quest for domination over all the Seven Sisters—she'd given it to him. She hadn't even known what it meant herself, at the time. The words came so easily back then, rising from her throat of their own accord, blooming like flowers from a garden she could never remember planting.

But the Dark Lord was as cunning as he was fearsome. He took from Vivienne's words exactly what he needed. He discovered the secret to binding his only real rival on the mountain—the one creature that, if it were so inclined, could stop his violent ascendance: the unicorn.

Vivienne carried the guilt still. She knew it was not her fault. She knew that her magic—that most magic, in fact—did not operate in such clear-cut terms as good and evil, dark and light. She knew that as soon as the Dark Lord Morcerous came over the mountains, seeking his new place in the world, few things would have stopped him. But each night as she looked up at the Lady in White, and now, as she gazed into the eyes of the unicorn—eyes that made her dizzy with all of the past, present, and future whirling in their depths—Vivienne could not help but wish there was some way to undo the harm she had done.

Vivienne blinked and leaned back in the water, which was already turning darker and earthier at the unicorn horn's absence. The unicorn backed away, expertly picking through the graveyard of swords. They were grim reminders of Vivienne's vain attempts to bag a hero—any hero would do—whose good deeds might reverse some of her terrible legacy. What aspiring hero or gallant knight could resist a mystical woman rising out of a lake and bestowing a sword destined for greatness upon them?

But that was before the Dark Lord Morcerous had come to the mountains.

The Dark Lord Morcerous had been no hero on a great quest—he'd been a villain, and his descendants had been villains, and would always *be* villains.

Just like the Lady of the Lake would always look for a hero to guide.

Just like Castle Brack would always loom over the Seven Sisters Valley.

Just like the heart of the unicorn would always be trapped, forever frozen, in the snow of the Fourth Sister.

Their fates were unavoidable.

And yet.

The last words Vivienne had said to Clementine rose up in her mind.

Think happy thoughts.

And very suddenly, a small seed of hope began to grow in the Lady of the Lake's mind. This time, she promised herself, she would remember.

It was funny to think that her hero might not need a sword at all.

CHAPTER 7

STOCK AND TRADE

or

The Importance of Keeping All Your Bits about You

Halfway up the steep mountain staircase to Castle Brack, Clementine and the black sheep were quite startled to see someone else coming down. Clementine froze on the steps, squinting at the short and squat figure muttering angrily as it made slow progress down the mountain, coaxing a cloth-covered wooden cart down after it.

Oh, for evilness' sake, thought Clementine with alarm, all fatigue from their long hike gone. *I've forgotten about Stan!*

The figure paused in its abuse of the cart when it saw Clementine, and waved at her cheerily.

"Halloo!" called Stanley Glen. "Is that the Dark Lady of the house herself, now?" Clementine smiled despite herself. She'd been acquainted with Stan since she was a very little girl. He was grumpy and smoked a stinky pipe and always complained about the mountains being murder on his old hooves, but he was one of the few peddlers who traded with her father who didn't look like he'd rather be anywhere else on earth than Castle Brack. He snuck Clementine peppermints under his cloak when Lord Elithor wasn't looking and winked a lot, and generally seemed like what a grandfather might be like (if Clementine had known any grandfathers) or perhaps an eccentric uncle.

Clementine hurried up the steps to help Stan with his cart. The black sheep trailed behind, thankfully silent for the time being. It should have occurred to her to forbid the sheep from speaking in front of strangers, lest he give away any hint of the Dark Lord's fading magic, but it was too late for that now.

"That's a good girl," said Stan, panting as they set the cart to rights. "Blast, it's hotter than a witch's cauldron!"

Clementine caught a glimpse of an extremely hairy goat's leg, ending in a cloven hoof, before Stan swept his cloak in front of it. Stan was a satyr—a creature with a man's face and body, and a goat's legs, tail, and horns. Clementine had only ever seen him in disguise, with his cloak and a large floppy felt hat to cover his horns and pointed ears, though he assured her there were other lands where he could walk about without them, "as free as the day I was born." (Clementine tried her best not to dwell on that particular image.)

The lumpy packages under the canvas of his cart clinked against one another, and Clementine heard a sound that might have been a *meow* from within.

"You caught me at just the moment," explained Stan, giving one of the lumps an affectionate thwack. "Here I was, swearing you hoity-toity Morcerouses up and down for making an old goat go leagues out of his way only to leave me standing at the front door like a beggar, knocking that fearsome dragon-skull knocker with the clacking teeth, and naught but an empty castle to receive me. Your timing was quite impeccable, young lady. I was sure you'd forgotten your old friend Stan!" He clucked his tongue.

Clementine had, in fact, forgotten her old friend Stan.

"Now, why don't you take me to the Dark Lord," asked Stan, looking with resignation at the steps above him, "and we can see if the merry glint of silver is enough to coax the old curmudgeon out of whatever study he's barricaded himself in today."

Clementine's stomach dropped, but Stan only winked at her, as if nothing were amiss. It was true that it wasn't unusual for Lord Elithor to be immersed in his work for days at a time, and her father had been known to miss appointments because his head was buried in a book.

There was no reason to assume Stan knew about his condition.

"Father is away," Clementine said.

Stan's furry eyebrows shot up under the brim of his hat.

"He has given me leave to conduct lordly business on his behalf," Clementine explained, the words coming out a little too quickly.

The latest dismal reports from the Decimaker discouraged her from spending any of her father's money—and Lord Elithor rarely paid Stan in coin, anyway. The Dark Lord usually traded goods for goods, and supplied Stan with his latest inventions, elixirs, and poisons, or magical artifacts from his personal collection. But with the Lord Elithor focused on finding a cure for the whittling curse, there hadn't been time for him to perfect any new products. While Clementine might be able to disguise her father's condition, there was no disguising the fact that she had nothing to trade.

"Grooming you for command already?" joked Stan as they reached the top of the stairs.

Clementine ignored him. "We have . . . quite a good harvest coming in this year," she lied, racking her brains for something—anything—that could tempt Stan to buy. They made their way through the gate and into the inner courtyard. "A handful of magic beans sprouted early. I'd be happy to give you—"

"The early ones are runts," said Stan with a wave of his hand. "Never grow tall enough to reach the sky. Which you know perfectly well, my dear." The satyr fumbled in his cloak for his pipe, and Clementine wrinkled her nose in anticipation of the stinky smoke.

"Father's been working on his truth serum," said Clementine. "He would love to offer you a sample—"

"'Working on?'" asked Stan. "I've been working on a boat for ten years. It's still in my garage. Does the stuff work or not?"

"On white lies," admitted Clementine. "But just think! Your customers could protect themselves from all sorts of . . . um, false compliments."

Stan merely snorted and lit up his pipe. Clementine coughed at the purple smoke. The great steel-banded doors of the castle opened before them. She tried other offers as she led Stan down the candlelit entry hall: that door knocker—didn't he always say he liked the skull door knocker?—and some of the snakes for breeding; her best cutting of strangling vines; and even the youngest nightmare. But the satyr remained unimpressed.

"Honestly, my dear," said Stan, shaking his head. "I expected at *least* a cannibalistic crystal ball, which your father swore to me he'd have in hand this time last year. So unless he's got something special to offer . . ." Stan turned back down the hall, stomping toward the doors.

"Wait!" cried Clementine. The flames flared in their sconces along the walls. Lord Elithor might not have anything special to offer Stan Glen—but Clementine did. "Wait right there. I'll . . . I'll be right back."

And with the barest acknowledgment of the merchant's nod, Clementine bolted down the hall in quite the undignified manner. She turned left and right and left again, going up one staircase and down two others and through the maze of Castle Brack, which she knew better than anyone, until she skidded to a stop in the moist earth of her secret garden—sparing a quickly blown kiss to the Lady in White—and plucked a single pale blue rose. It was the fullest on the young bush, and the other blossoms trembled as she cut it away.

"I'm sorry," Clementine whispered to the flower. "But I need you."

She ran back to the entry hall only to see one of the giant doors swinging shut and hear Stan Glen swearing at his cart outside. Clementine burst through the door, nearly running straight into the satyr on the other side. She cupped her hand protectively around the blossom.

"Ho!" exclaimed Stan, grabbing Clementine's shoulders to stop her from bowling into him. But he wasn't yelling at her. His eyes were fixed on the flower in her hands.

"Now what have we here?" he asked, lowering his voice.

Clementine took a step back. "An everlasting rose," she said, holding the flower out with one hand and surreptitiously wiping her other on her black skirt, where the thorns had drawn blood. "It changes color in the presence of poison."

At least, it was supposed to. This was Clementine's third attempt at the flowers, and this rose was barely ready to be picked as it was.

"Now *that* is something you don't see every day," said Stan. He fished around in his cloak again—how many pockets did the thing have?—and pulled out a small vial of ominous-looking black liquid. Clementine took a step back. She was starting to understand that she'd been lucky it was only harmless peppermints Stan had been sneaking her as a child.

"May I?" Stan asked, giving the bottle a swish.

Clementine nodded. "Of course." Reluctantly, she held out the flower toward the satyr, hoping he didn't see the trembling of her hand. He uncorked the vial—careful to keep any of the fumes away from his face—and as soon as the rose came within a few inches of the poison, its petals began to turn as black as the liquid it had detected.

"Ho, isn't that a pretty bit of magic?" exclaimed Stan. Clementine withdrew the rose, and almost instantly, it brightened back to its usual sky blue. She did not know whether to be happy or offended; nothing about her magic was supposed to be "pretty." Stan carefully corked the bottle and slipped it back inside his cloak. "Not old Elithor's usual style, though, is it?" He rubbed his hairy chin.

"*Lord* Elithor," Clementine corrected, "is always pushing the boundaries of his craft. I don't doubt one of your noble clients would appreciate such a useful artifact?"

Stan rubbed his chin again, and Clementine started to worry he'd take out his smelly pipe again to mull it over.

"You're right enough about that," Stan said with a wink, crossing to the front of his cart to pull out his ledger. "I'll take it. Now, will that be trade or coin?"

"Coin," said Clementine, hoping she didn't sound too eager. She ignored the brief, and admittedly insane, impulse to ask Stan for bananas instead.

By the time she had finished escorting the peddler back down to the foot of the Fourth Sister and past the outer gatehouse, Clementine had decided to give an entirely different insane impulse a chance. There was simply no one else she knew to ask.

"Stan," Clementine said to the merchant, who was now stringing up a lantern to hang from his cart in the slowly fading light. "Have you ever heard of the Whittle Witch?"

Stan paused, the flickering flames casting curious little shadows that danced across his weathered face. "Aye," he said, his brow furrowed. "I've heard of her."

"And?" she asked. "What does she . . . Why do they call her that?"

Stan sighed and narrowed his eyes at Clementine. "I'm not sure your father'd want me filling your pretty little head with scary stories, my lady."

"My father and I *are* scary stories, Mr. Glen," countered Clementine. "Who is this witch?"

"Well, she calls *herself* 'the Witch of the Woods,'" answered Stan. "But that don't account for her special proclivities, exactly."

Proclivities? wondered Clementine, suddenly wishing she kept volume M–Z of the dictionary even closer at hand.

"She makes wooden simulacra of her enemies," explained Stan. "Or anybody who gets in her way, really."

"Simulacra?" asked Clementine. She remembered the definition: *Image. Representation. Copy.*

"Dolls," said Stan with a small shudder. "Little wooden dolls she carves herself, with magic. All she needs is a bit of you—hair, nails, skin, you know—to bond to the simulacrum, and then, bippety-boppety-boo, your real body's tied to your doll. That's when she starts whittling away. I trust you don't need me to explain that."

"No," said Clementine softly. "I don't. But why would . . . anyone . . . let such a witch near them?" she asked, crossing her arms. Her father certainly knew better than to leave bits of himself lying around for any wily witch to grab.

"Well, they don't always know it's her, do they?" asked Stan. "Disguises herself, she does. Mostly like a beautiful young woman, though I hear she's old enough to rival the Seven Sisters."

Clementine groaned inwardly. She could guess exactly how Lord Elithor had been fooled into getting close enough for the Whittle Witch to a snag a bit of him, and she didn't care to dwell on it too much.

"It's getting dark," said Clementine. "Thank you for stopping by. You should be on your way, if you're sure you don't want to spend the night." She couldn't imagine it would be comfortable for Stan to stay in the village, having to keep his hooves and horns hidden, but she also didn't relish the thought of an outsider prowling around Castle Brack when her father was still ill.

"Ah, but I'd best be on my way," said Stan, tipping his hat to Clementine. "I'll be sure to find a good home for that flower."

But he had only gone a few steps down the crumbling path, his cart trundling behind him, when he stopped.

"You should not have asked me about her," warned Stan, his voice gruff but kind. Clementine did not have to ask whom he meant. "A lesser gentleman than I might think you were asking for help."

And that, they both knew, could prove very dangerous indeed.

CHAPTER 8

THE THREE RULES OF EVILDOING

or

Unfriendly Reminders That Also Molt on the Carpet

Clementine watched Stan make his slow way down to the village until he was but a mere dark speck in the twilight. The black sheep had said his own brief good night and trundled off to his preferred barn. Clementine sighed, thinking she ought to check on her poor rosebush before turning in herself, when she glimpsed a flash of movement from the corner of her eye—across the way, on the Third Sister. The figure picking a path through the cliffs was a bright, blinding white, as pure as the Lady in White's skirts after a fresh snowfall. There was only one creature with as brilliant a coat on all of the Seven Sisters.

Clementine froze where she stood. She watched the unicorn amble along the rocky ledges, its horn bobbing up and down with each step, until it stopped, too. And even though it was half a mountain away, Clementine could have sworn that it looked right at her.

The unicorn was regarded as a legend by the townspeople, and even, Clementine had to admit, by herself. In all of her twelve years, she had laid eyes on it only twice before. It was real, she knew, but in the same way she thought of the other side of the mountains as being real; they existed, but in a world so far removed from her own that it didn't pay to think of it.

But staring at the creature across the mountains, she couldn't believe she hadn't thought of it before now. In all the hours she'd spent studying poisonous plants and potions and curses in her father's laboratory, she'd also studied their cures, both magical and mundane. And there was no cure-all more legendary than the horn of a unicorn.

Clementine shivered before she'd even finished the thought. She wanted to look away from the unicorn in shame for even considering such a thing, but she couldn't tear her gaze from the beautiful creature, though it was hardly more than a white blur at this distance.

There were not many rules for Evil Overlords. As one might imagine, practitioners of the trade were rather inclined to rule-*breaking* on the whole. But even as Clementine's father had groomed her in the ways of terror and threats and general menacing, he had also taught her that there were certain lines that should never be crossed—both for the preservation of the sorcerer in question and for the entire world. He had instilled in her from birth his most important Three Rules of Evildoing:

1. Never travel through time.
2. Never try to bring back the dead.
3. Never, ever kill a unicorn.

The first two were fairly obvious. Terrible things had happened to wizards who meddled with time—they accidentally erased themselves from history or brought back the dinosaurs or created time loops that were a headache and a half for everyone else to sort out. Reviving the dead wasn't even possible, no matter what some of the nutty self-styled necromancers might say, and any attempts to do so were usually dangerous failures. Lord Elithor had once passed by a town under zombie quarantine on his travels; catching a whiff of the smell as he rode by had been enough to turn him off the idea of any and all necromantic pursuits. (Though the screams and guttural chomping sounds had likely helped, too.)

But unicorns were another matter entirely. They were the rarest of the rare in the magical animal kingdom, though even calling them "animals" seemed to do them an injustice. Clementine could not think of the unicorn the same way she thought of the nightmares or the fire-breathing chickens. The unicorn did not inspire fear or disgust—and yet it did not make her exactly happy, either. Even now, as goose bumps rose on her skin despite the warm evening, Clementine felt the presence of the unicorn like an ache around her heart. It felt like crying with her head against her father's knobby knees, but also like the glow of moonlight on her favorite flowers as she talked to the Lady in White, or like hearing snatches of songs forgotten so long ago they were barely memories.

Though unicorn horns were said to possess amazing magical properties—they could cure any disease, break any curse, or even grant immortality—few hunted them. Legend told that many years ago, the land had been full of unicorns, but that greedy humans had hunted them nearly to extinction, and discovered an unpleasant side effect in the process: anyone who killed a unicorn would be cursed for life, their every step dogged by violence and misfortune. It was the sort of underreported, vaguely worded curse her father would usually describe as "moralizing twaddle," but even he did not take any lore regarding unicorns lightly.

Even if one didn't believe in the curse or have any qualms about slaughtering innocent, shining beings of pure magic and light, Clementine had a more practical concern: the presence of the unicorn was what kept the Seven Sisters thriving. Lord Elithor's influence wasn't the only force nurturing his silent farm. Her father had told her long ago that the unicorn's powerful magic seeped into the earth itself, making the mountains and their surrounding valleys uniquely suited to raising magical plants and animals. If the unicorn were to die, like so many of its fellows, the magic of the Seven Sisters would fade, too . . . and with it, much of the Morcerous legacy.

But this knowledge did not stop a small, dark corner of Clementine's heart from skipping a beat at that sudden glimmer of hope. If by some miracle she could capture and kill the unicorn—though she nearly burst into tears, right there and then, at the thought of hurting something so beautiful—she could use the horn to cure her father . . .

And she would doom the entire valley in the process. How would they live without the earnings from the farm? How would her father's subjects, so accustomed to living with magic—even in small ways—fare without it? Would they realize the unicorn's presence had affected them, too—that their crops never seemed to fail as often as the villages on the other side of the mountains, that the potions they bought from their hedgewitches actually worked (even if only about half the time) for a reason? What kind of a world would it be without enchanted blue roses and Grickens and poison apples, and satyrs named Stan? The mere thought of it terrified Clementine. If she were to kill the unicorn, life as she knew it would be over. The Morcerouses and the mountains would be ruined.

If you looked at it that way, then the curse was real, after all.

* * *

Darka Wesk-Starzec was eighteen when she met her first unicorn hunter.

She didn't know that's what he was at the time, of course. After swaggering into her small town with nothing but a deadly-looking crossbow and the clothes on his back, Alaric had introduced himself as an "expert tracker, habitual woodsman, and professional adventurer." She'd snorted in his face. He'd asked to sleep in her family's barn. (The barn was one of the biggest in town, and as Alaric noted with a grin, "a gentleman of his caliber deserved the finest accommodations." He said most things with a grin. Darka couldn't help but laugh.) It was, as the stories always said, love at first sight.

Though he professed only to be passing through, Alaric's stay at the Wesk-Starzec household extended from a few days to a few weeks, and finally to several months. None of them minded . . . Not until the very end, at least. With his sandy hair and bright blue eyes, his tall and wiry build, and, most of all, that mischievous yet good-natured grin, he was generally impossible to be cross with.

He did more than his fair share to earn his keep. He hunted for the family's table, and it was here that his true gifts lay. Deer, rabbits—even a wild boar once, which they shared with half the town; no prey was swift enough once Alaric caught its trail. And one afternoon, after he caught Darka watching him practice shooting at impossibly difficult targets (or so they seemed to her then), he offered to show her how to use a bow, too. It surprised both of them when she caught on quickly, and soon (with minor protestations from her parents) she was accompanying him on his hunts.

He taught her everything he knew—how to move soundlessly through the forest, how to mask her scent, how to rig traps and follow her prey's trail for days. How to use her bow and arrow as well as the crossbow and the spear. And finally, he taught her how to hunt for monsters.

The first time Darka made a kill bigger than a buck, she didn't even know what she'd hit. When Alaric rolled the prone animal over, it had the head of a lion, the body of something like a goat, and a spiked, barbed tail covered in scales.

"A chimaera," Alaric explained while watching Darka's face carefully.

She had never seen a creature like it in her life. She'd assumed chimaeras were fairy tales, mythical creatures that had never existed or gone extinct long ago. Her blood pounded in her ears, her heart still beating with the thrill of the chase.

Alaric bent down and withdrew the knife at his belt. With one fluid motion, he severed the creature's tail from its body. It twitched for a moment before flopping to the forest floor, oozing green blood.

"It's the scales you want," he said. "But you have to harvest them while they're fresh. Otherwise, they lose their potency." He sat down next to the carcass and began shimmying one of his smaller knives under one of the scales, as casually as one might shuck a clam. "Used for poisons, mostly, but what can you do. These'll fetch a fair price on the magical markets. Well done, Darka."

The magical markets? Darka thought. Her head buzzed like the flies that were already surrounding them, attracted to the chimaera's fresh corpse.

This was how Alaric really made his living, she realized. Not by hunting deer or rabbits or foxes or even wolves—but by hunting monsters like this one. And now he was letting her in on his secret.

"Does it bother you?" he asked, watching her face again. Darka understood, though she did not know why, that her answer was of the utmost importance. Alaric had let her in. It was up to her to accept his invitation—and accept him, knowing that from here forward, her life would be much more dangerous than she'd ever imagined.

Her chest still heaving from running after the chimaera, Darka plucked her knife from her belt. She looked at the green blood smeared on Alaric's hands. It scared her. And it thrilled her.

"Show me how," she said.

***

Almost as suddenly as it had begun, the quiet moment between Clementine and the unicorn was shattered. A strange, fast-moving cloud had appeared on the horizon, a dark blur against the fading orange of the sunset. The unicorn's head twitched toward the movement, breaking Clementine's gaze. And though she looked back a second later, the unicorn was gone, nothing more than a white flash galloping through the cliffs and into the growing darkness.

Clementine took a shaky breath and looked back at the strange cloud, trying to clear her head of all thoughts of unicorns and the Three Rules of Evildoing. It did not take much effort, because she quickly realized the dark cloud was not a cloud at all, but a giant flock of birds—and it was headed straight for Castle Brack.

Was this the frontal assault the Whittle Witch had been building up to? Clementine stood frozen to the spot, unable to tear her eyes from the fast-approaching swarm. But no, she assured herself. Those red-eyed ravens were all too familiar. They had not been sent by the Whittle Witch, but by men Clementine feared almost as much: the Council of Evil Overlords.

The Council clearly thought its earlier messenger birds had not been properly received.

Clementine ducked as the ravens soared overhead—but they did not fly to her father's tower, as she had anticipated. Rather, they flew through *her* open window.

She ran into the castle and up to her room, her heart thudding with each pounding step against the stone stairs.

The Council of Evil Overlords had finally taken notice of Clementine Morcerous—and for all of the wrong reasons.

***

In the absence of any blank parchment lying about, the birds chose to deposit themselves on the next best thing: Clementine's bedroom wall. The message loomed over the entire room, each shining black letter dripping spindly dark drops onto the line of text below.

To Lady Clementine Morcerous,
heir to the Dark Lordship of the Seven Sisters:

It has come to our attention that your father, the Dark Lord Elithor Morcerous, has neglected to

submit sufficient evidence of a qualifying Dastardly Deed for over six months. As our previous attempts at contacting Lord Elithor have been unsuccessful, we hope this letter finds you both well (and by "well," we of course mean "terrible").

The Council wishes to remind you that the primary function of Dark Lords is to terrorize lesser beings through Dastardly Deeds. Failure to execute this sacred duty may result in revocation of Dark Lord status, requisition of Dark Lands, and/or transfiguration of the guilty parties into many small insects, which will then be individually squished.

Should the Dark Lord be temporarily indisposed, imprisoned, stuck in an alternate dimension, or otherwise occupied, it is permissible for his heir—in this case, you—to carry out Dastardly Deeds on his behalf and/or temporarily assume the title of Acting Dark Lord. See the helpful list below for Dastardly Deed suggestions to get those creative juices flowing:

1. A poisoning
2. An unfortunate transfiguration
3. A racket*
4. A stampede

5. A frame-up
6. A murder
7. A tempest**
8. A kidnapping
9. A plague

*Tennis equipment is unacceptable.
**Or other magically enhanced weather phenomena.

We request that you, the Dark Lord Elithor, or any previously acknowledged avatars of darkness licensed to speak on his behalf, submit proof of a Dastardly Deed within a month of receipt of this letter. As official Council investigators may be sent to the scene of the Dastardly Deed to confirm any questionable reports, we recommend that you leave between one and three witnesses alive and in a suitable condition to give testimony.

Yours in infamy,
The Council of Evil Overlords

CHAPTER 9

A SICKLY SHADE OF VIOLET

or

When Trees Attack!

Clementine evaluated her Dastardly Deed options carefully, poring over old Morcerous records in the library until late into the night. She woke up the next morning on the stone floor, a novel-length account of old Dark Lord Poringrar Morcerous's instigation of mass hysteria in the village still open on her lap. (It was an expert Dastardly Deed, which had resulted in the burning at the stake of three innocent women and two men on suspicion of being witches, not to mention generations of suspicious grudges between various families—but the prep work sounded like a nightmare.) Clementine sat up and spat a tuft of wool out of her mouth; she'd fallen asleep leaning against the black sheep, who was still snoring softly.

No, a plan as complicated as Poringrar's wouldn't do. She needed something simple, straightforward, and with a quick turnaround time. Extra points for easily quantifiable results. These were her father's preferred qualifications, anyway. She yawned and stretched, piling her tangled hair into a messy bun, and returned Poringrar's diary to the shelf (thankfully, no ladders were involved). The moonstones in the ceiling shimmered, giving the sleeping sheep's black coat a blue-purple cast.

Purple. That was it! Clementine immediately remembered a potion her father had made a few years ago to poison the village water supply. It had made several villagers queasy and turned them slightly purple for days. Surely, enough time had passed that a repeat Dastardly Deed wouldn't be too frowned-upon. Besides, for all the Council of Evil Overlords knew, the purple poisonings could be practice for a much larger plan to make the villagers of the Seven Sisters Valley permanently sickly and violet.

There was only one problem. The key ingredient for the poisonous potion was a mushroom called the amethyst deceiver—and there were no amethyst deceivers on the silent farm. They grew best out in the woods, feeding off the decay of the forest floor. The most potent ones were full of arsenic they'd absorbed from the soil around them.

But Clementine had never ventured into the woods without her father by her side. The woods were home to creatures—both magical and mundane—outside his command, as well as (though he never openly admitted this) the camps of the local hedgewitches.

Clementine wandered out of the library, padding along the corridors through the quiet castle until she came to the entry hall. It was lined with the still and silent sentries she hardly took notice of anymore—suit upon suit of shining black armor, each armed with a spear or sword. They looked menacing enough, but Clementine knew they were empty, and not even animated, as the scarecrows were. How long had it been since these suits had real men inside them, eager to wreak havoc and destruction, and defend the Dark Lord with their lives? If only she had a Brack Knight to call upon to accompany her into the forest—if only she had *anyone* to accompany her—she might not feel so nervous.

Clementine considered bringing one of the scarecrows with her but decided against it. The scarecrows were getting unreliable enough on the farm; she didn't imagine the magic animating them would last long outside the borders of the estate. The Brack Butler was busy attending to her father, and she certainly didn't want to leave Elithor alone up there in his tower. There was no getting around it. She would have to go into the forest alone. She *needed* to find those mushrooms.

And maybe—though she would never admit this was the purpose of the exercise, as that really would be breaking her father's rules—she would find some hint of the witch so determined to destroy her family.

* * *

Bulbous clouds hung thick and gray in the sky as Clementine, the black sheep, the Gricken, and a young nightmare set off into the woods. Clementine hoped that the sight of the future Dark Lord Morcerous riding a jet-black nightmare would be enough to intimidate any potential adversaries, even if the nightmare in question was only old enough to inspire slight feelings of unease and disconcerting stress dreams about forgetting to turn the oven off. She would go in, find the amethyst deceivers, and get out. Simple and straightforward.

The weather, unfortunately, seemed to have other ideas. The sky grew darker the deeper Clementine rode into the forest, and the air was humming with the pressure that comes right before a summer storm. Thunder rumbled above, and the wind grew strong enough that the Gricken stopped its haphazard hopping from tree branch to tree branch and perched on the back of the nightmare's saddle, its tiny talons digging into the stiff leather. A few raindrops started to fall, dampening the Gricken's papery wings. (Fortunately, said wings appeared to dry almost instantly, much to Clementine's relief.)

"Have you ever worn a wool sweater out in the rain?" mused the black sheep, blinking mournfully into the dripping sky. "That is what I'm going to smell like. A wet sheep. I will be a wet sheep. For days."

Clementine ignored his complaining. The wind and the rain picked up, slapping smaller branches across their path and in Clementine's face. The nightmare whinnied.

"Maybe we should turn back," suggested the black sheep.

"It's not much farther," Clementine said, but in the growing darkness and with the landscape rendered murky in the rain, was she so sure? It had been a while since her father had taken her into the woods. Suddenly, with the wind howling and the tree branches whipping at her face—one stung her hard enough she was sure it would leave a scratch—the entire landscape seemed more alien, more hostile. How was she going to spot a cluster of mushrooms in all this mess?

It was almost as if the forest *wanted* to get in her way. Clementine hopped off the nightmare's bony back and led the horse by its bridle, looking for any sign of the small bright purple mushrooms. Lightning flashed, and with a great *crack*, a small tree limb fell from overhead. Clementine was forced to let go of the nightmare to duck out of the way, and the horse scampered off in a panic, its shrill screams raising goose bumps on Clementine's already chilled flesh.

"Wait!" cried Clementine, but her view of the retreating nightmare was soon blocked by a great feathery mass launching itself at her head. The Gricken squawked and screeched along with the wind, desperately seeking shelter in the folds of Clementine's cloak, for which it was much too big. Clementine grabbed the Gricken around the middle and tucked it under one of her arms as best she could, using the other to whack aside the branches blowing in their path.

"Still think we shouldn't have turned back?" asked the sheep, his quavering voice even shakier than usual.

Clementine turned to glare at him, pushing another branch out of their way, when *smack*—the branch whacked back. Clementine yanked her arm away in surprise and blinked, sure the flashing lights of the storm were playing tricks on her eyes. But she hadn't imagined it. The trees were hitting her on *purpose*.

She remembered that page in the Witchionary, with all of its "Unknowns"—and the one entry that wasn't blank at all.

* * *

Specialties: Simulacra, arbomancy

* * *

Clementine stomped her foot in the mud. "We have to get out of the forest," she muttered. The Whittle Witch had been this close this whole time, she realized, and Clementine hadn't taken two steps out of her own front door before falling right into the Witch's trap.

"Oh, *now* she agrees with me!" groused the sheep, who was responding to the growing chaos by trying to curl himself into as small a crouch as possible. As he was very woolly—Clementine would have to see about shearing him if they survived—this was not very small. Clementine clutched the squirming, clucking Gricken and kneed the sheep in the behind, prodding him back the way they had come.

But the trees pressed thicker and thicker on both sides of the already barely detectable path, hemming them in. These trees had no intention of letting Clementine go.

"Ugh, it's no use!" spat Clementine. She nudged the sheep again. "Get out of here while you can, and get back to the farm!" she told him. "It's me she wants to stop!"

But that didn't mean Clementine planned on making it easy for the Whittle Witch. She turned on her heel, ignoring the black sheep's cries for her to come back, and ran deeper into the forest, trying to zigzag between the grasping, thumping limbs of the trees.

She tripped on a gnarled root and went sprawling, rolling down a shallow embankment until she came to a dizzying stop against the rocks of a dry creek bed. The Gricken let out an indignant *squawk* and hopped down after her, pecking at rogue roots.

Clementine looked up—willing her head to stop spinning—and saw that the trees were *chasing* her. The soil at their roots shifted as they shuffled down the embankment. Some of them simply toppled over, but others popped right out of the ground, marching like wooden soldiers using their large roots for feet. They would soon be upon her.

The closest white birch reached out, its limbs lengthening and stretching, transforming into grasping wooden hands, and—

Thunk. An ax soared through the air, cutting one of the hands off at the wrist. Something grabbed Clementine from behind, and she screamed. She felt a tingling sensation from the top of her head down to her toes and released the magic building inside of her; there was a bright flash and the faint smell of something burning, and the grip on her arm immediately went away.

She whipped around to see Sebastien Frawley swearing, his eyebrows visibly singed.

"Whoa! Relax! I'm not going to hurt you!" he exclaimed, shaking out his arms and legs from the effects of Clementine's magical shock. He hurriedly picked up his ax and gripped it tightly. "It looks like *they* might, though."

He looked at the rest of the approaching trees, gulped, and extended a hand to Clementine. She didn't know if he was more scared of the murderous trees or of her, by the look on his face, but the fact remained that he had an ax and she did not. She took his hand—it was freckled and tan and still warm despite the cold wind and rain—and allowed herself to be hauled to her feet by one of her lowly subjects. The day just kept getting better and better.

Sebastien swung at another branch as Clementine scooped up the Gricken. They ran along the creek bed, Clementine trying not to slip on the damp rocks and Sebastien seeming a little too excited about the chance to wave an ax around.

The trees fell back at Sebastien's swings, and those that were still rooted at the top of the embankments on either side seemed content enough to stay put. All they had to do was wait, after all—Clementine and Sebastien couldn't stay in the creek bed forever.

Clementine noted with mild embarrassment that her hair had turned bright white, presumably from the various ugly shocks of the afternoon. She could only hope it wasn't stuck that way forever. Assuming she survived.

"Where are we going?" asked Clementine, her lungs starting to burn. Dark Lords in training were *not* used to being the ones running for their lives.

"The loggers' paths aren't far from here," said Sebastien. At Clementine's mutter of confusion, he explained, "They're sections of the forest that've been cut down. They'll be clearer!" He suddenly swung the ax downward, smashing a sneaky root that had been about to snatch at their ankles. He yanked on Clementine's hand. "Keep moving, will you?"

Sebastien led her toward the tree line again.

"Now wait just a minute," Clementine fumed. You—"

Sebastien cocked his head. The branches waved at them in an eerily cheerful salute.

"You . . . you . . . extremely knowledgeable woodsman," she finished through pursed lips.

The boy snorted, and seemed to notice he was still holding Clementine's hand. He dropped it. "We'll have to cut our way through to get there," he said, hefting the ax—he truly seemed very fond of doing that—and rolling his shoulders. "I don't suppose you could blast those trees like you did me back there?"

Clementine blanched. "I, um . . . I . . ."

Sebastien rolled his eyes. "Stay behind me, then. And keep that chicken out of the way."

The Gricken squawked indignantly. Clementine agreed with the sentiment, but she had little choice. She followed the boy up the rocky bank and back into the trees.

CHAPTER 10

WOMEN WITH HYPHENATED NAMES

or

The Ultimate Betrayal of All of One's (Im)moral Principles, with an Egg

Their progress was slow, what with the roaring wind, spitting rain, flying debris, and trees throwing punches. Clementine did in fact manage to zap a few feisty boughs, but battle magic was not exactly in her repertoire—who knew that it would ever need to be, what with the comfortable Morcerous reign lasting hundreds of years?—and so Sebastien did most of the hacking. But soon his reactions began to slow, and his swings lost some of their wild enthusiasm. He was tiring.

"How much farther do we have to go?" asked Clementine. Now that she had a second to think about it, she was not so sure it would be wise to follow Sebastien all the way to the village. She could not allow herself to be seen wet and bedraggled, and depending on a mere boy for safety.

"Not far," Sebastien said with a grunt. He sounded about as confident as Clementine had regarding the location of the long-abandoned mushrooms.

"Do you even know where you're going?" asked Clementine, aiming another burst of energy at an evergreen that shot its needles at them. Sebastien and Clementine covered their faces as the resulting ashes scattered in the wind.

"Do you want to get out of this storm by yourself?" countered Sebastien, breathing heavily.

And then an arrow shot out of the trees, straight at Clementine's head, and she barely had time to scream.

She did not know it was an arrow at the time. She only knew that one second she was standing up, about to curse that impudent village boy and all of his descendants, and then the next, her head had been yanked back so quickly her neck would be sore for days, and she was suddenly lying on the damp ground, the side of her head feeling very much like it was on fire. (It was not. But she *had* lost a sizable hank of white hair.)

Clementine lay flat on her back, clutching her head. She tentatively took her hand away and saw a few smears of blood on her fingers. Black spots danced in front of her vision. She was dimly aware of the Gricken shrieking nearby.

"You will have to go on without me, Sebastien," she said as calmly as she could. "I have been killed."

Sebastien hovered over her and said, "Um."

Another voice said, "Oh, Seven Sisters."

Clementine saw a pair of legs run out of the trees, nimbly dodge Sebastien, and kneel by Clementine's side. Clementine squeezed her eyes shut, preparing for a killing blow.

But said killing blow never came.

"Oh, no, no, no," said the stranger—a woman, Clementine thought. The woman shuffled around and cradled Clementine's throbbing skull in her lap, gently prodding—though it did not feel all that gentle to Clementine—until she found the patch of hair the arrow had so cruelly ripped out. Clementine yelped at her touch, but she felt the woman sigh with relief.

"It's just a graze," said the woman. "I'm so sorry. I thought—I was out, um, hunting, and I thought you were . . ."

Clementine blinked the tears out of her eyes, taking great gulps of air, and looked up into the worried, upside-down face of the scarred young traveler from the village square.

The woman's gray eyes were still wide with concern as she helped Clementine sit up.

“I’m Darka,” she said. “Darka Wesk-Starzec. And I’m very sorry I shot at you.” She turned to Sebastien, who still had one eye on the encroaching trees. “Both of you.”

“Sebastien,” said the boy, extending his hand over Clementine for a firm handshake with Darka. He seemed to be forcing himself to meet the young woman’s gaze, but Clementine saw no hint of the revulsion his comrades had so clearly expressed.

Clementine, however, was less sure of how to introduce herself. The woman had just shot her, after all. Who would be out hunting in a storm like this? And though the woman hadn’t spelled out her two last names, Clementine could practically hear the hyphen between them. Her father had warned her to be wary of all signs of witchcraft; things like hyphenated names, controlling wild animals with one’s will, and the ability to fold fitted sheets were all quite high on the list.

“I . . . I’m . . .” said Clementine. Her decision-making ability seemed to have been yanked out of her head along with that unfortunate chunk of her scalp.

“We’ve got to get you two out of this storm,” Darka said, squinting up into the rain. “There’s a cave not far from here we can shelter in. Come on!” And without waiting for so much as a nod of encouragement from either of them, Darka hoisted up Clementine, grabbed Sebastien’s ax, and shoved Clementine into the boy’s arms.

"Hey!" protested Sebastien.

He had barely propped up Clementine before her shaky knees collapsed again. The Gricken leapt into Clementine's arms, nearly bowling both of them over.

Sebastien glared at the ax in Darka's hands. "That's mine!" he said.

Darka merely flexed her fingers, took a practice swing at an encroaching branch, and set off into the forest. "I trust you don't mind if I borrow it."

* * *

Darka's cave really was only a few (harrowing) minutes away, and she was much better at navigating through the storm than either Clementine or Sebastien had been. Had she been staying in the forest since being driven out of the village?

Unfortunately, as the three of them stumbled into the cave, the storm rushed in after them. The wind howled even louder, and great sheets of rain poured sideways through the cave opening, spraying them with icy water. Darka rushed into the shallow interior—Clementine saw a few piles of supplies and blankets on the floor—and hurriedly lit a lantern. The meager light was mostly drowned out by the darkness from outside.

"You, help me with this!" said Darka, gesturing to Sebastien.

Clementine leaned against the wall while Darka and

Sebastien rolled a large stone in front of the cave opening, blocking out the worst of the rain. The Gricken flew out of Clementine's arms and proceeded to careen against the cave walls, clucking with agitation. Darka and Sebastien collapsed against the stone, panting and soaked to the skin with rain. Clementine supposed she didn't look much better.

But just as entering the cave hadn't deterred the storm, neither, it seemed, would the boulder in front of it. Thunder crashed and the wind roared, strong enough to make the rock shudder. Clementine, for one, was beginning to suspect it was useless to hide. This storm was magical.

"What's happening?" asked Sebastien, staring at the lightning flashing around the entryway. Darka, however, seemed less surprised that a storm was literally chasing them. She merely wiped her sodden hair out of her face and shook her head, the unscarred half of her lips twisting upward, as if she were laughing at some dark private joke.

"She's not going to stop," said Clementine, more to herself than anyone else. "I should never have left the farm. Who knows how long she's been waiting?"

Sebastien looked at Clementine like she had suddenly sprouted two heads, but when Darka looked up, her eyes were sharp and bright in the flickering lantern light.

"What are you talking about?" Sebastien said. "And what does it have to do with—"

Crash. The thunder sounded again, and the rock covering the cave mouth quaked. Dust and pebbles rained down from the ceiling, making everyone cough.

"With *that*?" finished Sebastien, pointing outside.

Darka's gaze never wavered from Clementine.

"Who?" asked Darka. "Who is doing this?"

Clementine almost answered her but stopped herself just in time. She didn't even *know* these people. She was most certainly not going to go blabbing about how her Evil Overlord father's sworn enemy had managed to charm her way right to the edge of his lands.

"A . . . a witch," allowed Clementine, trying to get ahold of herself. "It has to be. This is a magical storm." There was no sense pretending otherwise.

Sebastien blanched under his freckles, but then looked hopefully at Clementine. "If it's magical, that means you can stop it, right?"

Clementine glared at him. *Oh, sure, just go bragging about my magic to every stranger who may or may not decide to murder us at such a declaration*, she thought. But she supposed that her bright white hair was a big enough hint that she wasn't exactly a normal village girl. Still . . . stopping the storm? Clementine didn't know about such things. She knew how to feed fire-breathing chickens without getting a singed bum for her troubles, how to measure out poisons for maximum effect without actually murdering one's victim, and how to do basic tax returns. But to fight brute magical force with brute magical force . . . that was a job for the darkest magic. Magic Clementine had never used—especially since the family grimoire's transformation into an overprotective chicken.

"I . . . I don't really . . ." Clementine looked around. Behind her, the Gricken had stopped its panicked hopping and settled down into Darka's blankets.

Another rumble of thunder shook the cave, and freezing water started to shoot through the cracks between the cave mouth and the boulder in front of it.

"Are you a future Dark Lord or not?" demanded Sebastien.

Clementine froze. The cat was out of the bag now. Darka Wesk-Starzec, however, did not look terrified, horrified, or any other *-ified* usually associated with the revelation that one was in the presence of an evil sorceress. Instead, she raised a delicate eyebrow and looked over Clementine's shoulder.

"I think your mutant chicken is in distress," she said dryly.

Clementine whipped around. Sure enough, the Gricken was fidgeting and making the fast, low clucks that usually meant—

"Is it . . . laying an egg?" Sebastien asked, his expression caught between disgust and wonder.

Clementine noticed that the ax had somehow made its way back into his possession. She backed protectively in front of the Gricken.

And sure enough, when she crouched down and reached a hand under its paper feathers, she came away with a single smooth, bright golden egg. It was warm in her palm and pulsed faintly with tiny bursts of heat.

Ignoring Sebastien's hysterical questioning about how exactly an *egg* was supposed to help them, Clementine dashed the egg against the cave wall with all her might. The boy shouted, and even Darka nocked an arrow, as glowing gold letters and symbols appeared on the stone. Clementine rushed forward to read it, hurriedly translating runes and rearranging the nursery-rhyme gibberish of the protective cipher, grasping for any clue as to what the spell might be for: A tornado? Her own lightning blast? Perhaps a miniature volcanic eruption? But the end result was murkily described at best. And there were enough key words like "light" and "bright" and "warmth" to set alarm bells off in Clementine's head before she even got to the key ingredient, when suddenly, all hope shattered as easily as the egg against the cave wall.

"What is it? What is she doing?" Sebastien asked, looking to Darka. He crouched in the corner of the cave, one eye on the water and wind shooting through the entryway with increasing severity.

"It's . . . a spell," said Darka, stepping forward to examine the wall. She nodded to Clementine. "Isn't it?"

But Clementine could barely speak around the lump in her throat. Her father was dying, she'd been shot in the head, they were about to be blown to pieces by a magical storm, and her stupid grimoire chicken had *finally* decided to lay her a spell, and it was one she couldn't even *use*.

"It doesn't matter," said Clementine finally, sniffling. "I can't use it."

Sebastien started to complain again, but Darka cut him off with an icy glare. Clementine would have to ask her for tips, if they survived this.

"And why not?" asked Darka, her tone still even.

"Because . . . because it's *light* magic!" cried Clementine.

"Seven Sisters," sputtered Sebastien. "I didn't even know there was a difference!"

"Clementine," said Darka, leaning against the boulder as it rattled to keep it in place even as her feet slipped in the mud. "Is that magical chicken yours?"

Clementine nodded, still sniffling. Her head had started to throb again.

"And it . . . lays spells just for you?" Darka guessed.

Another nod.

"I don't know much about magic," Darka admitted, wincing as a wave of icy water ran over her feet from outside. "But it sounds like if your . . ."

"Gricken," Clementine said. "Grimoire chicken."

Sebastien snorted.

"Naturally," said Darka. "If your Gricken laid this egg for you, then that spell was *meant* for you."

Clementine wiped her eyes and took another look at the shimmering spell on the cave wall. Maybe Darka had a point about the Gricken, but the huntress could never truly understand. Clementine had never, ever cast light magic before—for obvious reasons. She didn't know *how* that spell had come to exist in the family grimoire. To attempt to cast such a spell, even in self-defense, was unthinkable. Dark Lords did *not* use light magic.

And even if she wanted to do the spell, Clementine wasn't so sure she could. The final ingredient, the *key* ingredient, made her heart go cold.

The spell required a happy memory.

Think happy thoughts, the Lady of the Lake had warned her. *You're going to need them.*

Clementine could have cursed herself, if she weren't quite sure they were all about to die already.

"*Well?*" asked Darka. She practically had to yell over the howling wind.

Sebastien jumped back from the cave mouth at another crash of thunder, and the boulder covering the door nearly fell over with the absence of his weight. He rushed to help Darka push it back into place.

How could Clementine explain why she couldn't do the spell? How could she tell them that she felt just as frozen by the idea of having to think of a happy memory as by the rain and the wind? That looking back on her whole life, all that stood out to her was her father's angry face—always judging her, always scolding her, or acting like she wasn't there at all? How could she explain that when she tried to think of a happy memory, her mind drew a complete blank?

She'd experienced positive emotions and experiences before, she was fairly certain. She'd felt victorious, and relieved, and even smug on occasion. But a moment when she'd simply been . . . happy?

Dark Lords were not *happy*. Her father would never forgive her for casting this spell—for straying from the path of darkness. Perhaps it was better to die than to cross over into the light.

But Darka and Sebastien were in danger, too, and they *hadn't* chosen the path of darkness. (Well, she wasn't sure about Darka, what with a name like that, but one never wanted to make assumptions about people.) They were trapped here because the storm was chasing Clementine, and they'd only tried to help her. Was it fair to let them die, too, all so Clementine could stick to her convictions? She was the one who had gotten them into this situation—and not on purpose, either, so there was no counting *that* as a Dastardly Deed.

Clementine looked around the now-muddy cave floor and picked up the sharpest rock she could find. She stepped forward, right in front of the trembling boulder, and began tracing the symbols from the spell in a circle in the dirt around her.

"When I say 'now,'" Clementine said, unable to meet Darka's or Sebastien's gaze, "roll the rock away from the opening." She could not *believe* she was actually doing this.

Sebastien's eyes nearly bugged out of his head. "Are you serious—"

"Just do it, you impertinent boy," snapped Clementine.

Sebastien opened his mouth again, but Darka beat him to the punch.

"We're ready when you are," she said with a nod, though her eyes did dart to the cave mouth, as if she, for one, couldn't quite believe Clementine could stop the maelstrom waiting for them. Clementine wasn't sure she could stop it, either.

But she had to try. And so, for the first time in her life, Clementine Morcerous closed her eyes and tried to think happy thoughts.

It was not easy. The sounds of Sebastien's annoying, panicky mouth-breathing, along with the rain practically boring holes through the cave wall, did not help her concentration. Her feet were cold and wet, sticky blood was still pouring from her burning head, and shame was burning through her even hotter than that. Yet still, she tried her hardest to dredge up some memory—any memory—that might suffice. She started with memories of her father's successful Dastardly Deeds—surely, she'd been happy for him—and then moved on to her own magical triumphs, like the first time she'd conjured flesh-eating rot all by herself. But nothing seemed to fit—at least, not well enough to activate the spell. There was no click in her brain, no surge of power to signal the spell's effect.

Sifting through memory after memory as fast as she could, she almost missed it. But as soon as she saw the image of the Lady in White—the very first time she'd *ever* seen the Lady in White—Clementine knew this memory was the one.

What a relief it had been, to find someone to talk to—someone she could say anything to without fear of reprisal. Someone who was calm, and steady, and always there. How . . . yes, how genuinely *happy* she'd been to find the hidden garden. It was a secret place, a safe place—a place all her own.

Clementine held on to the memory tightly, cupping her hands where she stood, as if it were water she was trying to keep from seeping through her fingers. Her fingers *were* tingling with warmth—the same warmth that had pulsed from the Gricken's egg. And suddenly,

Clementine knew exactly what the spell was for, and why the Gricken had chosen this moment to lay it for her: it was a spell for sunlight.

Energy pulsing inside her from head to toe, Clementine knew the spell *was* like water in her palms—she couldn't hold on to it forever. She could only throw what little light she had into the world and hope it was enough.

"Now," she said, drawing her hands in toward her chest and spinning around, tracing another circle in the dirt with the toe of her boot. As she turned, she heard Darka and Sebastien grunting as they pushed the stone away from the mouth of the cave. Clementine faced the stabbing rain and the howling wind, thrust out her hands, and let her happy memory go.

Beams of light erupted from her fingertips, and then from behind her in the cave, and then from the very sky itself. White hot and blinding, they stopped the raindrops in their tracks, turning them to harmless mist. The light cut through the darkened sky, mingling with the lightning, until the dome of it looked like one of the Gricken's shining eggs, crisscrossed with golden cracks.

Darka and Sebastien threw their arms in front of their faces to shield their eyes, but Clementine couldn't look away. She was part of the light.

She noted, in a detached sort of way, that her face was wet, and thought perhaps the rain had started up again and her spell was failing—and then she realized it wasn't the rain at all. She was crying.

She was crying because she was ashamed. Not about the light magic—although there would be plenty of time to feel bad about that later. No. Clementine was ashamed because out of all the memories in her entire life, her happiest moment had not been a victory over her enemies or satisfaction at the completion of one of her father's Dastardly Deeds. Her happiest memory had nothing to do with her father or her very calling in life, at all. Her happiest memory had been escaping them.

With sunlight streaming down around her, Clementine lowered her hands. She looked down, blinking away her tears, and noticed that her eyelids felt suddenly very, very heavy, and that her hair had turned a glowing burnished yellow to match the occasion. It was a positively cheerful color.

How embarrassing, she thought, and promptly fainted.

CHAPTER 11

IN ENEMY TERRITORY

or

The Probability of Being Baked in a Pie Increases Exponentially

The bed that Clementine slept on was soft, and smelled of moss and campfire smoke and something that was quite possibly duck. It was not an unpleasant smell, but it was an unfamiliar one. The feathers in her mattress did not usually smell as if they had only recently departed their owners.

The smell was not the only unfamiliar thing. Clementine slowly opened her eyes and found that she was on the floor of what appeared to be a tent, just tall enough in the center for a smallish grown-up to stand in. Above her, tiny wind chimes and strange creations of knotted twine strung with gems and stones hung from the ceiling. Light snuck in through the tent flap and played across the crystals and the colored glass, casting little rainbow flecks across the tent walls and on Clementine herself.

She tilted her head to see more and winced at the spike of pain that skittered along her scalp. She extricated her hand from underneath the multicolored quilt that covered her and tentatively prodded at her head. Her fingers came away sticky with some sort of half-dried ointment.

Though it should have alarmed her to wake up alone and injured, in a strange tent, with an unidentifiable substance surely winding its way through her bloodstream, Clementine was too tired to worry about it very much. She didn't think she'd ever *been* this tired. Even just shifting under the blanket made her feel feverish and queasy with fatigue, and she resigned herself to staring up at the ceiling until her body felt like waking up along with her brain. She closed her eyes—just for a moment, she assured herself—and when she opened them again, the light was different and Darka Wesk-Starzec was hovering inches from her face.

"Oh, good," Darka said with a sigh of relief. "You're awake."

And suddenly, the reasons *why* Clementine was lying injured in a strange tent came rushing back to her. She cleared her throat, preparing to unleash every curse she could think of on this hyphenated-named wild woman who apparently thought it was completely acceptable behavior to run around wearing pants and shooting people in their own forests . . . but Clementine's body *still* seemed to be catching up with her brain, because all that came out was a rather petulant, "You *shot* me."

"Yes," said Darka, the hint of a blush blooming across her face. She tucked her bow farther behind her, out of Clementine's sight. "Awfully sorry about that."

"You *shot* me," said Clementine again. The charms hanging in the air—and they *were* charms, she realized—started to vibrate, ever so slightly.

"I did *miss*," said Darka. Her eyes flicked to Clementine's matted hair. "Mostly."

"You can't just go around shooting people and . . . and bringing them . . ." Bringing them where? Where was she? Clementine looked around. Along with the charms, strings of dried herbs hung from the ceiling, and bunches of colorful candles littered the floor, though they were unlit at the moment. Clementine knew of only one place that would be home to such an eclectic and dangerous mix of objects.

She was in a hedgewitch's tent. And by the sounds she now noticed filtering in from outside, she was in a hedgewitch's tent in a hedgewitches' *camp*.

Clementine grabbed Darka's wrist in a viselike grip, too suddenly for Darka to move away, and unsteadily raised herself to a half-sitting position.

"We have to get out of here," Clementine whispered fiercely. "They'll flay our flesh from our bones. They'll pluck out our eyes and pickle them for afternoon snacks. They'll bake us in *pies*."

Darka slowly pried Clementine's fingers off her wrist, her face suddenly twisted by what Clementine strongly suspected was a smirk. It pulled at the jagged edges of her scar.

"I don't think you'd make a very good pie," Darka said. "Not much meat on you at all, is there?"

Clementine got the distinct impression that the smirk was, in fact, genuine, and that Darka Wesk-Starzec was most definitely making fun of her.

"You don't understand," Clementine said, shoving off her blankets and ignoring the way her hands trembled as she did so. "It's not safe here." She lowered her voice even more. "This is a *witches' camp*."

Darka tilted her head, as if to say, *And?*

"We have to get out of here," Clementine said again. "What were you *thinking*, bringing me to a place like this?"

Darka snorted and started to reply, but the answer hit Clementine hard enough to make her head throb all over again.

"Seven Sisters," Clementine said, scooting back against the tent wall. "You're one of them. You *are* a witch. That's why you were staying in the woods. That's why you shot at me. How couldn't I have sensed it? And now you're going to use my bones for stew and make charms out of my hair and sell my blood by the vial for much less than it's worth in a competitive market, and—"

"I'm not a witch," said Darka, sitting back on her heels.

Clementine paused. "What?"

"I'm not a witch," repeated Darka. She slapped her hands on her thighs and looked thoughtful. "Well, my grandmother was one, supposedly, but as neither my mother nor myself decided to continue that colorful bit of family tradition, I don't think I count."

Clementine wasn't so sure. "Well, if you aren't a witch, why did you bring me here?"

Darka threw up her hands and snorted. "I'm sorry, *Your Highness*, but I didn't exactly have a lot of options when faced with the question 'Hmm, what do I do with this unconscious mystery child out in the middle of the woods?'"

"My lady," corrected Clementine.

"What?"

"You may address me as 'my lady,'" said Clementine. "'Your Highness' is typically reserved for princes and princesses."

Darka stared at Clementine, mouth agape, as if she couldn't believe what nonsense she was hearing. It was clear she really *wasn't* from around Lord Elithor's lands.

"Noted," Darka said. She shook her head as she stood up. "Well, my lady, you might be a little more thankful to someone who just saved your life."

No, no, thought Clementine. *This would not do at all.* Future Dark Lords could not be saved by commoners. It simply wasn't done.

"Excuse me," snapped Clementine, "*you* saved *my* life?" She flicked her hair over her shoulder with her best dose of imperious disdain, though it was admittedly less effective with her accompanying yelp of discomfort. She'd forgotten about her sore head. "If I recall correctly, *I* was the one who saved us from that murderous maelstrom." Clementine silently congratulated herself on her use of the word "maelstrom." It was one of her favorites in volume M–Z.

"You did, at that," admitted Darka, scooping up her bow. Clementine pressed even farther back against the tent wall, but Darka simply slung the bow over her shoulder and fixed her piercing gray eyes on Clementine. "But I've been wondering, who exactly was that maelstrom so intent on murdering in the first place?" Darka turned and left the tent.

Clementine hauled herself up on shaky knees to follow. She would have to sneak out of the camp before any of the witches realized who she was—assuming they didn't know already. Clementine crept out of the tent, trying not to grip the tent flap as if it were the only thing holding her upright, and looked around.

It was a hedgewitches' camp, all right. The forest clearing was crowded with tents and cook fires. Protective amulets hung from the limbs of the trees, just as they had inside the tent Clementine awoke in. Clementine took a few fast, uncertain steps and bumped into someone walking by. When the woman noticed who Clementine was, she jumped back as if she'd been burned by Clementine's touch.

Clementine's head swam as she half stumbled away. More curious stares followed. Women of all ages milled about the camp—some barely older than Clementine, some wrinkly enough to have appeared in the earliest entries of the Witchionary—but they all stopped in their tracks when they saw Clementine approach. And most of them did *not* look friendly. One witch with a half-shaved head and bright red feathers threaded through the rest of her hair even spat as Clementine passed.

The events of the afternoon came rushing back to Clementine with more clarity, and she nearly groaned aloud at the possibility of the Gricken missing in the woods—or, worse, captured by the witches. And where was the black sheep, and the nightmare? Where was Sebastien? If anyone was a good candidate for witch stew, the village boy surely fit the bill. Those dimples of his just radiated well-fed childhood innocence. Not that she thought about his dimples at all, ever.

I have to get out, I have to get out, I have to get out, thought Clementine, panicking as the trees started to wave and shimmer before her eyes. She heard footsteps trailing after her and walked faster. She thought she might be sick, and she could think of nothing more embarrassing—short of dying a grisly death—than losing her lunch in front of a coven of hedgewitches.

The world very inconsiderately tilted sideways, and Clementine stumbled again, but this time, a pair of hands reached out to steady her.

"And where do you think *you're* going?" asked Darka Wesk-Starzec.

"Unhand me this instant!" demanded Clementine.

"I'd like nothing better," said Darka, grunting a bit under Clementine's weight. "But you'd probably fall over."

"You have nothing to fear, child," another voice said.

An old witch—though not the oldest, Clementine noticed—approached them from the center of the camp. She was short and squat and walked with a carved birch walking stick. Her weathered skin was heavily freckled, though it did have a surprising lack of warts—a feature Clementine had come to expect from descriptions in the Witchionary. The witch's wispy shoulder-length hair sprouted haphazardly out of her head in gray and auburn tufts. She blew an errant strand out of her face with a short horselike huff.

The witch stopped a few feet from Clementine and Darka and rested her hands on her staff, panting slightly. Clementine felt rather guilty about making an old woman chase her around the woods, and then remembered she was dealing with a witch, and then felt guilty about feeling guilty.

"My name is Kat Marie Grice," said the witch. "And you have my word that no harm will come to you in this camp today."

A few of the witches, including the shaved-headed one, looked disappointed at this declaration, but none of them challenged it. Clementine did notice that the old witch had specified *today*.

"Please, stay and rest for a while," continued Kat Marie Grice. She looked beyond Clementine and into the trees, where just at the camp's edge, Clementine could see the stark line between the wards around the witch's camp and the devastation in the forest outside. Broken branches littered the forest floor. Shattered eggs from smashed birds' nests oozed down the bruised and battered bark of fallen trees. The trunks leaned crisscrossed against one another, propped up like wounded soldiers after a battle.

Clementine reluctantly took Darka's offered arm.

"The woods are no place for a little girl walking alone," said Kat Marie, narrowing her eyes at the trees. "Especially not today."

* * *

Clementine stroked the Gricken's feathers as she took a tentative sip from a steaming mug of tea that Kat Marie had pressed into her hands. She sat next to the old woman on a bench outside her tent—the same tent Clementine had woken up in. Taking food or drink from strangers—especially strange witches—would have gotten her a tongue-lashing for the ages from her father at best, and been suicidal at worst, under normal circumstances. But considering the events of the day, and the fact that the witches had had multiple chances to kill her and had so far chosen not to, Clementine did not think these could be considered normal circumstances. She still felt ill and tired, and tea was nice, and Kat Marie hadn't given her much choice in the matter, anyway.

Amazingly, the hedgewitches seemed more inclined to *avoid* the Gricken than to steal it. They walked past the creature on tiptoe—if they dared to walk past at all. Average folk would have noticed *something* off about the giant chicken in their midst, but its disguise didn't seem to fool the hedgewitches in the slightest. Clementine knew she wouldn't be much interested in a book of spells that had been used against her family or friends for generations, either.

The nightmare was busy terrifying two fat ponies in the horse pen by baring its teeth and whinnying in a pitch so high only the other animals could hear, and the black sheep was chomping on a patch of grass with a few of his lighter-coated brethren. A little girl with four crooked pigtails shyly offered him a bunch of celery, which he ate with gusto. Sebastien, she'd been told (and then double-checked with the black sheep) had gone home to the village while Clementine slept, eager to check on his parents' farm after the storm.

Kat Marie seemed to be keeping to her word. No harm had come to Clementine or any of her companions—yet.

"That was quite a piece of magic you entertained back there," Kat Marie said, as if Clementine's sunshine spell had been an unruly guest who showed up to dinner uninvited. Clementine nearly choked on her tea. Had the whole mountain seen her cast that light magic?

"I don't know what you're talking about," said Clementine, gripping her mug tightly.

"If I were that chicken of yours, though," said Kat Marie, scratching her chin, "I'd be a bit more careful. Sun summoning's powerful magic. Quite risky for one so young—and so unfamiliar with light magic."

Clementine took a prim sip from her cup and said nothing. But questions *had* started to bubble up in her mind—questions that Kat Marie Grice, whatever her professional failings, might have some idea how to answer.

"No wonder it knocked you flat," said Kat Marie with a shrug.

"I was perfectly in control," said Clementine, knowing full well that she had indeed been knocked flat.

"You're lucky it didn't kill you."

Clementine gulped. Perhaps she *had* been lucky that Darka had thought to bring her here.

"Did *everyone* see?" asked Clementine quietly.

"See what?" asked Kat Marie with the hint of a smile. "The apocalyptic storm clouds rolling over half the forest? The trees marching of their own accord? Or the blinding streams of sunlight cutting through the churning black sky like divine swords of retribution?" She winked. "No, I'm not sure anyone else noticed."

Clementine took a deep breath through her nose. "I meant . . . did anyone else . . ."

"Know it was you?" Kat Marie suggested, looking down her bespectacled nose at Clementine.

Clementine nodded.

"You were deep in the caves when you cast it, yes?" asked Kat Marie. At another nod from Clementine, she sighed, and said, "I'd say your secret is safe, my child."

Clementine let out a sigh of her own, but hers was of relief. Her reputation might not have to suffer as much as she'd feared. All she needed to do was threaten the witches into silence, and then she could go back to the drawing board for Dastardly Deeds. The Whittle Witch's encroachment on the forest complicated matters, of course, but still. (Clementine assumed it was the Whittle Witch, though now with so many witches apparently running amok, she couldn't be certain.) Her brief flirtation with light magic could fade into distant memory—a mere hiccup in the course of her magical education. And yet . . .

"It felt . . . different," Clementine found herself saying. "From other spells I've done."

Kat Marie Grice gave her a long look. "I imagine it would."

The urge to ask Kat Marie Grice about the spell—and especially, the reason she'd had to cast it in the first place—was so powerful Clementine was sure she would burst with the effort of keeping silent. What did the hedgewitches know of the Whittle Witch? Was the Whittle Witch one of them? (This seemed unlikely, given how heavily warded the camp was, but you could never be too sure with witches.) How long had she been in the forest? Why had Clementine been able to even *use* light magic?

And why had it felt so right?

But her father's warnings—and Stan Glen's—echoed in her mind. Asking for help was dangerous. Asking for help might reveal how help*less* she really was.

Clementine also couldn't help but notice that Kat Marie wasn't exactly volunteering information. Either the old woman supported the Whittle Witch, or—as seemed increasingly likely—she, too, did not want to admit to being chased around her own forest by another witch.

My father's forest, Clementine corrected herself. Kat Marie Grice and her coven had no claim to anything in it at all.

With some effort, Clementine turned from the witch's gaze and surveyed the camp. Now that most of the coven wasn't preoccupied with a raving Dark Lord's daughter stumbling through their camp, they'd mostly gone about their business—and it *was* a business, Clementine soon realized, at least partly. She was surprised to see people who were almost certainly not hedgewitches themselves ambling through the camp, approaching one witch or another. Not all the charms here were for the camp itself—they were for sale.

Clementine was shocked to recognize a few of the villagers among the hedgewitches' customers. Wasn't that the baker's wife, sniffing a proffered sack of herbs from one of the witches and gossiping about the storm? Wasn't that one of the men she'd seen building the roof in town, now blushing and stumbling over his words as he shyly asked for . . . a love potion? Clementine snorted into her tea.

And was that . . . No, it couldn't be. But it was. Clementine would recognize that head of stupidly perfect, bouncy blond curls anywhere: it was Henrietta Turnacliff, the village mayor's teenaged daughter! She held up a bumpy coral-colored stone on a string and spoke to a middle-aged witch with a mass of turquoise braids that fell to her waist.

"Please, I need something that will help me locate my brother," Clementine heard Henrietta tell the witch. "He's been missing for . . ."

But the turquoise-haired witch put a hand on Henrietta's shoulder and turned her to face the other way, and their conversation faded from Clementine's ears. None of the villagers seemed to notice Clementine in their midst, and she wondered if the charms around Kat Marie's tent were to thank for that.

A chorus of *baah*s arose from the sheep pen, and Clementine looked over to see the black sheep pawing the ground and scampering behind the witches' flock. She hoped none of the witches were giving him a hard time—and that those white sheep were really as plain and innocent as they looked.

Clementine frowned at the townspeople weaving through the witches hawking their wares.

"Why would they come here?" Clementine wondered aloud, watching Henrietta Turnacliff purposefully stride over to another witch's stall, where shelves of potions stood on display. "My father would never allow this if he knew."

Kat Marie Grice let out a soft sound that might have been a snort, but Clementine ignored it.

"The villagers hate witches!" pointed out Clementine. "They chased Darka all the way out of town just because they thought she was one."

"Ah, but *do* they hate us?" asked Kat Marie. "I think it's more that they *fear* us, and hate does follow fear more often than not. But not always. And we fascinate them. Just as we fascinate you."

Clementine dropped her gaze—she really had been staring at as much of the camp as she could—and muttered something about simply being curious. Kat Marie smiled, revealing an incomplete set of lumpy teeth that was far more in line with Clementine's mental image of witches than anything else she'd seen that day.

"They come to us for things they can't get anywhere else, Clementine," explained the old woman.

Clementine supposed she should have been offended at a witch addressing her so informally, but she found she rather liked the sound of her name in Kat Marie's full, low voice.

"They may not accept us, but they need us," Kat Marie said. "They come to us for little bits of hope, or healing . . . even a small adventure. How many can say they've been to a witch's hut and survived to tell the tale?" Kat Marie waggled her eyebrows, and Clementine had to bite her own lip to keep from smiling. (*This was* no *laughing matter*, she told herself. Not that anything was a laughing matter.)

They come to us for things they can't get anywhere else. For things they could not expect from Lord Elithor, the witch meant. Clementine tried to picture her father taking petitions or healing the sick or giving away any of his priceless and powerful magical artifacts to his subjects. The idea was laughable. But Clementine reminded herself that the welfare of her father's subjects was none of his concern—in fact, it was the opposite of his concern. Lord Elithor's duty was to inflict as much misery and terror as he could on the villagers without leading to statistically significant population decline. It was a delicate balance—quite a bit harder than handing out minced garlic in the woods and claiming you were a gift to society. Everyone had his or her place in the world, and evildoing was the Dark Lord's responsibility. That was just the way things were.

Clementine shook her head. "They shouldn't be coming here," she said. "They shouldn't be coming here, and you shouldn't be here. Witchcraft is outlawed in my father's lands."

Kat Marie looked around the lively camp. "Clearly," she said dryly.

Clementine sighed. She had finished her tea and

was finally feeling much better, and she shouldn't have even been having this conversation, anyway. It was time to brave the forest again before she lost the light—and before the Whittle Witch had a chance to rally.

But Kat Marie cleared her throat and went on. "Imagine, if you will, living a sad, short, and often violent life that is entirely out of your control. Imagine being governed by the whims of a seemingly all-powerful ruler who oscillates between willful neglect one moment, and unreasonable, unpredictable demands and blind rages the next. Imagine that even though there are days he barely enters your thoughts at all—and those days are a blessed few—that his influence is always there. That there is no part of your life that he could not touch, nothing and no one too precious for him to destroy—not if he really wanted to. Imagine being trapped by that fear for your whole life." Kat Marie took a deep breath in through her nose, as if she were forcing herself to be calm. "Imagine what that might do to a person—and what lengths they might go to for even a moment's relief."

Clementine looked away, thumbing at a chip in her mug. Though Kat Marie might never have believed her . . . she didn't have to try very hard to imagine such a life at all.

"I might be able to talk to my father about . . ." Clementine's voice trailed off. What sort of promise could she hope to extract out of Lord Elithor? *"Please, Father, don't persecute the people you're required to persecute so very much"?* "Some things," she finished lamely. "But don't get your hopes up. He'd only take great delight in dashing them to pieces, and that's an end unto itself for Dark Lords. Best not to have any expectations at all."

Kat Marie Grice nodded and held out her hand for Clementine's cup. Clementine gave it to her.

"I do wonder what to expect from *you*, Clementine," said the witch. "As I said, not many could have cast the spell you did. Even a Good Witch in training might've had trouble—"

Clementine started. "I'm not a witch," she said sharply, "and if I were, I most certainly wouldn't be a good one." Clementine had to fight the bile rising in her throat at the mere thought: Clementine Morcerous, Good Witch of the Seven Sisters, prancing about in gowns made out of flower petals and whistling along with songbirds and aiding plucky heroes on quests? She'd rather have her head mounted on the library wall.

Kat Marie held up a hand. "I didn't mean to suggest—"

"Thank you for giving me shelter and a place to rest," said Clementine in a clipped voice. She stood up. "And for the tea. But my . . . associates and I really should be going."

And without meeting Kat Marie's eyes, Clementine scooped up the Gricken and strode away.

CHAPTER 12
INTERESTING COMPANY
or
Necessary Qualifications for a Murderous Line of Work

Darka Wesk-Starzec had never seen so many witches in one place, and she was the granddaughter of a witch. Perhaps it *was* true what they said about magic on this side of the Seven Sisters—that there was just infinitely *more* of it.

Not all of the hedgewitches' trade was magical, just as not all of the hedgewitches had magic—of that she was sure. But as she trailed her fingers along the crystals dangling from protective amulets, or along the bumpy rune-carved surfaces of hazel dowsing rods, Darka could feel the difference. She could feel the magic, a pulse that started as a tingling in her fingers or a chill on the back of her neck that sometimes crept all the way inside her old wound, making her scar burn.

Would her whole life have been different, on this side of the mountains? If she and Alaric had had this many magical tools at their disposal, might they have succeeded? Would Alaric still be alive? Would Darka's face still be unharmed? It was impossible to know, and it wasn't worth dwelling on, Darka knew. She could never bring Alaric back.

But she could recognize the resources at her disposal. She could use them. Alaric had taught her everything he knew, and that hadn't been enough. Five years of hunting on her own, and she was better than he'd ever been. He'd told her, once, that one needed a dark heart in his—their—line of work.

"Because of the killing?" she'd asked quietly, her face pressed into his neck as they lay next to each other, looking up at the stars.

But he'd told her no, not because they killed—but because they needed to survive. As hunters of magical artifacts and creatures both, they walked in all the places most mortals didn't dare to tread: the deepest caves, the ghostliest ruins, the darkest parts of the forest. One needed a heart dark enough to blend in.

Five years and two dead unicorns later, Darka was sure her dark heart made her almost invisible.

Darka peered at a row of tiny bottles stuffed with pebbles, feathers, and impossibly tightly rolled scraps of paper displayed on a table at one of the witch's stalls.

"Genuine curses," said the proprietress, coming to stand with her arms crossed on the other side of the table. Darka looked up to see a young woman with a half-shaved head, brilliant red feathers winding through the rest of it. "Guaranteed to make the object of your spurned affections vomit slugs—or any other small invertebrate of your choosing—for one to three days."

Darka peered behind the young witch to the more mundane supplies hanging near the back of her stall.

"I'm more interested in that length of rope back there, to be honest," Darka said.

The witch cocked her head, bemused. "Anything else?" she asked. "Lamp oil? Soap? Shoe polish?"

"I'm sorry," said Darka, ducking her head and letting her bangs fall in front of her face. "I'm just passing through, and I tried to get supplies in the village, but . . ."

The witch immediately uncrossed her arms and sighed. "The local yokels thought you were about to eat their young?" she said. She turned around, grabbed the length of rope, and plunked it down on the table.

"It felt more like their young were about to eat *me*," said Darka. "But that sounds about right."

"Those people," muttered the witch, shaking her head. "Rope it is. Free of charge."

"Oh, I couldn't—"

"Shirin Kirrane," said the witch, holding out her

hand. Darka held out her own, and the witch—Shirin—gave it a firm shake. "And I won't hear any more about it. Nice to meet you, child eater."

Darka let out a small laugh. "Darka," she said, and then hesitated. Shirin's friendliness (and feathered hair and big brown eyes) had made Darka let down her guard, but she knew better than to give her full name to someone in a coven of hedgewitches. If any of them had heard of her exploits beyond the valley, they might be just as likely as the villagers to come at her with pitchforks raised. "Darka Millbrook," she lied.

"And what brings Darka Millbrook to the Seven Sisters?" asked Shirin with a smile, leaning with her palms against the table.

Darka was about to make up an answer when the *baah*ing of sheep turned her attention toward the other end of the clearing. She could just see Clementine's bright gold head—now fading to a light peachy orange—bobbing up and down in close conversation with the witch who seemed to be the coven's leader.

Shirin followed Darka's gaze, but her expression immediately soured at the sight of Clementine. "And keeping such interesting company?" Shirin asked archly, busying herself with rearranging her "genuine curses."

"I only just met her today, in the woods," said Darka honestly. Shirin's posture relaxed somewhat. Darka considered her next words carefully. “Is she really the Dark Lord’s daughter?”

“The one and only,” said Shirin, shooting another glare in Clementine’s direction.

Darka could hardly believe her luck. If she absolutely had to nearly kill a kid, she couldn’t have picked a better one. Clementine herself seemed far too softhearted to be sympathetic to Darka’s cause—the girl had just been shooting actual sunshine out of her fingertips, after all—but her father was a different story. She’d heard of the Dark Lord Elithor, of course, but her initial plan had been to avoid him at all costs. He didn’t take kindly to visitors, she’d guessed from the rumors on both sides of the mountains, and Darka didn’t exactly have a letter of introduction from some other Evil Overlord to get her foot in the door of Castle Brack. But Clementine could be her ticket to an audience with him—and if anyone would want the unicorn dead, surely the Dark Lord would be at the top of the list. Taking down a unicorn would be a display of cruelty that no Dark Lord could resist. Surely, Lord Elithor would want to at least aid Darka in her quest.

“You’re staying in the caves, aren’t you?” asked Shirin, changing the subject. When Darka nodded, Shirin said, “These mountains can be dangerous. Why don’t you stay with us?”

Across the camp, Clementine was striding away from the coven leader and making a beeline for the black, skeletal filly that Darka had heard the witches whisper was an *actual* nightmare. Darka couldn't let her get away.

"Oh, but . . . I'm not a witch," she said hurriedly to Shirin.

The young woman tossed her feather-bestrewn hair over her shoulder and smiled. "Don't be silly—"

"Thanks for the rope," Darka said, ducking her head and hooking the rope onto her belt as she turned away. She didn't miss the puzzled frown that crossed Shirin's face.

"So what are you then?" called Shirin after her.

Darka didn't know what made her say it, and she wasn't even sure Shirin heard her. But she stopped just long enough to say, "A huntress."

And she followed the girl who would lead her to her prey.

* * *

After that day in the forest seven years ago, Darka and Alaric began to hunt together—*really* hunt. Alaric taught her how to lure selkies to the shoreline and capture their precious seal-like skins. He taught her how to shoot a griffin right out of the sky, and how to steal eggs from under the nose of a sleeping dragon (though they never actually tested this last one together). Their journeys took them away from her village and her farm, away from her family, for days and then weeks at a time. Her mother, father, brothers, and sisters were at first a bit annoyed—even one less pair of hands on their land made a difference—and then they were concerned. Her little sisters whined that they never saw her anymore. Her parents cautioned Darka against spending so much time with Alaric, and then against spending any time with him at all. And when that didn't work, they promptly threw him out of the house.

And then *that* didn't work, either, because Darka promptly declared her intention to marry him.

It was shortly after slamming the door to her parents' house for what she thought was the last time that Alaric first mentioned unicorns.

They were some of the most powerful magical creatures on earth, he told her. They could detect poisons or impurities in water just by touching their horn to it—and could purify that same water in seconds. They could cure any illness. They were attracted to suffering, especially that of young maidens, and their mere presence could bring comfort and solace to even the most broken of hearts. They could cast powerful magic without spells or incantations. They could manipulate the elements and the landscape around them, leaving the lands they traveled over more fertile than others. Unless they were felled by unnatural causes, they did not age past maturity. In short, they were incredible and immortal beings.

But unicorns were rare and solitary creatures. They were nearly impossible to track, and more impossible to capture. And even when they *were* captured, they refused to do their masters' bidding. They withered and wasted away in captivity, their magic draining along with their lives. The crushing force of their despair was usually enough to drive their captors mad, too.

"Why are you telling me this?" Darka had asked, rubbing her shoulders as a sudden chill overcame her. She could not rid her mind of the image of a captive unicorn, its wildness and wonder being stifled day by day until it died. This was not the quick, easy death she preferred to deliver—or would prefer to receive herself, when the time came.

Alaric kissed each of her shoulders. The most important thing to remember about unicorns, he said, was that much of their magic did not come from the unicorn itself, but from its horn.

To hunt a unicorn in its prime, to kill it swiftly and extract its horn, preserving all of the wondrous magical properties therein . . . well, one kill could make a man rich for life.

"A man," Alaric said, with that crooked smile of his, "or a woman."

***

"Wait!" Darka called, rushing to Clementine's side as the girl mounted her nightmare. A shiver went down Darka's spine as she approached, but Clementine seemed unaffected by the beast.

"I'm sorry," said Darka. "You were right. I didn't realize who you were when I brought you here. I apologize for leading you into danger."

Kat Marie Grice approached from the other side of the horse, her slow, uneven gait a stronger indicator of her age than the streaks of gray in her hair. Her keen gaze followed Darka, who looked away. She would have to be careful of a witch like that. Darka was more afraid of Kat Marie Grice than any of Shirin Kirrane's purported curses-in-a-bottle.

Clementine sniffed, and Darka suppressed an eye roll. How long would she have to suck up to this snobby, pampered little tyrant before she got what she really wanted?

"You saved our lives, stopping that storm like you did," said Darka as Clementine busied herself with the reins. "Thank you. I'd like to repay you, if there's any way I can." The girl's black sheep had ambled over and was peering up at Darka, who got the distinct impression that if it could, the sheep would have been raising an eyebrow at her. Darka ignored it.

"That won't be necessary," said Clementine, clicking

her heels against the nightmare's sides. "Do try not to shoot anyone else while you're in my father's forest." And with a last nod to Kat Marie, Clementine started to lead the horse and the sheep back toward the forest.

"I heard your family's got a farm!" Darka called after the girl, trying to think of something—anything—that might get her in the door of Castle Brack. "Any chance you could use an extra hand?"

Darka had expected Clementine to laugh at her with a stuck-up little titter, or simply to keep on riding without sparing Darka another thought. But much to Darka's surprise, the girl pulled up on the reins and stopped. The surrounding witches had gone quiet, all pretense of trying not to stare given up entirely. Shirin Kirrane stared at Darka with a hand on her hip and a far-from-friendly expression on her face.

Oh well, thought Darka. *At least I have the rope.* There was no going back to the hedgewitches now. She'd offered the Dark Lord's daughter her help, and that was something they would not soon forget.

"And what skills do you have that I might put to use?" asked Clementine, her back still to Darka.

"Mostly? I kill things," said Darka, and a murmur swept through the crowd. "But I'm not bad at coaxing milk out of a cow, either, or so I've been told." Darka watched Clementine set her shoulders.

"Come then, if you must," said Clementine, and she urged the nightmare forward once more. "Do try to keep up. I won't wait for you if the trees decide to get . . . feisty . . . again."

Darka sighed and started to follow Clementine out of the camp. She reached around to grab her bow—it wouldn't hurt to keep it at the ready in the forest—when a surprisingly strong hand gripped her wrist. She whipped around and came face-to-face with Kat Marie Grice.

"I'll ask you to draw that weapon *outside* this camp," said Kat Marie.

Darka shrugged away from the old woman's grip.

"Oh, and Darka?" said Kat Marie, lowering her voice as they watched Clementine, the nightmare, and the black sheep disappear beyond the tree line. "A small warning for you: do not let your heart be consumed by revenge."

Darka looked around, but no one else seemed to have heard Kat Marie's words. The camp was returning to business as usual. But Kat Marie's piercing gaze never wavered.

Rubbing her wrist where the old woman had grabbed it, Darka hurried after Clementine. And her dark heart beat against her ribs, thumping like a drum, echoing through the trees. This time, Darka did not feel invisible at all. She felt as if the shadows themselves were watching.

* * *

After the future Dark Lord of the Seven Sisters left the coven's camp, Kat Marie Grice's gaze wandered up and over the trees, up to the Fourth Sister, and finally to a very particular patch of snow. It sparkled and flashed in the sunset, rays of sunlight from Clementine's spell still dancing around it, light drawn to light.

The Lady in White, the villagers called it. If only they knew.

Kat Marie Grice watched the last remnants of the spell fade away, the lights swallowed by the mountain's shadows, and willed her hope to fade away, too. She told herself it was a fruitless hope. The little girl was still a Morcerous, through and through.

And yet, Kat Marie could not help but think of that brilliant light magic and wonder . . .

What if Clementine was the one?

* * *

Darka Wesk-Starzec would never do anything but curse the day that the love of her life was taken from her. But she had to admit that seven years of experience hunting mythical beasts had prepared her as well as could be expected for the reality of Dark Lord Elithor Morcerous's silent farm. If she were still the innocent farmer's daughter she'd been when she'd met Alaric, she would have run screaming from the looming shadow of Castle Brack before she'd even had a chance to see the fire-breathing chickens, poison apple orchard, or creepy animated scarecrows. The scarecrows were what really almost got to her. It took quite a bit of resolve not to set them alight with a few flaming arrows and run for the other side of the Seven Sisters like her life depended on it.

"How are you with plants?" Clementine asked as they entered one of the greenhouses.

"I know which ones not to eat in the forest," said Darka, just as a fanged flower with petals as big as her hands made a lunge for her head. She drew her dagger from her waist and slashed without thinking, cleanly slicing off the blossom. It let out a distressingly human cry as it tumbled to the ground, where it lolled around like a severed head, fangs still snapping at Darka's ankles, before it went still.

Clementine gave Darka a withering look.

"Best you not come in here alone, then," said the black sheep, trotting alongside them.

Darka nearly jumped into a prickle bush in surprise at hearing it speak.

"Don't worry," said the sheep quietly, when Clementine had gone on a few steps ahead. "No one really buys the carnivorous ones anymore, anyway. More of a niche item."

Darka nodded, but she did not sheathe her knife again until they left the greenhouse.

* * *

The sun had nearly set by the time they wrapped up the tour of the farm, completing their circuit at the foot of the mountain by a slightly crumbling gatehouse attached to a creaking drawbridge. (Darka did not ask what was in the moat below. She had a feeling she did not want to know the answer.) Castle Brack loomed over them. For a moment, Darka feared the little girl was about to send her right back across the drawbridge and away, but her worries were unfounded.

"It's getting late," said Clementine. "I must attend to . . . other business. We'll discuss your duties in more detail in the morning. You . . . I want to thank you. For staying with me in the cave and making sure I was all right."

"I did shoot you," Darka said with a shrug.

Clementine's hand drifted to her head before she snapped it back down to her side. "You may stay here," said Clementine, nodding to the gatehouse, "if . . . if you like. It was—is—the captain of the guard's quarters, but it's been unoccupied for several years . . . Not that we don't have guards! We do. Of course we do. But they are stationed in the castle at the moment. My father's magical wards are strong enough to protect us from any invaders." Clementine smoothed her skirts and held herself up to her full height. "A security presence this far down the mountain was deemed unnecessary."

"Naturally," said Darka, though she did wonder at the profound absence of another living soul throughout their entire tour. She'd assumed the servants or prisoners or whoever did the real work on the farm had been stashed away from their mistress's view, and that she'd have a chance to meet who was really in charge of the day-to-day operations later. Now, though, Darka wasn't so sure she *wasn't* the only other person on the grounds.

"It's not much," warned Clementine. "The gatehouse hasn't been looked after in a while, but I expect it's better than anywhere you've ever stayed. And you'll have to look out for yourself out here, you know."

Darka flipped up the straw doormat in front of the old oak door, bent down, and picked up the dented brass key she found under it. She raised an eyebrow at Clementine, who blushed.

Darka tested the key in the rickety lock and, with a little elbow grease, managed to wedge open the sticky door.

"I'm sure it will be fine," she said. She looked back to find Clementine staring at her. The girl looked sharply away, as everyone did when Darka caught them staring. Darka was rather impressed that Clementine had lasted this long without saying something. Most children—Seven Sisters, most adults—didn't have such self-control.

"You can ask, you know. It doesn't bother me."

Well, that wasn't strictly true. It did bother Darka, sometimes more often than not, when people asked about her scar. It just depended on how they asked, and who was doing the asking. But the curiosity of children tended not to offend her as much as others' hostile stares.

"What happened?" Clementine asked softly. A lot of people asked softly, as if scared of summoning ill fortune onto themselves by merely speaking of it. "To your face?"

"I was attacked," Darka said, trying to keep her voice light. But she squeezed the key tighter in her hands. "By a monster."

It was all she could say at the moment, and fortunately, Clementine didn't press for details. Darka hadn't pinned her for the type who would.

"Now I've got a question for you," said Darka. "If I'm to do work around his farm, your father should know about it. I don't want to get shot at with fireballs for trespassing. When can I meet him? So we can finalize the . . . details of this arrangement?"

"Father is away on business," said Clementine, her voice suddenly clipped and proper again. "He'll be away for at least a month. And hopefully . . . you'll have satisfied your debt long before then, anyway. Good night." She gave a curt nod and walked *through* the heavy metal portcullis that barred entry to the path leading up to the Castle, the iron bars bending around her like wet noodles.

Darka approached the portcullis after her, but the bars had already snapped back into place by the time she reached it.

Clementine turned on her heel to face Darka once more. “Oh,” she said. “Remember to keep your doors and windows locked at night. And for your own safety . . . please make as little noise as possible.”

CHAPTER 13

MAGICALLY ENHANCED WEATHER PHENOMENA

or

The Value of Lies of Omission

Despite Clementine's fear that her father would immediately sense the presence of light magic around her as if it were a reeking, rotting stench emanating from the rapidly decomposing corpse of her reputation, he said nothing to her that evening. She caught a glimpse of his hunched shoulders as the Brack Butler slipped out the tower door, but that was all. She exchanged the dirty dishes balanced on the Butler's shiny black top for a fresh dinner plate and some clean sheets, but when she made to linger, the Butler flashed its red lights at her and hummed angrily until she retreated. Whatever magic made *it* work appeared to be doing just fine, curse or not.

That night, as Clementine lay down for bed, she could still feel the sunshine thrumming through her fingers. Through her veins. Through her soul. And just this once—for it would only ever be this once—she let its pleasant warmth lull her to sleep.

* * *

"What do you think you're doing?" Clementine demanded. A few yards ahead, a familiar-looking brown-haired figure jumped off the fence surrounding the horse pen.

When Clementine caught up to him, Sebastien held up his hands in surrender, still clutching a half-eaten apple. The nightmare she'd ridden into the woods happily chomped down the rest of it.

Sebastien said quickly, "I was just—"

"You shouldn't feed a nightmare regular apples," Clementine explained. She was surprised Sebastien had even approached the horse voluntarily. She reached into one of the many new pockets she'd installed in her work dress and pulled out a clean handkerchief. She rummaged in another for one of the poison apples she'd picked to feed to the Decimaker. "Give her this instead," she told Sebastien, offering him the fruit in the handkerchief. "Be careful to hold it in the cloth. It's very fresh. The sap will burn right through your fingers."

Sebastien's fingers shook a little as he took the apple (Clementine politely pretended not to notice), but he did take it. The nightmare nuzzled his hand before gobbling down the new treat.

"You can't be too careful," said Clementine. She knew she was starting to babble, but she couldn't seem to help herself. It wasn't every day a boy from the village just showed up outside her stables. "Too much coddling, and they might just grow up into a daymare. Or worse, a regular old pony!"

"Uh-huh," said Sebastien. He gingerly handed the handkerchief back to Clementine.

"What are you doing here, anyway?" Clementine asked. It came out a tad sharper than she meant it to. "Sharp" was sort of the Morcerous default mode of communication.

Much to her surprise, Sebastien blushed. He hopped back onto the fence, facing away from Clementine. They watched the nightmare frolic around the pen, practicing shooting fire from its nostrils.

"I . . . I just wanted to make sure you were all right, I guess," the boy said. "You didn't look so great after that spell . . ."

The sun spell. The *light magic*. Clementine's heart sank.

"Have you told anyone?" she asked—and that time, she was sharp on purpose. "Did anyone else see the—"

"'Blinding sunstorm?'" finished Sebastien. "That's what folks in the village are calling it. Not sure they know it was you—I certainly wasn't going to brag about palling around with . . . um, well, that is to say—"

"Yes, yes, that's as it should be. Go on."

"Oh," said Sebastien, putting his hands on his hips.

Clementine stopped herself from rushing forward to stop him from toppling off the fence rail. Boys seemed to have their own magical powers when it came to posing about in precarious positions.

"Um, well, it terrified everyone, didn't it?" he said. "Great big streams of sunlight shooting around the sky willy-nilly. The shadows swept through the whole village. The schoolmistress thought the Dark Lord was making the sky fall."

Clementine could have sworn Sebastien let out a small snort. He didn't seem to realize he'd said exactly the words that Clementine needed to hear.

The villagers had been—and she could even quote—"terrified."

They thought her father had been the one doing the terrifying.

Perhaps it hadn't been such a disaster not to find those mushrooms, after all.

"Sebastien," Clementine said, "do you think a sunstorm counts as a 'magically enhanced weather phenomenon'?"

* * *

Somehow, it did not surprise Clementine that the next spell the Gricken laid was the one to conjure messenger birds.

It also did not surprise her as much as it might have that she had no trouble with the enchantment at all.

* * *

* * *

Dear Council of Least Esteemed Evil Overlords,

I write this letter on behalf of my father, the Dark Lord Elithor Morcerous, who is far too busy with nefarious plotting at the moment to spare even a minute for bureaucratic niceties. It is my pleasure to inform you that the Dark Lord Morcerous has successfully completed a qualifying Dastardly Deed, in the form of a blinding sunstorm that froze his subjects with the fear that the very sky itself was falling and also reportedly blinded an old man who was already three-quarters blind anyway and happened to look at one of the light beams at just the wrong angle.

Testimonials of this Dastardly Deed are available upon request. I will thank you to make sure that no more friendly reminders of the Morcerous family duties grace the threshold of Castle Brack. As anyone can see—or not, if you happen to be that unfortunate man—such concern was completely unnecessary.

I look forward to communicating further reports of my father's dastardliness.

Insincerely yours,

Lady Clementine Morcerous

* * *

* * *

Clementine knocked, softly this time. She was sure her father could hear it.

"Father, it's me . . . I just wanted to let you know . . . well, I managed to carry off a small Dastardly Deed, and I've . . . I've written the Council to let them know, so . . . they should stop bothering us for a while. You can just focus on getting well again, all right?"

She had not yet told him about her run-in with the Whittle Witch's storm, or about Kat Marie Grice's coven. There was no need to upset him unnecessarily.

* * *

* * *

Was there?

* * *

Darka Wesk-Starzec had been warned not to go wandering around the Dark Lord Elithor Morcerous's silent farm and castle grounds unsupervised. Naturally, during the breaks between curing cheese made of black milk from blood-red cows, pitching hay in the stables for the full-grown nightmares (which always left her jumping at shadows), and dodging the spark-shooting beaks of ungrateful fire-breathing chickens as she fed them live crickets, she did exactly that.

This led to the discovery of a few of the more colorful parts of Castle Brack, including a grand ballroom that appeared to be literally frozen in time—the tables were magnificently set for a feast for over a hundred people, but a thick layer of dust and frost covered everything, from the teacups to the tabletops to the iced-over dance floor. She'd also found a musty dungeon with torture devices so complicated Darka wondered if they came with instruction manuals, along with a few long-forgotten skeletons; a library lit by moonstones and filled with what appeared to be thrones; and most exciting of all, a poisonous snake pit. Darka had found that one through what she assumed was the "guest entrance"—a trapdoor hidden in the middle of an otherwise unremarkable hallway. She barely made it out alive.

And yet, throughout all of her sneaky—and not so sneaky—adventures, she did not see another single living soul. Some doors were locked to her, of course, and resisted all of her attempts to pick their locks. Sometimes she simply walked into invisible barriers—she'd smacked her nose good and proper on a few of these—and could go no farther. But she had expected a bustling castle full of evil knights and ill-used servants (either human or otherwise), court members, and captives. What she got was a creepily quiet, decaying spectacle of former glory, an awful lot of mundane farmwork, and two square meals a day, which Darka strongly suspected were prepared by a twelve-year-old girl. For whatever reason, the Morcerous estate had not been what anyone would call "bustling" for quite some time—fortunately, that meant that Darka could steal basically any supplies she needed without anyone noticing.

When she stumbled upon the hidden garden, Darka immediately knew it was different from the other parts of the castle. Colorful blossoms, silken-looking ivy, and forsythias in full bloom greeted her between the crumbling stone walls. She took a deep breath, savoring the surprisingly crisp smell of the blue roses, but did not linger. Unlike much of the grounds, this garden was well tended to—and not, Darka suspected, by Lord Elithor.

She did not always feel alone. She did not know if it was the creatures that lived on the farm, or the obvious magic in the air, or even the ghosts of long-dead castle inhabitants. But sometimes, even if she knew Clementine was on the other side of the farm, Darka felt . . . watched. Watched by a gaze that was decidedly disapproving.

Darka Wesk-Starzec began to suspect that the Dark Lord Elithor Morcerous was not as far away as she had been led to believe.

CHAPTER 14

SHELTER FROM THE STORM

or

Myths of Time-Traveling Cordelias

Early fall came to the Seven Sisters, and with it came the rain. Darka was not sure if it was the downpour, the thunder, or the pounding on the door that woke her in the middle of the night, but she was awake all the same. She leapt out of bed and grabbed the crossbow she'd stashed under the bed frame, pointing it at the door.

"Darka!" called a small voice on the other side. "It's me. Let me in!" The pounding increased, and Darka had just enough time to set aside the crossbow before lightning flashed, thunder roared, the door flung open of its own accord, and a sopping-wet Clementine flung herself inside—and straight into Darka's arms.

"It's her, it's her. It's got to be her. She's come for me

again," Clementine babbled, tears running down her face and onto Darka's nightshirt.

Darka stiffened for a moment—how long had it been since she'd been hugged by anyone?—but before she knew it, she found herself patting the back of the future Dark Lord of the Seven Sisters.

"Who's 'her'? What are you talking about, Clementine?" Darka put her hands on Clementine's shoulders.

A few seconds later, the black sheep ambled through the door, bleating and attempting to shake the water out of his wool.

"Let's just make it a party then, shall we?" Darka muttered.

"Th-the Whittle Witch," said Clementine. "She's sent another storm. We have to . . ." Clementine's voice trailed off with a wet hiccup.

Darka looked out at the rain lashing the window—and in through the open door—and sighed. She gave Clementine's shoulders an extra squeeze and moved to close the door.

"I tried to tell her it was nothing," whispered the sheep, "but . . ." The sheep shrugged—well, it was as close to a shrug as sheep could manage, Darka thought.

She nodded and nudged the sheep over a bit so he could drip freely on the entry rug instead of the floor. She couldn't see much in the driving rain, but she also didn't feel any of that strange tingling she'd experienced in the forest. The Whittle Witch—or whoever Clementine seemed so afraid of—had likely stayed home that night. Darka closed the door with a firm yank.

"I'm no expert," said Darka, leaning for a better look out the window, "but I think that's just a regular thunderstorm, Clem." Darka winced at her unintended shortening of the girl's name, but Clementine, thankfully, seemed not to notice. Darka yanked at the handles on the windowsills, shutting them as tightly as she could, and frowned at a small leak that had just started dripping from the ceiling. Clementine stood stock-still, soaked and shivering from her run down the mountain in the rain.

"How can you be sure?" Clementine whispered.

"Let's say I've got a sense for these kinds of things," said Darka. "As I'm sure you do, too."

Clementine blushed and looked down at her boots, shifting from one foot to the other. Water oozed out of them.

"If you like," said Darka, choosing her words carefully, "you can stay here and ride out the storm with me. Just to make sure."

Clementine looked up at Darka, eyes wide and unsure. Now that her panic had passed, she looked ready to bolt all the way back to the castle.

"We are the first line of defense, after all," said Darka, gesturing to the stone walls around them.

Slowly, Clementine nodded.

* * *

Darka built up the fire to dry Clementine's clothes—as well as the girl herself—and lent Clementine one of the musty but clean shirts Darka had discovered among the old guard captain's belongings. It was black, with a silly red velvet trim. The shirt fell past the girl's knees.

They curled up on the bed with cups of tea while the sheep scooted as close as he could to the fire without accidentally setting his woolly behind aflame. Darka stared into the flames, wondering at the strange journey that had taken her from farmer's daughter to traveling adventurer, to unicorn huntress—and now, apparently, to dark heiress babysitter. Which made her wonder, not for the first time, that if the Dark Lord really was away on business . . .

"Clementine," said Darka. "Where is your mother?"

It was not the question either of them had been expecting her to ask. But Darka had asked it, and Clementine, even more surprisingly, answered.

"I don't know much," Clementine admitted with a small sigh. "Father doesn't . . . he doesn't talk about her often. I know she told him her name was Cordelia, but Father had his doubts."

"No one knows for sure where the Dark Lords' brides come from," piped up the black sheep.

Darka raised an eyebrow.

"At least, the people don't," he added. "The villagers

say they've never seen any of the Lady Morcerouses . . . Well, I don't mean to be indelicate now . . ."

Clementine shrugged. "It can't be anything worse than what I've heard already."

The sheep cleared his throat. "Well, it seems no one sees the Lady Morcerouses after they give birth to the heir. And Clementine's the first-ever female heir to the title."

Or the first allowed to live, thought Darka grimly, but she did not say so.

"There are *some* female Dark Lords," Clementine said. "Just not very many. And they're still called 'Lords,' anyway." Clementine twisted her lips.

"Some say the brides come from the other side of the mountains—or even from inside the mountain itself," said the sheep, clearly relishing the chance for a bit of unchecked gossip while Clementine seemed in a forgiving mood.

"They all come out of the mountain. They are all sorceresses. They are all time travelers," Clementine said with a sad little smile. She sighed. "I've heard all of the stories. Some of them might even be true." She shrugged and then crinkled up her nose. "Though I don't think Father would *ever* marry a time traveler."

Darka let out a short laugh. The conversation had taken a decidedly surreal turn. "And why not?" she asked. She might as well play along.

"Because it's one of the Three Rules of Evildoing," said

Clementine, as if this were one of the most obvious things in the world. She counted off on her fingers. "Never travel through time. Never try to bring back the dead. And never, ever—" She stopped abruptly and set her tea down on the bedside table with a clank. "I shouldn't be telling you this. Either of you," she said, with a pointed look at the sheep. "It isn't proper. We should all just go to sleep. I apologize for interrupting yours." She nodded to Darka and turned over on her side, yanking the blankets over her face.

The girl had been close to telling her something important; Darka was sure of it. She set her own cup down.

"Clementine," she said, giving the blanket-covered lump next to her a gentle poke.

"I'm *asleep*."

"Clearly. Sit up—your hair's still soaked." Darka got out of the bed and retrieved her comb from the bureau.

"So?"

"So, sleep on it loose and wet like that and you'll wake up with a head full of knots."

Clementine grumbled but sat up, yanking her hair out from under the collar of the oversized shirt. The gold strands from the sunlight spell had since darkened all the way to purplish black. Though even now, the firelight's warm glow seemed to want to stay in Clementine's hair, highlighting it in burnished bronzes and oranges.

"May I?" asked Darka, holding out her hand.

Clementine looked at her warily.

"It's a comb," Darka said. "I can hardly shoot you with it."

"Somehow, I think that if anyone could commit murder with a comb, it would be you," mused the black sheep. Darka shot him a glare, but Clementine merely shrugged and scooted around to sit in front of Darka. That was probably a compliment in her world.

Darka was careful with the comb—it had been years since she'd had hair long enough to braid properly, and even longer since she'd done this for her younger sisters, and she didn't want to irritate Clementine's head wound. But after a few minutes of gentle strokes, she saw Clementine's shoulders relax, and she thought the time might be right to open up their earlier conversation.

"I was wondering about something," Darka said as she tied off the end of the braid. "Clementine?"

But there was no answer. The poor child had fallen asleep sitting up. Darka sighed and tried to shift Clementine over, but the girl merely lay down where she was, settling with her head in Darka's lap. She stirred only when the thunder gave a distant rumble. The storm was leaving.

The black sheep was dozing off, too, in front of the slowly dying fire, but Darka was far from sleep.

"Where is the Dark Lord Elithor?" Darka whispered into the growing darkness.

One of the sheep's yellow eyes flicked open. He shut it again when he saw Darka watching him.

"Where is he *really*?" Darka asked again.

"Away on business," croaked the sheep in his tremulous voice. It was hard to understand his throaty whisper. "As the Lady Clementine said."

Lightning flashed, and Clementine scrunched up her face in her sleep but did not wake. Darka changed tack.

"You seem to know a lot about the local legends," she said conversationally, stroking the ends of Clementine's hair. "Are you from the valley as well?"

But the sheep seemed even less inclined to answer *that* question than the one about Lord Elithor, and he shifted farther into the shadows. And that, coupled with all of the strange things that had happened on this strange evening, made Darka even more curious than before.

* * *

That night, Clementine dreamed of the unicorn.

She watched it from across the mountain, just as she had the night Stan Glen came to call. But this time, they were not alone.

A tall figure dressed in black stood on a ledge high on the Fourth Sister, arms extended. The wind whipped, and dark clouds swirled overhead. The white glow of the unicorn looked even brighter in comparison. Rain lashed the mountain, but the figure in black stayed dry, as if some invisible force were keeping the very sky at bay.

"YOU CANNOT ESCAPE," the figure roared. Its face was a blur in the rain. One moment it was a dark-haired man with piercing eyes and a thick black beard. Then, it was Lord Elithor, scowling, his face whole and human. The next moment, it was Darka Wesk-Starzec. Then another sandy-haired man Clementine didn't know, who grinned against the wind as if he were having the time of his life. And finally, it was Clementine herself.

"No!" the real Clementine cried. She did not know why, but she knew she must stop the sorcerer on the ledge, no matter whose face the sorcerer wore. She turned in desperation to the unicorn and shouted over the wind, "Run! You must run!"

But the unicorn could not run—it was trapped, somehow, by the force of the sorcerer's spell. And though she was half a mountain away, Clementine could feel its panicked breathing, the sweat rolling down its white coat. She could practically *see* its heart thundering in its powerful chest, pounding with such force it must surely be about to break through muscle and skin in its fearful quest to escape the fate that awaited it.

And Clementine knew, just as the figure on the mountain knew, that the world had been wrong about unicorns. The key to their magnificent power was not their horns.

It was their hearts.

CHAPTER 15

THE NEW NORMAL

or

The Intellectual Property Disputes of Evil Overlords, Explained

Clementine Morcerous awoke the next morning to discover that other than a few murky dreams she could barely remember, she had slept soundly for the first time in weeks. Sunlight streamed into the gatehouse from the high windows and the door, which had been left wide-open—presumably to dry up the remaining water on the floor from the night before. A warm breeze wafted in. Clementine stretched, yawning, and realized how warm she was already. She shucked aside the quilt she'd been lying under. She must have slept in late, if the heat of the day had already arrived. She knew she should feel panicked at getting such a late start on her chores—the demonic cows would be beyond testy—but it was hard for anything to pierce her feeling of contentment.

Darka was gone, but a note had been left on the small kitchen table, along with a glass of milk, a nonpoisonous apple, and a roll with a generous slice of cheese.

Thought you could use the sleep, the note read. *I'll take care of the cows. —D*

Clementine was busy eating her breakfast when Darka returned. Darka paused in the doorway, leaning against the frame.

Clementine daintily wiped her lips with her napkin. "Thank you for the breakfast," she said, "and for . . . letting me stay. When I was frightened." It all seemed terribly foolish now, of course. But the thunder had been so loud and the wind so strong it was like being right back in the woods the day the Whittle Witch's storm had attacked. Clementine hadn't known where else to go.

"It's your house," said Darka gruffly, stepping inside and brushing dust off her trousers. She rinsed her hands in a bucket and dropped down to the table for her own breakfast. She cut herself a slice of cheese with a knife drawn from her belt, but then proceeded to tear the cheese—and her roll—into several smaller, bite-sized pieces. Darka glanced at Clementine, who quickly realized she was staring, and dropped her gaze.

"Does that . . . make it easier to eat?" Clementine

asked. She figured that if she was going to stare anyway, she might as well just ask.

Darka paused only briefly, nodded, and popped the piece of bread into her mouth. After they had both eaten, she filled Clementine in on the chores she'd completed that morning, as well as the slight damage the farm had sustained from the storm. (The stable roofs had lost a few shingles, and what remained of the chicken fence had fallen over completely.)

Despite the prospect of even more work, Clementine's to-do list suddenly seemed far more manageable, with an extra set of hands around. It wouldn't solve everything—only a cure for her father would do that—but it was certainly a help.

Clementine started. Her father! She'd forgotten to check on him and the Brack Butler this morning, as she usually did.

"I'm sorry," said Clementine, "I just remembered . . . something. I've got to go. We'll discuss the rest of the repairs later."

She folded her napkin and hurried for the door. She paused only for the briefest of moments to look up at the castle. It loomed dark and foreboding, a stark contrast with the clear blue sky behind and the warm breeze dancing through the valley. For the first time, the thought of returning there offered Clementine little comfort.

"You know," called Darka from inside the gatehouse. Clementine turned around to see her standing in the doorway once more. "You could stay here in the guards' quarters for a bit, if you like. Much easier to keep an eye on things around the farm from down here, in case that witch of yours really does attack." Darka shrugged. "Unless you're really enjoying the trudge halfway up the mountain ten times a day."

Darka had a point. Of course, she'd still have to return to the castle to help the Butler and her father, but perhaps . . . perhaps it wasn't such a bad idea. And if Clementine stayed with Darka, she could keep an eye on the traveler, too, and keep the woman's attention away from the castle while her father continued his search for a cure.

"I'll think about it," said Clementine.

By that afternoon, she had returned with her toiletries, a few changes of clothes, the Gricken (which had insisted on following her), and the black sheep in tow.

* * *

Sebastien Frawley took the longest, most rambling route he could through the Seven Sisters Valley on his way to Castle Brack. Perhaps part of him hoped that more time would give him more chances to change his mind and turn around, but instead, he'd gotten distracted by the many interesting aspects of the mountains that he'd never dared explore before, from the babbling brooks rolling down the Fifth Sister to the fields upon fields of wildflowers that had sprung up at the foot of the mountains. He could almost forget that his ultimate destination was a cursed castle home to the daughter of an Evil Overlord.

It was only right that Sebastien should check on Clementine after that thunderstorm, after all. All of that wind and thunder had reminded him of their terrible time in the woods, the trees snatching and grabbing at them. While last night's storm seemed normal enough, even the memory had certainly made him hide under his covers! And if Sebastien, a young man destined to be a brave knight, had been scared, then Clementine must have been terrified. He was only doing what any chivalrous knight would do for a lady.

He didn't know when exactly he'd started thinking of Clementine as a lady, but it seemed rather late to change his mind, now that he'd made the distinction.

Wrapped up in his thoughts, Sebastien failed to notice the sword sticking up out of the ground until he'd tripped over it, stubbing his toe good and proper. He hopped around, clutching his foot, until he realized that hopping wasn't a very good idea, either—the damp, sandy ground was littered with swords.

"What the . . ." Sebastien said.

He spotted the rippling and winking of water in the sunlight up ahead and realized he was approaching a lake of some sort, though he hadn't even known there was one here. A strange sound emanated from the water as he approached, like someone gargling, or wailing, or possibly both.

"AAAAAAAAAAHHHHHHHH."

The wailing sound exploded out of the center of the lake, along with a fountain spout of water at least a dozen feet high—and those weren't the only things flying through the air. A sword flew out of the lake and straight for Sebastien's head. He threw up his arms to protect his face and, by some miracle, caught the sword by the handle.

Sebastien stared at the gleaming blade and bejeweled pommel, breathing hard, and though he knew he should be quite alarmed that someone had just thrown a sword at him, he just couldn't help his very first thought, which was, *Wow. Cool.*

Sebastien hefted the sword—it was actually pretty heavy—and advanced cautiously toward the water. The form of a woman emerged—the most beautiful woman Sebastien had ever seen, with dark green hair that flowed to her knees, and eyes as pale blue as ice crystals.

"What brave traveler comes this way?" the woman asked, her voice just as thunderous as when she had been singing, though quite a deal more pleasant-sounding. "Who dares to seek what the future may bring? What hero of ages will wield this mighty sword?"

Sebastien edged forward.

"Um, do you mean this one?" Sebastien asked, holding up the sword he had caught. He couldn't be sure. There were a lot of other available options.

The woman gasped and turned to Sebastien as if she had just noticed he was standing there.

"Oh, goodness!" she said, suddenly fretting and smoothing her hair. "I wasn't expecting anyone to—well, of course I was expecting someone, for *I see all*, but you know, it's been a while, and . . ." Her eyes turned to the sword in his hand. "Boy, where did you get that sword?"

Though a wrong answer seemed likely to end with Sebastien at the bottom of the lake, judging by the woman's expression, he thought it best to tell the truth.

"Um, I caught it?" He cringed at the frightened crack in his voice.

But this lady of the lake didn't seem to mind. In fact, she looked positively ecstatic.

"You caught it?" she asked. "You really caught one?" At Sebastien's nod, she shrieked and clapped her hands with excitement. Spouts of water began shooting out in impossibly high arcs above lake—joined, even more impossibly, by multiple rainbows crisscrossing one another.

"You caught one, you caught one!" exclaimed the woman. "A hero of ages, a brave knight on a quest, finally come to me at last!"

Sebastien rather liked the sound of being called a hero of ages, but he was also a bit distracted by the shooting rainbows. If the Dark Lord Elithor saw a hint of anything so charming as a rainbow over his mountain range, he'd likely curse them all to months of darkness as punishment. Sebastien's sword would be of no use at all against a wrathful Dark Lord.

"It's very exciting," Sebastien said. "But do you think you could be just a little quieter?"

The Lady of the Lake did not seem to hear him and was now making the fish and various other grumpy-looking inhabitants of the lake join her in a circle dance as she sang a painfully out-of-tune ballad, occasionally interrupting herself to exclaim once again about Sebastien's future great feats.

Somehow, this was not how he imagined being given his first quest. To begin with, he'd thought it might entail learning what his quest even was.

Sebastien's hopes of going unnoticed in the Dark Lord's lands were dashed when he saw a flying shape appear in the distance, barreling around the edge of the mountain. Sebastien's heart leapt up into his throat as vigorously as the jumping rainbows around him, until the figure grew close enough for him to realize it was not a leathery-winged bird of some sort come to peck out his eyes, but Clementine. The wind whipped her hair out behind her in a bright orange stream, looking like a flame against her black dress. She circled the lake a few times on her broomstick, then spotted Sebastien. From his spot on the ground, he thought he could feel her scowl, and he cringed.

She touched down gracefully at the lake's edge, pausing to nudge a beached baby kraken back into the water with the end of the broomstick.

"Would you care to explain yourself?" she asked acidly, but Sebastien noticed with no small amount of relief that she did not appear to be addressing him. The Lady of the Lake, however, seemed a bit occupied with muttering to herself about coming up with a good prophecy for her "new protégé." Sebastien gulped.

"She threw a sword at me," he confessed to Clementine, wondering what sort of punishment would be in store for someone caught trying to take a magical sword from the Dark Lord's own lands.

But Clementine merely squinted at the woman in the water and said, "Oh, is that it?"

Sebastien nodded.

"Don't worry," said Clementine. "The Lady of the Lake throws swords at everyone."

Clementine's utter lack of interest disappointed Sebastien. Surely, he must be destined for *something* significant, what with the way the Lady of the Lake was carrying on.

"I did catch it," he said hopefully.

Clementine looked at him as if she didn't quite believe it, but she nodded appraisingly all the same. "Huh," she said. "I think it's been a long time since that's happened. That might explain the rainbows."

"So, I'm *not* going to get a great quest today?" He just wanted to be absolutely clear.

The Lady of the Lake floated right up to the edge of the lake, beaming, but then frowned a little when she finally set eyes on Sebastien.

"Ooh, you're a little young, aren't you?" she asked, crossing her arms and tapping her chin with her finger. "A bit on the short and scrawny side, too, but there's time, there's time!" she assured him. "Rome wasn't built in twenty minutes, as they say."

Sebastien sighed. He didn't know what Rome was, but he did understand the lady's tone of disappointment.

"Keep your skin up. There's a good lad," said the Lady.

"Chin," corrected Clementine quickly. "She means 'chin.'"

"Yes, yes, that," said the Lady. "Come back when you're done cooking!" And with that, she dove back into the water.

The lake was motionless mere moments later, the rainbows faded into the warm air and blue sky.

"I'm not sure what to make of that one," admitted Clementine, still watching the lake with her hand on her hip.

Sebastien let out a deep breath and sighed, swinging his sword along the ground.

"I should have known," he said, shaking his head. The sword clanged off the side of another blade, nearly sending Sebastien off-balance. Clementine regarded him with a delicately raised ginger eyebrow.

Sebastien righted himself and turned away from her, scowling. He wasn't destined for greatness, *and* he'd looked like a fool in front Clementine, as well. This visit had been a total mistake.

"It was silly to think I'd ever . . . that anyone would let someone like me be . . ."

"Be what?" Clementine asked.

"A . . . a knight," Sebastien said defiantly. It was the first time he'd ever admitted his dream to anyone. There didn't seem to be much point in hiding it, since now he knew it to be a silly idea.

He didn't wait for Clementine to answer, and instead

started picking his way through the swords, using his own as a walking stick. He stopped when he remembered that he would have about as much use for a sword as the eels in the lake, and turned around to toss it back in, when Clementine called out to him.

"Wait!" she said.

He paused midthrow.

"The villagers might not have use for a knight," she said, "but . . . I might."

"What?"

Clementine dug her heels into the damp shoreline, shifting from foot to foot.

"As the heir to the Dark Lordship and a lady of House Morcerous, I can name you a Brack Knight."

"A Black Knight?" Sebastien asked.

"No, a *Brack* Knight," corrected Clementine. Sebastien detected the hint of exasperation in her voice. "For Castle Brack. Some Dark Lord in the west claimed the *Black* Knight title for his men ages ago. He's been hoarding it quite selfishly for years. It's caused no end of creative strife for the rest of us . . . but, well, the suits are still black, if that was a big selling point."

She said this all so very quickly that Sebastien could barely keep track.

"Really?" Sebastien asked. "I could . . . be a knight?"

"A Brack Knight."

"'Brack' doesn't really sound all that different, does it?" Sebastien mused.

"I've always thought so." Clementine shrugged. "So . . ." She held out her hand, and Sebastien almost reached out with his own before he realized it was the sword she wanted. He held it out to her hilt first, hoping his ears weren't blushing, and knelt before her.

"Ahem." Clementine cleared her throat, struggling to lift the sword over his head. He kept very, very still, hoping that Brack Knighthood did not entail, say, being a headless huntsman. "I, Lady Clementine Morcerous of House Morcerous, future Dark Lord of the Seven Sisters Mountains, dub thee Sir Sebastien . . ."

"Erm, Frawley."

"You haven't a middle name or anything?"

"Not one I want to be reminded of," said Sebastien. "Can we get on with it?"

Clementine huffed but went on. "Sir Sebastien Frawley of Castle Brack, and entrust to you the sacred rights, privileges, and responsibilities of the Order of the Brack Knights."

She did not elaborate as to what these rights and responsibilities might be, but Sebastien supposed that might ruin the important and symbolic mood. With some difficulty, she touched the sword to one of his shoulders, and then the other, and finally backed up a few steps to touch the tip to his chest. The metal brushed like a dangerous kiss across his shirt.

"Now please take this," she said, her wrists shaking. "It's very heavy."

Sebastien happily obliged.

"My lady," he said with a low bow, planting the sword at his side. "What will my first quest be in your service?" It was a little formal, but he felt he should speak the part from now on.

"Well . . ." said Clementine, shaking out her hands from the effort of holding the sword. "Is there any chance you know how to build a chicken fence?"

CHAPTER 16

KNIGHTS IN SHINING ARMOR

or

Cheerfully Trampling over Hundreds of Years of Dark Lord Tradition

Much to Clementine's surprise, Sebastien Frawley—*Sir* Sebastien Frawley now—did know how to build a chicken fence. And so, apparently, did about half a dozen other boys from the village, who all appeared with him at the front door of Castle Brack, panting slightly from their trek up the mountainside. They looked at the castle grounds and at each other with wide eyes, like cats who could not quite believe how high they'd climbed in a particular tree and had just realized they did not know how to get down.

Sebastien shrugged at Clementine, his hands shoved in his pockets.

"Er, sorry," he said. "But, it looked like you could use a few extra hands, and—"

"And we want to be knights, too!" piped up one of the boys, a curly-headed, dirty-faced creature Clementine thought she recognized as Curly Cab. A chorus of grunts of agreement followed.

Clementine did not allow herself the completely justified moment of horror that such a declaration would have normally warranted. (Commoners strolling through the gates of Castle Brack? Commoners becoming *knights*?) Here she was, surrounded by a peasant mob of the like her family had threatened and intimidated and cursed for hundreds of years, and they were . . . clamoring to pledge themselves to her service for life?

Clementine doubted they understood it to be that much of a commitment. But they were fairly excited about the swords.

Sebastien was right. She *did* need the help. The formerly silent farm was now teeming with noise—chickens clucking, nightmares and horses neighing, chimaera heads on the wall sneezing at the dust collecting on their noses. The snakes in the snake pit had even started hissing; they were surprisingly loud, all bunched together like that, which Clementine thought sort of ruined the "surprise" element of said trap. The poison apples would need to be harvested soon, carefully picked by hand, as any that fell to the ground would be contaminated and their absolute perfection lost. It was a lot of work for her and Darka alone.

And so Brack Knights they became. The chicken fence was completed in an afternoon with only two singed buttocks from the fire-breathing chickens, which Clementine thought qualified as a success. They mucked out the stables, replaced the shingles that had blown off the roof, and fixed the leaks in the gatehouse ceiling. They pitched hay and picked hellebore and caught mice to feed to the snakes. How they had the energy to do this after their schoolwork and their work on their own farms was a mystery to Clementine, but it appeared that the allure of knighthood was enough to lift any of their spirits.

At least, it was at first. But it did not take long for the village boys to figure out that the tasks their Lady had set them to were not very much like quests at all, and an awful lot like chores.

"When do we get to do *real* knightly things?" asked Gregor one afternoon as the boys and Clementine weeded the kitchen garden. He was a thin-faced boy with wispy blond hair, who Clementine remembered had been one of the first to heckle Darka in the village. (Darka tended to keep herself scarce when the boys were around. Clementine didn't really blame her.)

Clementine did as any Dark Lady of standing would do, and simply ignored him. Unfortunately, he did not seem to take the hint.

"Helloooooo," he said to Clementine, sitting on his heels and wiping his brow with the back of his wrist. "I said, when are we going to do *real* knightly things?"

"I'm sure I don't know what you mean." Clementine continued her own fight with a particularly strong dandelion. "It is your duty as a knight to protect and preserve the House Morcerous. What better way to support your lord than by growing the very food that sustains him?"

This was not the answer that wispy-haired, whiny Gregor wanted.

"That's *servant* stuff," said Gregor. Some of the other boys nodded, pausing in their work. "I mean *real* knightly things. Hunting dragons, saving *you* from dragons, going to war with, uh . . ."

"Dragons?" Clementine suggested. Gregor scowled.

"Or . . . tracking lost relics!" a redheaded boy said, holding up his spade.

"Or jousting!" called another.

"Feasting!"

"Hunting!"

"I expect we'll have to do the hunting before the feasting," Sebastien observed.

"Now, really—" said Clementine, but the boys cut

her off with their protests that they absolutely *would not* lift one more finger at farmwork. And suddenly, they were all on their feet, garden implements in hand—even the youngest, Little Ian, who couldn't have been more than seven—and despite a few half-hearted attempts by Sebastien to quiet them, a chant of "We want a quest! We want a quest!" soon rose into the air. Feet stomped along to the rhythm, carelessly crushing perfectly good vegetables under their dirty soles.

"Please," Clementine begged with a fleeting look toward her father's tower. "I must ask you to be quiet, or I shall—"

"We want a quest! We want a quest!"

"Come on, lads," said Sebastien. "Let's all just—"

"We want a quest! We want a quest!"

Clementine scooted backward, tripping over the hem of her dress, as Roderick, the nearest boy, took a step toward her. This was exactly the sort of mob violence her father had warned her about, and she hadn't listened, and now she was going to be murdered by angry peasants in her own vegetable patch.

"We want a quest! We want a quest!"

"What in Seven Sisters is going on here?"

Darka stepped into the garden. She had not yelled, had not threatened, had barely raised her voice—and yet absolute silence fell in her wake. That sort of talent,

Clementine thought ruefully, was not something that could be taught, no matter how many times one practiced in front of the mirror.

Gregor the Whiny did not seem as inclined to speak up now that a purported witch was in their midst.

"Lady Clementine," said Darka with a short bow. Clementine nearly laughed—she didn't think Darka had ever bothered to call her by her title, and it sounded a bit silly now. "Are these schoolboys causing you trouble?"

"We're not just *schoolboys*," said Roderick indignantly. He puffed up his chest. "We're *knights*."

"And . . . some of us did think there might be more adventuring involved," explained Sebastien with a grimace.

"Oh," said Darka, striding among the rows of plants. "I see." Most of the boys tried (and failed) to keep from flinching as she passed. Curly Cab's eyes darted to her scar so often he looked as if he were having a fit.

"And you have been knights for . . . how long, exactly?"

A few of them shifted uncomfortably.

"About three days, ma'am," Sebastien finally said.

"Ah," said Darka. "And you think you should be doing more . . . what did you say, 'knightly things,' is that right? Fighting battles and rescuing princesses from towers?"

A few nods.

"Have any of you ever used a sword?" asked Darka, stopping to look each of the boys in the eye. More silence. "A bow, then?" Darka held up her own. Three hands tentatively went up, but no one volunteered any more than that. "Trained in hand-to-hand combat? Military strategy?"

She really is very good, thought Clementine. The knights were practically squirming under Darka's skeptical stare.

"I didn't think so," Darka said, crossing her arms as she came to stand next to Clementine. "If you lot want to be 'real' knights, as you say"—she looked pointedly at Gregor, who gulped—"then you'll have to prove you're up to the task. First, you'll have to train."

"Er, train with who?" Sebastien asked. The boys looked around as if they expected big, hairy warriors to sprout up right out of the ground like cabbages. Unfortunately, that was a trick even the Dark Lord Elithor had not yet mastered.

"With me," said Darka Wesk-Starzec. "This castle's captain of the guard."

For the first time, the silence that followed after Darka spoke was punctuated with a handful of snickers. Clementine, for one, wished that Darka had thought to discuss this change in job description with her, but she was not about to argue with her now and look the fool.

“Is there something funny I should be aware of?” Clementine demanded, which made the boys laugh even more.

“It’s just, well . . .” said Sebastien.

“She’s a girl!” blurted Curly Cab.

“And a witch,” muttered Roderick.

Sebastien cuffed Curly Cab, who was closest, around the head. Clementine wanted to point out that young as she was, Darka Wesk-Starzec was most definitely a *woman*, and not a *girl*, but another boy had already piped up.

“Curly’s right,” said Gregor the Whiny, who seemed to have regained some of his courage. “*You* can’t train knights. How are we supposed to learn to fight from a *girl*?”

Darka twisted her mouth in a way that made even Clementine nervous.

“Lady Clementine,” Darka said, looking straight ahead, “do you happen to have any of those charming letters of yours on you?”

Clementine stared at Darka blankly. *Charming letters?* And then Darka’s meaning hit her: the messenger birds. Darka wanted Clementine to conjure one of the flying letters.

Fortunately, Clementine had a piece of parchment on her already, though it was only a list of items she’d been meaning to pick up in the village. She rummaged through her pockets and smoothed out the wrinkled list, murmuring the words that would lift the ink from the pages. It was harder, with the letter not being fresh, but she managed.

The boys gasped as a gray-eyed blackbird formed before them. It shrieked, and a few jumped back.

"Thank you," said Darka. "Now just a moment, please." Darka jumped over the rows of the garden and ran until she was over a hundred yards away—leaving Clementine to the mercy of the boys' growing mutterings.

"Go ahead, my lady!" called Darka.

Clementine leaned in toward the bird she had created, which was perched lightly on her forearm, and whispered, "Darka Wesk-Starzec."

The messenger bird launched itself from Clementine's forearm, leaving little pinpricks in her skin, but Clementine barely noticed. She watched the bird fly straight for Darka, who drew her bow and aimed it . . . straight up in the air?

"What is she *doing*?" Clementine muttered to herself, but Darka had already loosed the first arrow. The boys watched it sail high overhead until finally, it could do nothing but drop—but Clementine's eyes were on Darka. Quicker than Clementine could imagine, Darka had fired a second arrow, this time straight into the bird's path.

Both arrows hit the messenger bird at the exact same time. It exploded in a shower of ink, utterly obliterated.

"Seven Sisters," breathed Sebastien.

"She *is* a witch!" exclaimed Roderick, but it sounded strangely like a compliment. The boys turned back to face Darka and Clementine, eyes wide.

There was the look of fearful respect that Clementine liked to see.

By the time Darka sauntered back to the garden, the messenger bird had reformed and perched on Darka's shoulder; the birds were, in the end, impervious to such mundane intervention, but that didn't seem to dampen the boys' shock.

"Are there any further questions?" asked Darka, shouldering her bow.

"Yeah," said Curly Cab. "How long before we get to do *that*?"

* * *

And so Darka Wesk-Starzec, the new captain of the guard of Castle Brack, came to a deal with her raw recruits. For every task they completed on the farm for Clementine, they received a training session with her in return. The knights practiced shooting at targets and hacking at scarecrows who had finally lost the last of their magic with the swords they had all chosen with the help of the Lady of the Lake. (Fortunately, the Lady listened to Clementine's stern warning not to actually *throw* any more swords at the boys, as not all of them were as coordinated as Sebastien.)

The knights often practiced in a courtyard near Clementine's garden, as far from her father's tower as possible. Clementine would peek around her garden wall and watch Darka drilling them on balance, endurance, and proper stance. Far from minding the disturbance to her work, she found she rather liked the sound of Darka's voice and the boys' shuffling feet and the thudding blows and grunts of exertion. For the first time Clementine could remember, Castle Brack felt like more than a dusty, silent relic of days gone by. It felt . . . alive.

But even as the Brack Knights brought life to one part of the castle, Clementine knew that in another, a different life was fading fast.

She was no closer to finding a cure than she had been since her father had shut himself in his laboratory. And considering that Lord Elithor no longer let Clementine see him as she helped the Brack Butler with his meals . . . she didn't think he was any closer, either. She continued to scour the library for references to the Whittle Witch, but other than an introduction to arbomancy, she found little that would help her. The gaps in the shelves told her that Lord Elithor must have taken all the texts on witches, woodworking, and curses—and barricaded them, along with himself, in the tower.

There seemed to be so little she could do, even as she did . . . well, everything. She woke up at dawn with Darka and worked until dusk just to keep the farm afloat, rushing to carve out enough time to keep an eye on the training knights and squint at the reams of complicated reports spewing from the Decimaker. In the evenings, she practiced her spellwork with the Gricken until she was so tired that she fell over, accidentally set something on fire, was forcefully scolded by Darka, or some combination of all three.

She and Darka would sit down to a simple supper of fried fish from the lake, or sausages from her father's stores, and look up at the mountains together. And with each passing day, Clementine began to wonder . . . was this what other people did? Did they always get up in the morning and have breakfast with their families without fear that they might be poisoned by some rival for power? Did they grow food without worrying their plants might eat *them* instead? Did they sometimes laugh when they did their chores together, and sometimes grouch at one another, and more often than not, a little bit of both? When they gathered in front of the fire at the end of a long day, did they, too, have someone to brush and braid their hair and tuck them into bed?

Clementine had not ventured out beyond the estate since the Whittle Witch's storm. She told herself that she was merely abiding by her promise to her father not to seek out the Whittle Witch, that she would only put both of their lives in jeopardy by putting herself in harm's way. And she had plenty of time before the Council of Evil Overlords would expect another Dastardly Deed. It was easy—easier than she would have ever hoped—to lose herself in the whirlwind of her days, in the physical hardship of the work itself, or the companionable silence of meals shared with Darka, or the rambunctious antics of the Brack Knights. It was easy to forget that just outside her father's wards was someone waiting for the right moment to snatch it all away.

But in those rare moments when Clementine did find herself alone, she couldn't escape the real reason she didn't fly her broomstick straight into the forest and scour the land until she found the Whittle Witch's hiding place. She was afraid—and not just of what would happen if she failed. She was afraid of what might happen if she succeeded. She was afraid of what would happen to her life as it was now, crushingly exhausting as it was, because for the first time, it was a life she had built for herself—a tiny, delicate rose she had somehow coaxed into growing out of the darkness.

A small, traitorous part of her heart—that same part that made her grow flowers in her secret garden, and dwelled a little too much on a certain Sebastien Frawley's freckles, and delighted in the giggles that bubbled up inside her when the black sheep tried to "help" her feed the chickens and got a singed backside for his trouble—wished that somehow, she *could* break the Second Rule of Evildoing and travel through time, if only to freeze herself in this moment forever. No Dastardly Deeds to worry about completing (at least not for a while). No constant glowering and disappointment and unpredictable rages, or equally unpredictable cold silences from her father. No lessons in how to kidnap princesses for ransom, or conjure a plague of locusts, or how to look down her nose with just the right amount of disdain.

She would think back, sometimes, to her conversation with Kat Marie Grice. The mere suggestion that Clementine—future Dark Lord Clementine Morcerous!—could ever be a Good Witch was preposterous. Because, spewing sunbeams or not, good people did not think the sharp, wicked thoughts that flitted across Clementine's mind.

Good people did not feel relieved at the thought that their fathers might die.

And as Clementine stood in the main hall of Castle Brack, surveying the still, silent jet-black suits of armor that lined the walls on either side of her, she could not help but feel judged by their empty, unseeing helms. She could not help but feel that they knew her secret, just as they knew about the village boys running around their castle, playing at being knights. How could the likes of Sebastien and Curly Cab and Gregor the Whiny ever fill these suits of armor? How could they ever compare to the long-dead Brack Knights, servants of the earliest Dark Lords, who had conquered the Seven Sisters with sword and fire and dark magic? How could she, Clementine, ever live up to the legacy of Dark Lords past?

The empty suits looked decidedly skeptical.

But when Darka called for help carrying some rusty maces up from the dungeon, Clementine went. And for a while, at least, she left the thoughts of her disapproving ancestors behind.

CHAPTER 17

THE MONSTER IN THE TOWER

or

How to Lose Every Friend You've Ever Made in Three Minutes

"MAN YOUR POSTS," shouted Sebastien, raising his sword in the air. "WE'RE BEING ATTACKED!"

Darka gingerly took the flat of his blade in two fingers and pointed it toward the ground. "You're going to take someone's eye out," she said. "Your knights can hear you just fine."

Sebastien looked like he was about to protest that it was more fun to do things his way, but by then, the "invaders" had breached the gatehouse at the foot of the mountain, and he was preoccupied with other duties.

From her perch up high on the battlements facing the courtyard, Clementine suppressed a giggle at

Sebastien's enthusiasm, then returned her own attention to the fight at hand. It had been Darka's idea to stage a mock defense of Castle Brack, and in the absence of real adversaries (at least for the moment), it was Clementine's job to supply the invaders. She'd spent much of the day before practicing a spell for animating the scarecrows that the Gricken had laid for her, to create the attacking army. The Brack Knights had had a grand old time tying together old tools and rusted weapons and bits of scrap wood to make the dummies, and Clementine had added her own finishing touches by furnishing a few of the opposing "generals" with chimaera heads she'd swiped from the castle walls.

"You're only collecting dust sitting up here, anyway," she told one of the heads, a scaly combination of lion and snake, when it scowled at her for moving it from its mount. "It's time to live a little!"

It tried to bite her hand off.

"Well, I supposed you're a bit past that stage," she'd admitted.

Now, the cobbled-together creations really did look intimidating as they lurched toward the second gate, propelled by Clementine's spell. She hoped her brave knights wouldn't lose their nerve—and that she wouldn't lose hers. Not only did she have to animate the fake invaders, but she also had to keep an extensive soundproofing spell running. She could not risk her father hearing the racket their practice was making.

"Nock, draw, loose!" cried Sebastien, and a hail of arrows rained down on the dummies. Clementine was pleased to note that a few of them even hit their targets.

Two other boys ran to the gatehouse's murder holes. They perched over the openings carved into the stone and prepared to dump vats of boiling oil onto the heads of any stragglers below who made it past the archers and attempted to take the gate. (It wasn't really boiling oil, because that would have been terribly unsafe, but plain well water. Clementine, however, would stop any scarecrows she saw struck by it, so the end result was the same.)

A few of the invaders, including the scaly-headed general, made it past the murder holes unscathed. They pushed through the giant wooden doors far too easily—had one of the boys left the blasted things *unlocked*?—and came galumphing into the inner courtyard, scythe hands waving about and generally looking menacing. (Clementine was quite proud of their motor skills, if she did say so herself.) At this, Sebastien and his best knights left the gatehouse battlements and came charging down the stone steps, swords and spears in hand. It gave Clementine quite a thrill to see them all rushing to defend her castle like that, even if it was only pretend, and even if she was a little bit distracted by the fear that the boys might poke one another with the spears.

She rushed to the edge of the wall as the knights let out their battle cries.

"FOR YOUR LADY!" Sebastien cried at the head of the formation, sword glinting in the sunlight.

"Go! Go get them!" Clementine shouted, pumping her fist in the air. There was a sudden crackling sound, and the dummies stumbled; Clementine refocused on keeping them marching along.

Darka looked up at her with a smirk, which left Clementine fighting a smile of her own. She did not think the sacking of one's castle was supposed to be quite this much fun.

The dummies had not been spelled to fight back—merely to advance on the castle—and so they did not put up much resistance against the knights' defense. Still, the boys rushed at them with gusto, and the sounds of swords clashing filled the courtyard.

"Watch your left flank!" Darka shouted to the boys as they fought. "Widen your stance!"

Gregor and the few boys who remained on the walls heckled the invaders from above, pelting them with strangling vine clippings.

"Isn't it over yet?" moaned the black sheep from next to Clementine. He had plastered himself against the wall and refused to look over the side. "You know what Vivienne would say: it's all fun and games until someone loses—"

Ploink. The chimaera heads snarled as the strangling vines wound themselves in and around their skulls, popping out their glass eyes.

"You were saying?" Clementine said to the sheep, though she cringed a little at the sight. Still, she could always put the heads back together again.

The sounds of the battle began to die down as the last of the dummies succumbed to the knights. A great cheer went up as Sebastien lopped off the head of the scaly chimaera, sending Clementine into fits of giggles—of all the heads least likely to approve of being killed twice!—and only the twitching remains of the artificial invaders remained.

"Sebastien! Sebastien!" chanted the boys, still riled up from their fight.

"Yes, yes, you were all amazing," said Darka with a bit of a grumble. "Except for the small error of *leaving the door unlocked.*" But no one paid her much heed.

Clementine rushed down the stairs two at a time to join the knights, the black sheep at her heels. The boys continued their cheering, and Roderick and Sebastien hauled one of the heads over and presented it at Clementine's feet with a bow.

"For you, my lady," Sebastien said, and though she

knew it was not quite ladylike to be so pleased by being presented with a severed head, she did feel a bit of a thrill.

"*Yuck*," said the black sheep.

"You fought very bravely, my Brack Knights," Clementine said, trying to be as serious and solemn as she really would be on such an occasion, but the effect was rather ruined when Little Ian skipped over to her, grabbed her hand, and insisted on leading her in a victory dance around the courtyard.

"Oh, this really isn't the time," Clementine said, breathless with laughter, as Little Ian spun her around, and the rest of the boys joined in, jumping and kicking aside the spare parts of the dummies. "We've still so much work to do!" she protested, but her heart wasn't really in it.

It wasn't until the sound of thunder boomed across the sky that any of them noticed something was amiss.

"WHAT. IS. THIS. NOISE."

Clementine froze at once, her heart leaping into her throat. She thought at first it was the Whittle Witch, come to attack with another storm, as Clementine had feared since that day in the woods. But though the sky had darkened, it was a darkness she recognized all too well; the thunder had not really been thunder at all, but the sound of every door in the castle being opened and slammed at once. The very walls seemed to shake in the aftermath. The remains of the dummies went terribly still, all thought of keeping the spell going swept from Clementine's mind. The crackling she'd heard earlier hadn't been her scarecrow spell stuttering. It had been her soundproofing spell *breaking.*

And standing above them on the battlements, hardly recognizable even to Clementine, was her father.

"WHAT IS THE MEANING OF THIS?" Lord Elithor screamed, his voice high and rasping. Even the effort of standing seemed to be difficult for him, and it was easy to see why. He was little more than a walking wooden skeleton. Normally over six feet tall, he was now hardly taller than Clementine—everything about him had shrunk to doll-sized proportions. He could barely take a step without tripping on the oversized black robes that were nearly falling off his tiny, pointed shoulders. His hair was gone, replaced by patchy dark paint. His eyes were filmy and huge in the emaciated triangle that was his face.

A chorus of gasps arose from the children as they registered Lord Elithor's arrival.

"Did we miss one?" Little Ian whispered, pointing to the discarded dummies strewn about the courtyard.

Roderick shushed him with a hand over his mouth and pulled him close.

Her father had heard everything. How could Clementine have been so *stupid*? How could she have lost focus like that? She'd been caught up in the moment, caught up with her silly friends—her *knights*—and now . . .

"WHO ARE THESE INTRUDERS WHO DARE TO DISTURB MY PEACE?" roared Lord Elithor, waving his spindly arm in a slicing motion. Lightning bolts zigzagged down from the sky, along with more thunder—real thunder, this time—and landed within feet of the terrified knights. Some of the boys screamed, dropping their weapons. The black sheep scampered into the shadows of the gate.

Clementine ran forward. "Father, stop!"

Lord Elithor's eyes focused slowly on Clementine.

"Clementine!" he said. "What . . . what is the meaning of this?" He swayed on his feet.

"Father, these are . . ." Clementine looked around at the white-faced village boys, half of whom had dropped their weapons in fear. "These young men are your knights."

"MY WHAT."

"Your new Brack Knights," explained Clementine, taking slow steps forward. "I thought that the Castle could use some . . . ex-extra protection, given . . . your current condition, and—"

"You told these . . . commoners of my affliction?" Lord Elithor's eyes blazed white, and more lightning crashed to the earth, accompanied now by a light rain.

The knights fell, crying, to their knees.

"No, Father," shouted Clementine over the thunder and Little Ian's wailing. "I'd never—"

"GET OUT OF MY SIGHT," roared Lord Elithor at the knights. Dark clouds swirled overhead, blocking out the afternoon sun. "AND IF YOU DARE TO ENTER THIS CASTLE AGAIN . . . IF YOU DARE TO . . . IF YOU . . ." The Dark Lord Elithor stuttered, stumbled, and fell flat on his face.

"Father!" Clementine exclaimed, rushing into the castle and up the steps. It was lucky he hadn't fallen right off the edge.

Behind her, the boys were staggering to their feet—to seize their chance to run as far away from Castle Brack as they could get.

"Come on," Roderick urged, hauling Little Ian up. "Let's scram!"

"Before that monster roasts us like marshmallows!" Gregor agreed, eyeing the scorch marks on the ground left by the lightning.

Weapons abandoned, the boys scrambled through the gate and down the steep mountain stairs as fast as they could, sparing a glance backward only to be sure that the monster that had appeared on the balcony wasn't following them.

The monster in question was lying facedown in a rain puddle of his own making. Clementine skidded to his side and turned him over, choking down her revulsion at how shockingly easy it was to lift him. She hoped the rest of his face—or Seven Sisters, his neck—had survived the fall better than when he'd banged his arm on the table.

Fortunately, other than a few dents and smears of mud, he seemed to be all right—or at least as intact as he had been before. But his eyes were wild, darting this way and that, and he hardly seemed to see Clementine.

"Father, please say something," she said, holding his head in her lap.

She looked up to see Darka Wesk-Starzec on the battlement with her, inching along the wall like a cat, her expression as wary as Clementine had ever seen it. Behind Darka was Sebastien—Sebastien, who was the only knight to stay behind when *real* trouble arose, but whose disgusted expression she could see even through the falling rain.

He was still holding his sword.

"Don't come any closer!" she snapped.

Sebastien flinched. Darka held up her open hands higher.

"Clementine," rasped Lord Elithor, finally seeming to notice her. He held up a shaky, skeletal hand in front of his face.

"Father, we need to get you inside," said Clementine. "You should not have exerted yourself so . . ."

But *how* would she get him inside? As light as he was, Clementine still wasn't strong enough to carry him back to the tower by herself.

Darka squatted down, her hands still up in surrender, to bring herself to Clementine's level.

There was no getting around it. Slowly, Clementine nodded, and Darka helped her get the Dark Lord Elithor to his feet. If Darka thought anything of being so close to a Dark Lord, she did not show it, and if that Dark Lord thought anything of being half carried by a strange peasant woman, well . . . he did not seem alert enough to be thinking much about anything.

The three of them faced Sebastien, who still stood there trembling, his sword raised. But he did not attack them, or scream, or even run away—any of the things that Clementine might have expected. He wasn't even staring at Lord Elithor anymore. Instead, he raised his chin, his lip quivering, and looked right at Clementine.

"You could have told me, you know," he said, finally lowering the sword to his side. "I thought we were friends."

"Please," Clementine whispered through her the tightness in her throat. "Just leave."

Sebastien ran after the other knights, his shape disappearing down the mountain and into the mist. And just like that, Castle Brack was almost as empty and silent as it had been for Clementine's entire life.

CHAPTER 18

THE DARKEST HEART IN THE FOREST

or

Reevaluating One's Options upon the Appearance of Wooden Stick People

It was funny, Darka reflected, how the weather in this land so conveniently changed according to the emotional state of its inhabitants. She wished, for the first time, that she, too, could have the power to make the world storm-cloud gray when she felt it should be. It was a convenient and effective mood setter.

Sunlight had been streaming from the sky the day that Alaric and Darka finally cornered the unicorn. After nearly a year of searching—of sleeping rough and following rumors to dead ends and hunting down other, smaller catches and artifacts just to keep themselves from starving—they had finally found it. And there, in the sun-dappled woods, Alaric had tried to kill it.

But the unicorn had killed him first.

It had been resting peacefully, its head in Darka's lap, when Alaric's arrow came whipping through the trees. By this point, they had both figured out that Darka was a better shot, but like it or not, she was the bait.

She had always been the bait.

Alaric missed.

The unicorn reared up in alarm, its great white head flailing. Darka tried to duck away, but she wasn't fast enough. The edge of the beast's horn caught her on the right side of her face, barely missing her eye. It was a glancing blow—if the point had gone through her cheek, she would have never made it out alive—but the edges of the horn's spiral cut deep and jagged.

There was so much blood she could hardly see through it. Or perhaps it was just that her hands were clutched so tightly to her face as she writhed on the ground. All she knew was that the world existed only in flashes of white and green, and hot, pulsing red. She could not remember all of it.

But she saw enough. She saw Alaric rush into the clearing, heard him screaming her name. She saw the unicorn charge. She tried to shout, to warn him or to scare off the creature—it didn't matter—but all that came out was a strangled cry.

She saw the unicorn impale the love of her life right through the chest.

If Darka Wesk-Starzec could have, she'd have made the sky itself split apart, too.

* * *

It was nearly sunset when the gatehouse door creaked open. Clementine looked surprised to see Darka still there at all. She hovered in the doorway.

"Come on in, then," said Darka. "It's your house, after all."

Clementine shook her head. "My *father's* house," she said, but she closed the door behind her. She leaned against it with a soft thud.

"Aye," was all Darka said. She was still trying to reconcile her mental image of a Dark Lord with the ranting, sickly stick man she'd just tucked into bed like a babe.

"I . . . I'm sorry I lied to you," said Clementine, suddenly quite fascinated by the floor.

Darka sighed. "I would've lied to me, too."

Clementine looked up at her in surprise. Darka shrugged. Little had the girl known of Darka's own plans. She almost laughed. And what plans had those even been? Her grand strategy of gaining the Dark

Lord's support had amounted to exactly zip. That man looked more ready to break in two than to go out hunting unicorns.

If Darka was being honest with herself, she knew she'd been letting her plan gather dust for weeks now. She'd had her suspicions about the Dark Lord's whereabouts from the start, and she'd done nothing. She'd played house with a lonely girl and a ragtag bunch of country boys no more fit to hold swords than the black sheep was. Sure, she'd explored the surrounding mountainside, learning the lay of the land and, she told herself, diligently looking for signs of the unicorn. But it had been just as easy—easier, even—to spend her days mending fences and milking demonic cows and teaching those boys to shoot. It had been easy to spend quiet evenings in the gatehouse with a cup of tea and Clementine's bloodcurdling stories about her ancestors, and the black sheep sitting at the foot of the bed, keeping their feet warm.

It had been easy to forget she had come here with the sole purpose of taking a life. And now, for the first time since Alaric had died, Darka wasn't so sure she wanted to remember.

"You should leave this place," Clementine said tightly. She rushed to the wardrobe, flung it open, and began folding up the few shirts that Darka had claimed as her own during her short stay at the castle. "I absolve you of any obligation to House Morcerous. The villagers will be back soon—I'm sure of it. They know about Father now. They know he's not fit to defend the castle . . ." Her hands shook as she scrambled for more of Darka's meager possessions to pack. Darka could practically see the image of the crowd with raised pitchforks reflected in Clementine's eyes.

Neither of them could forget where they came from, she realized. Clementine would always be the daughter of a Dark Lord, and Darka would always be the outcast—always the disfigured witch woman, to be shunned or reviled or hunted—unless they became the hunters.

And Darka wouldn't—couldn't—give up so easily, could she? Could she dishonor Alaric's memory, and let a single unicorn roam free, a danger to anyone who crossed its path?

No, she couldn't leave. And not just because of Clementine.

There was a very sick Dark Lord who could use her protection in his hour of need. She could hold off more than a few country bumpkins with torches in a fortress like Castle Brack. And once she'd firmly secured Lord Elithor's favor, she could be even surer of securing his permission to hunt on his lands. The man was clearly desperate, and whatever disease or curse was taking over him did not look likely to run its course anytime soon. He needed a miracle cure.

He needed the horn of a unicorn.

"Nonsense," said Darka, putting a hand over the shirt Clementine was folding on the bed. "What did I teach you to defend this castle for, if we were just going to abandon it?"

"You'll . . . You mean you'll stay?" Clementine asked, sitting on the bed with a *thump*.

"I didn't take care of all those giant pumpkins just to watch someone stomp all over them," said Darka.

"We have giant pumpkins?" Clementine cocked her head.

"Ah, that might've been a different kingdom," said Darka. "But you get the idea."

Clementine smiled, but her eyes darted to the window with a fearful glance. Darka reached out and tugged one of her braids.

"Hey," said Darka, thinking that they might not have any real Brack Knights to protect them anymore, but the townspeople had no reason to know that. "Any chance you can cast one of those fancy spells of yours on those suits of armor in the hall?"

* * *

They prepared for a siege. Clementine conducted drills with the suits of armor until she had them marching up and down the battlements like real knights on patrol. She whipped up an epic batch of a watery butter-yellow paste called "bee stings in a bottle," from one of her father's books, to pour through the murder holes; it kept well at room temperature, so she could have it at hand at a moment's notice. Darka spent hours making arrows, until Clementine was sure she must have enough for a whole army, never mind one woman. The black sheep surveyed all of the farm buildings and helped Darka and Clementine herd the animals into the closest and most secure. They harvested what they could from the kitchen garden and brought Darka's few possessions to the castle proper. Darka and Clementine made a bed for Lord Elithor in his laboratory—it was at the top of the tallest tower, which would be hardest to take—but Darka hardly saw him after that. Clementine insisted on taking care of her father alone.

It wasn't until late the next afternoon that the cry Darka had been expecting came.

"Someone's coming!" called Clementine, and Darka rushed to her side at the window. But there was only one lonely figure trudging up the mountain path—a hooded man with cloven-hoofed feet pulling a wooden cart laden with goods.

"Oh, it's just Stan," said Clementine with a sigh of relief. "He trades with father sometimes. I'd better see what he wants."

There was something about the man—and the name—that seemed vaguely familiar to Darka, but without seeing his face, she couldn't put her finger on it. "Clementine," she said, "we shouldn't let anyone in without—"

But the girl had already run for the door. Darka sighed and followed.

"Halloo, my lady!" called Stan as he huffed and puffed his way up the mountain. He stopped to rest outside the gate as Clementine bounded up to him.

Darka hung back in the courtyard, surreptitiously shaking her bangs in front of her face. It had been a while since she'd tried to hide her scar, but if the satyr seemed familiar to *her*, there was every chance she'd be familiar to him.

"Hello, Stan," said Clementine, helping him heave the back wheel of his cart over a loose stone in the steps. "We weren't expecting you."

"Well, I wasn't expecting me, either," said Stan with a wink. "But I picked up a few things in the Ensorcelled Sandbanks that I thought would just *tickle* your father, and since he and I haven't had a good sit-and-chat—or sit-and-scowl, since this is Elithor we're talking about—in a while, I figured I'd pop on by!" Stan wiped his brow, lowered his hood, and peered around the open gate, as if hoping to catch Lord Elithor right there in the courtyard.

What he caught instead, unfortunately, was the sight of Darka. "Ah, but I see you've already got company!"

"Oh, yes!" said Clementine. "But, no, not company, just . . . Darka, why don't you come and say hello to Stan?"

There was no way to avoid it now. Darka cursed herself for not staying behind, in the castle—and yet she'd had to make sure Clementine was all right.

"Hello," said Darka with a curt nod. She took just a few steps forward.

If this man was a trader . . . if he and Alaric had known each other from the magical artifacts circuit . . .

Darka didn't have to play the what-if game for long. Stan's eyes widened as he took in Darka's face.

"And such interesting company, too!" said Stan, slapping his knee. "I'm surprised the Dark Lord would deal with an . . . expert such as yourself." He nodded at Darka.

"You two know each other?" asked Clementine.

"We've passed in the same circles," Stan said with a shrug. He wouldn't stop staring at Darka with that shrewd look of his. She wished she could ram one of his packages down his throat before he opened his mouth to blab any more. "But I can't say I've had the pleasure. Not that's it's strictly a pleasure, mind. Folks do get a bit squeamish about your kind—"

"Your kind?" said Clementine.

"But it's not every day one meets the fiercest unicorn huntress in the known lands!"

Clementine froze, as utterly still as an animal in the path of a raised arrow. The color drained first from her face. Then her hair turned so black it seemed to suck the light from the air around them.

"Ah," said Stan, scratching his beard. He looked from Clementine to Darka and back again. "It seems I've gone and put my hoof in my mouth again, haven't I?"

* * *

"*The fiercest unicorn huntress in the known lands?*" repeated Clementine, breathing shallowly. She had been utterly silent until the gatehouse door shut behind them, leaving a slightly bewildered Stan to make his own way back through the valley.

Darka sat at the small table, her hands clasped before her. She had chosen the chair closest to the door—just in case.

"I told you I was a hunter," said Darka quietly. "You never asked what kind."

"*Why?*" asked Clementine. "Everyone knows that anyone who kills a unicorn is cursed—"

"An old wives' tale."

"And even if you could, *why*? How could you kill something so . . . innocent and powerful and perfect?"

"Innocent?" scoffed Darka, ignoring the accompanying twinge in her scar. "A unicorn *killed* the love of my life. Stabbed him to death with that shining, majestic horn everyone is always writing songs about—right in front of me."

Clementine flinched. "He must have done something," she insisted.

The girl was too smart for her own good.

"They're powerful, but they're just animals," Clementine said. "Just like the chimaeras and the nightmares. Just like you and me. I don't know any animal that won't attack when it's threatened."

Darka stared down at the table. This little girl could never understand. Not from her life of magic and privilege, and . . . who was *she* to talk about innocence, anyway?

"Well, aren't we Miss High-and-Mighty," snapped Darka. "Need I remind you that you're the daughter of a *Dark Lord*? When was the last time he let any 'innocent' creature be?"

"It . . . it's not the same," protested Clementine.

"Isn't it?" asked Darka sharply.

Clementine fiddled with the ends of her hair.

Darka took a deep breath. If she was to salvage any chance of obtaining the unicorn, she was going to have to get Clementine back on her side. She softened her tone. "Don't tell me you've never even considered it, to save your father? Everyone knows the legends about unicorn horns. That they can cure any ill? Reverse any curse?"

Clementine's eyes welled up. The girl did know the stories, after all.

"Don't you see, Clementine?" pleaded Darka. "If we work together—if we bring down this unicorn—we both win." Darka would be one step closer to avenging her true love, and Clementine would have a father again—for better or for worse.

For a moment, the girl seemed to be considering it—and then she went even paler.

"That's why you came here, isn't it?" whispered Clementine. "That's why we found you lurking about in the woods. You'd heard the stories about the unicorn of the Seven Sisters, and you just couldn't resist."

"Yes," admitted Darka, twisting her hands together on the table. "That is why I came here, but—"

"That's why you shot me," said Clementine, her eyes wide. "You thought I was the unicorn!"

"Yes," said Darka through gritted teeth, "but—"

"That's why you pretended to be my friend," finished Clementine, her voice breaking.

"No," said Darka, standing up. "No, Clementine."

Except that *was* why she had come to the farm, at first. Darka hadn't expected to care for Clementine. She hadn't expected to find comfort in the work, or camaraderie with the village boys, even if they couldn't tell the sharp end of a sword from the hilt. She hadn't expected to forget, just for a few moments, the thirst for revenge that had been driving her for the past five years.

Clementine backed away from her. "Everything—helping on the farm, and . . . and helping me. Living here. You were just trying to get closer to the unicorn, this whole time."

"In the beginning, I was," said Darka, her hands up. "But that changed. I—"

"LEAVE," said Clementine, and the door blasted open, swinging wildly on its hinges. Wind filled the guardhouse, tossing up the stray papers and cutlery on the table, and the clothes in the open wardrobe, until they swirled around the room. When Clementine spoke, her voice seemed unnaturally loud, as if amplified by the very mountains themselves. "I, Clementine Morcerous, future Dark Lord of the Seven Sisters, hereby banish you from Castle Brack and all of the Morcerous lands!" Clementine thrust out her hand toward Darka, tears streaming down her face.

Nothing happened. Darka was not thrown out the door by some invisible force, or burned to a crisp where she stood, or instantaneously transported to some far-off land. She did feel an unpleasant sort of tingling in her bones, but that always happened around the presence of strong magic.

"I said, 'I banish you'!" said Clementine, thrusting out her palm again.

She looked down at her hand, puzzled, as if she'd seen this done with much more success several times before. But either the Morcerous magic was too weak in the throes of the Dark Lord's sickness, or the full power of the Dark Lord's will was not yet Clementine's to wield.

This did not change the fact that the child had just attempted to throw Darka out the door—and Clementine's support or not, Darka had unfinished business on the Seven Sisters.

"You can't do it, can you?" Darka asked, crossing her arms. She knew her voice sounded taunting. She decided she didn't much care. There would be no more distractions from her quest. "You're not the true Dark Lord of the Seven Sisters."

Clementine glared at Darka, breathing heavily.

"At least, not yet," said Darka.

The girl gasped, as if physically wounded by Darka's cruel words, and spun on her heel. She fled the guardhouse, sobbing, and the wind fled with her, bowing and browning the unfortunate grass in her wake. The swirling papers floated gently to the floor, while the plates and cutlery fell with a discordant smash. Darka ground a piece of pottery under her heel, wishing she could stamp out the guilt that was rising up inside her just as easily.

The Evil Overlordship might not have been Clementine's yet, but her magic was now in every part of the farm. Darka stepped out into the kitchen garden and watched most of the vegetables wilt before her eyes. Dark clouds threatened overhead, and she could hear the nightmares shrieking from the stables. They knew when all was not right with their mistress. When Clementine's heart wept, so did the farm's.

For the first time, Darka Wesk-Starzec began to consider how she might use that gentle heart to her advantage.

* * *

Clementine had tried so very, very hard.

She had tried to keep her faith in her father. She had tried (mostly) to stay away from the Whittle Witch. She had tried to keep the farm going. She had tried to mend the ever-widening holes in Lord Elithor's magic, tried to make sense of the dismal numbers pouring out of the Decimaker, tried to keep the plants watered and the animals fed and the castle defended with all the means at her disposal—and none of it had been enough. None of it could ever be enough.

Clementine was not the Dark Lord of the Seven Sisters Mountains. (*Not yet*, Darka's cruel voice reminded her in her head.) She was not even a good Dark Lord in training. She had let outsiders in on the Morcerous magical secrets. She had let them parade around the estate, violating hundreds of years of precedent and her father's direct wishes. She could not seem to help that she was better at making flowers grow than weeds—that she felt more alive with sunshine shooting from her fingertips than performing any respectable act of dark magic. The silent farm was no longer silent, because her best hadn't been enough.

She had never felt less like a future Dark Lord in her life, and she had never felt more alone. And so just this once—just one more time before she was a grown-up, she promised herself—she did what any other twelve-year-old girl might do when utterly friendless and faced with an impossible choice: she ran to her father.

Up the higgledy-piggledy stone stairs and through the gate and across the courtyard, through the great wooden doors and down the candlelit corridors, up and up and up the tower stairs, Clementine ran. She knew there could not be much time left. The door flew open as she approached, and she could not even bring herself to be afraid of what her father might think, because at that particular moment, she cared what he thought only about one very specific thing.

Was Darka right?

Should they kill the unicorn?

She would do it, she told herself. She would do it if he asked. She wouldn't care about leaching the magic from the land, or being cursed forever, if he thought it was the only way. She would go crawling back to Darka and apologize, and promise to lend whatever magical help she could. She *would* break the Third Rule of Evildoing to save her father—but it wasn't her choice to make. She was not the Dark Lord of the Seven Sisters. She was not the one whose life hung in the balance. If one of the most inviolable rules was to be broken, she needed to hear it from the Dark Lord's lips.

But Clementine discovered, as she crept into the dark, deathly quiet tower, that she would not be able to hear anything from the Dark Lord's lips. Because he could no longer speak. He lay on top of his bedclothes, the size of a small wooden puppet. His face had been whittled away until his head could fit in Clementine's palms. His eyes had turned from glassy to *actual* glass, his jaw into a pointy painted wooden hinge, painfully stuck. Only by pressing her ear to his tiny chest could Clementine hear the faintest ticking of what remained of his heart. The Brack Butler did not even try to stop her, but merely huddled on a corner of the bed, its red lights pulsing dimly.

"Oh, Father," Clementine sobbed. How long did he have before even his heart was whittled away, turned to wood just like the rest of him? How long before he was not the Dark Lord at all—just another puppet in the Whittle Witch's collection of victims? Clementine took deep breaths, trying to quell her own crying, lest she miss any precious beat of that dying heart.

Clementine had broken many of her father's rules since he had become ill—and some even before. She had gone into town alone. She had let strangers—commoners—into the castle. She had violated his precious silence. She had ridden a broom and consorted with hedge-witches and, yes, made friends—even if only for a little while—that he would never have approved of (not that Dark Lords approved of friends, period). But she could not bring herself to break this rule—the last of the most sacred of rules—if she did not know for certain it was what he wished. And now, she would never know.

There was only one promise left to break if she had any hope of lifting the curse in time, and Clementine decided it was worth breaking. She would go into the forest and find the Whittle Witch herself.

CHAPTER 19

MUCH MORE SERIOUS THAN PURPLE

or

The Whittle Witch Strikes

"You're not supposed to be here anymore," scolded the black sheep. In truth, he did not look too surprised to see Darka still in the guard captain's quarters. "Clementine banished you."

"And yet here I stand," said Darka, shoving an extra canteen into her rucksack. The sheep's hooves clicked on the floor as he hovered in the doorway. "I could say the same for you, of course. Shouldn't you be with your family down in the village, David Turnacliff?"

The hooves froze.

"H-how do you know who I am?" the sheep bleated.

"I spent my afternoons wisely, David," said Darka, tying the top of her bag. "It doesn't take me too much effort to move about town without being seen if I don't want to. And those villagers do love to gossip. How many years has it been since the mayor's shy, bookish son went missing?"

"Please don't tell anyone," pleaded the sheep. "I can't go back to living under his roof. He doesn't even have a *library*."

Darka sighed. Did *anyone* on this side of the Seven Sisters know how to bargain?

"Look," said Darka, sitting down with a *thump* to tie her boots. "It's none of my business whether you want to be a sheep or not."

"Thank you," sniffed David.

"But I'm guessing that your . . . woolliness . . . depends quite a bit on whether the sorcerer who cursed you is still alive and kicking."

The sheep's nose twitched. "I'm not sure," he admitted. "But with the way the rest of the magic is going . . ." He sighed.

"You need Lord Elithor alive," said Darka. "And it just so happens I know how to save him. But I'll need you to do your part." She stood up and shouldered her rucksack and her bow. "What do you say, David? . . . Or do you prefer Dave?"

* * *

When Clementine entered the woods, she was wreathed in flame. She did not bring the black sheep, the nightmare, or even the Gricken. The black sheep had pleaded with her

not to go—had even tried physically blocking her with his woolly bulk—and she didn't blame him for not accompanying her, but he would never understand. Clementine could not risk the Whittle Witch getting her hands on the Morcerous grimoire, should Clementine be defeated. And the nightmare was too young, too untested. (At least, this was what Clementine told herself. It had nothing to do with wanting to keep the creature out of harm's way, of course.)

The flames from the grimoire's most recent fire spell wrapped around her wrists like fiery snakes, flickering and slithering around her hands and haloing above her head in all of the colors of the rainbow. They did not hurt her—at least, not much—but they would hurt who she wanted them to. In the pockets of her black cloak were other tools of her trade: a small bottle of the bee-sting potion, a cutting from her blue rose bush, a pouch with a sampling of herbs she might need in a pinch, as well as a few magic beans, and a small net woven from nightmare tail hair, which would plunge anyone caught in it into terrifying waking dreams. The magic thrummed in her gut, not quite light and not quite dark—but powerful. Clementine would see how much the Witch of the Woods liked to play with fire.

The trees, which had been ready and waiting for Clementine, shrank back in fear, a few unlucky branches singed and blackened. The wind hissed and sputtered, trying to douse Clementine's fire, but the enchanted

flames would not be extinguished. It would make her a visible target, she knew. For the first time ever, she did not care. For the first time ever, her veins pulsing with power and anger and grief—*no, not grief yet*—she felt ready to go into the woods alone.

Her father was dying. Darka was hunting the unicorn. And the Whittle Witch was after everything else that remained. What did she have to lose?

The air sizzled, and the flames popped and winked around her head. Clementine stopped. The leaves littering the path turned to piles of ash at her feet.

"Who's there?" she demanded.

A figure appeared on the path, and then another—and then even more. They walked out of the mist, out of the angry trees that they kept at bay with songs and charms strung between their fingers and through their hair.

Kat Marie Grice led the crowd. The angry young witch Clementine thought was called Shirin walked by her side, ready to offer an elbow to lean on or swipe at any branch that dared accost them. Clementine wondered why the hedgewitches—seemingly *all* the hedgewitches—were leaving the forest, but she didn't have the time to worry about them. There was only one witch she meant to deal with today.

"Clear the path, hedgewitch," commanded Clementine. "I've no quarrel with you."

Kat Marie stopped in the middle of the path. She looked older—more hunched and wrinkled—than the last time Clementine had seen her.

"I'm afraid we can't do that, Clementine," said Kat Marie. She gripped her staff firmly. "Our forest has suffered enough. We cannot allow you to bring yet more destruction here." She nodded to Clementine's flames.

"*You* cannot allow *me?*" said Clementine. Her flames flared, so strong she felt their searing heat even through her protective enchantments. "I will remind you that this is *my forest.* These are *my lands.* You stay here because *I* suffer you to stay, old woman. Now let. Me. Pass."

Smoke filled the path, making some of the witches cough. They shielded their eyes from Clementine's flames. But Kat Marie did not flinch.

"I warned Darka not to be consumed by revenge," said Kat Marie, shaking her head. "But it seems I should have extended that same warning to you."

A lump rose in Clementine's throat at the mention of Darka's name. She lowered her hands, and the smoke cleared a bit.

"You don't understand," Clementine said. "I *must* find the Whittle Witch. I must defeat her. My father will die if I don't."

"What a shame," scoffed Shirin. The words hit Clementine like an icy blow to her chest.

Kat Marie held up her hands. "Insensitive though she may be," she said with a sideways look at Shirin, "this young woman is right. Why should we stand aside and let you ravage this poor forest, to come to the aid of a man who has done nothing but hunt us to the edge of extinction?"

Clementine didn't have an answer for that.

"I'm not asking you to help me," she said. "I'm just asking you to *get out of my way.*"

"Clementine," said Kat Marie, "you must listen to reason. We have heard of this witch's curse—some of our sisters have fallen to it themselves. The Whittle Witch possesses your father's simulacrum. Only the one who possesses the doll can control the curse."

"That's why I must pass," pleaded Clementine. "I need to find her so I can find the doll, and . . . and . . ."

"And would you know what to do with it, even if you had it?" asked Kat Marie. "Even if you overpowered the Whittle Witch, how would you convince her to tell you the secret to reversing the spell? Would you torture her? Chop off little bits of her, just like she did to your father?"

"Stop!" said Clementine. "Stop talking!" Clementine's vision flashed red. She did not see the lightning bolt that crashed down into the path, but she did hear the witches' screams when it landed. A line of flame consumed the earth before them.

"See?" cried Shirin, backing away from the flaming

path. "She's just as bad as her father!" Some of the other witches shouted their agreement. Charms popped in the air, burning to crisps as they hit Clementine's wards.

"Stop!" cried Kat Marie, and Clementine could not tell if she meant her or Shirin. Clementine's breath came in shallow gasps. Her wrists blistered red.

Kat Marie slashed her staff, and the flames on the ground were extinguished. Clementine felt the cool sensation of trickling water flow over her body, but her fire still flickered. The flames outlined her fingers like glowing gloves.

"HELP!" a voice called.

And then, very suddenly, they were not alone. The trees to Clementine's left rustled as ungainly limbs crashed through the branches, and two people burst out onto the charred path: Sebastien Frawley and Henrietta Turnacliff.

"Oh, I'm so glad we found you," said Sebastien to the witches. He leaned over with his hands on his knees, breathing heavily. "We've been looking everywhere, but you weren't at your camp, and we need your help."

Henrietta Turnacliff had also stopped, leaning heavily against a tree that was probably too polite to whack the mayor's daughter. She looked pale and sweaty and—unless it was Clementine's imagination—slightly . . . violet?

They both noticed Clementine at the same time. At the look on Sebastien's face, Clementine felt her flames sputter out as suddenly as if she'd been dunked in the lake.

"It's her!" said Henrietta, pointing a finger at Clementine. "This pestilence comes from the Dark Lord!"

"Well, you don't know that," hedged Sebastien. He would not meet Clementine's eyes.

"Child, what is the matter?" asked Kat Marie, shuffling forward and putting her hand to Henrietta's brow, where her blond curls were lank and dark with sweat.

"The villagers are falling ill," explained Sebastien. "We don't know what it is. First they get the rash, and the fever."

Henrietta breathed out heavily through her nose as Kat Marie examined her. "When the rash gets over the throat and chest," Henrietta said, "they start to have trouble breathing. Some of our elderly are suffering dearly." Her eyes narrowed with loathing as she looked over Kat Marie's shoulder at Clementine.

"We thought you might have something that could help," said Sebastien. He addressed the witches, though his eyes flicked to Clementine. She barely noticed. She was remembering.

Clementine remembered purple mushrooms that grew only in the woods. She remembered a potion that had made the villagers just a little sick—if it affected them at all—and turned their skin a light shade of violet.

How her father had tried to muster an appropriately evil chuckle at the poor (slightly) purple people, but eventually just sighed and said, "Well, I suppose that's good enough."

"I have never seen a sickness exactly like this," Kat Marie said, turning Henrietta's head to the side to get a better look at the bright markings.

Clementine remembered the list, the list that was the second most important list in her life, outside of the Three Rules of Evildoing: the Qualifying Dastardly Deeds.

1. *A poisoning*
2. *An unfortunate transfiguration*
3. *A racket*
4. *A stampede*
5. *A frame-up*
6. *A murder*
7. *A tempest*
8. *A kidnapping*
9. *A plague*

Turning the villagers purple had never been the intended final result of the poisonous potion. Someone else had managed to execute it with far more success than the Dark Lord Elithor Morcerous ever had. Someone else had started racking up their own list of Dastardly Deeds.

The Whittle Witch didn't just want to kill Lord

Elithor. She wanted to be the next Dark Lord. And if she was attempting Dastardly Deeds, the Whittle Witch considered the title already won.

"I have," said Clementine. Everyone turned to look at her.

"She admits it!" cried Henrietta, wrenching herself away from Kat Marie's care. She stumbled, and Sebastien caught her under the elbow.

Clementine shook her head. "It's true I know this sickness—or at least, I think I do—but I'm not the one who poisoned you . . . and neither is my father." She locked eyes with Kat Marie, who nodded grimly.

"Can you help us?" asked Sebastien.

It was the first time he'd spoken directly to her since that day at the castle, and suddenly, nothing that had happened since mattered. It didn't matter that she'd lied, or that he'd been angry with her, or that he'd abandoned his post as a Brack Knight. All that mattered was that he was Sebastien, and he needed her help, and maybe—just maybe—she could give it.

But if she went with him, if she left to help the villagers, that meant losing more time to the Whittle Witch's schemes.

And it meant letting her father go.

Suddenly, Kat Marie was in front of her, hands gently resting on her shoulders. When she looked down at Clementine, her face was kind, but her voice was firm.

"Come with us, Clementine," she said. "Help us save those who still might be saved."

Clementine took a deep breath. She closed her eyes. She remembered, again. She remembered the smell of old parchment and fresh, pungent plants mashed with mortar and pestle, and swinging her feet on the stool next to her father until he scolded her to stop. She remembered his harsh words and his scowl, and how he never remembered to tie his robes back, even when the long, draping sleeves caught alight over the fire (which happened more than once). She remembered a man who was Dark Lord, and turned people into sheep and made children cry and enforced cold silence in his domain. A man who settled for slightly purple, rather than deathly ill.

Because his heart had never truly been that of a Dark Lord, either. And yet he had still chosen that life, ill-fitting as it was and with all the suffering it caused.

Clementine opened her eyes. She nodded. First, she had to be sure. They had to identify the source of the poison—if poison it really was—to stop the spread of the sickness as soon as possible. Fortunately, Clementine had just the magic flower for the job.

"Take me to the village," she said, and let the mayor's daughter, a disgraced knight in training, and a coven of hedgewitches lead her out of the woods.

CHAPTER 20

WHAT FRIENDS ARE FOR

or

The Real Siege of Castle Brack

The Whittle Witch was a woman of wood, of growing things and green things and things that take root. Castle Brack, on the other hand, was a thing of stone. It was hard and cold. It could not be molded by her hands—not slowly and gently, not as she liked. It was part of the mountain itself. She would not be able to go about this the way she'd like—a little sanding here, a little scraping there, a careful peeling with a sharp knife.

Today was not a day for waiting. She had been waiting for so long.

Her trees followed her out of the forest. They screamed as their roots tore from the ground, leaving great gaping wounds in the earth, but they followed. They dragged themselves across the moat and climbed up the stone path, trailing crumbling earth with each splintering step, until they reached the castle gate. They used their own brothers to make battering rams, bashing and bashing against the gate until the Whittle Witch could not tell the screams of pain from the battle cries.

Her wooden dolls came with her, too. Some were so small she wore them strung around her neck, some were lashed to the tail of her broomstick (these were usually the naughty ones), and some were large enough to limp along with the trees, like half-finished marionettes without strings.

The Dark Lord's wards prickled against her skin, even though he was nearly gone. They put wrinkles in her forehead and made her knees ache with the pain of a few hundred winters. It cost her more effort, more years of magic, than she'd planned. She would have to find the unicorn quickly.

The Whittle Witch had thought she would sense the creature's presence as soon as she entered Elithor's domain. She had been able to feel its magic only in fits and starts out in the woods, but there had always been a pull toward the epicenter of the Dark Lord's power—the Fourth Sister, and Castle Brack. And she had wondered—of course she had—what kind of unicorn would let a Dark Lord rule with impunity on its mountain. They were not known to be meddlesome creatures, and yet the unicorn's silence all these years was . . . troubling. And now, its power did not seem any nearer than it had before—except for that same pull.

The Whittle Witch had heard the stories, of course—the stories the hedgewitches whispered about the Dark Lords Morcerous and the unicorn. She never did know what to make of them, and now she found she didn't much care. She would take Castle Brack for her own, and if the unicorn became hers sooner rather than later—well, so much the better.

She found the scarecrows scattered across the farm, called to their wooden souls, and bid them follow, too. A few more soldiers would not hurt her cause.

By the time the Whittle Witch and her trees and her dolls and her scarecrows reached the front doors of Castle Brack, the Whittle Witch could see the edges of Elithor's magic stretched across it—thin, sad ribbons, as flimsy as spiderwebs. She pulled out her whittle. It was her oldest knife, her favorite knife. No other would do.

The ribbons of magic shivered, frayed bowstrings playing one last, feeble song.

The Whittle Witch raised her knife and did what she did best.

***

The black sheep could not believe what he was doing. If anyone had told him years ago, when he was still just a small lad in the village, that one day he'd be risking life and limb to *save* the Dark Lord Elithor Morcerous, he'd have said they were crazy. Now, he was quite certain he was the crazy one.

The sheep had been grazing in the valley when he saw the Whittle Witch emerge from the forest. In truth, he saw only the *signs* of her emergence from the forest, as a rush of deer and squirrels and owls and all manner of other woodland creatures fled from her destructive path. He heard the ripping and stomping of the trees next, and when the first of them mowed down their still stationary fellows to leave the forest behind completely, well, the black sheep knew it was time to say goodbye to his life on the Morcerous farm.

The sheep ran for the castle as fast as his short legs could carry him. (*Do sheep run?* he wondered. *Trot?* "Gallop" seemed like a word that belonged to horses.) He raced past the empty Brack Knight suits of armor that were swinging their weapons wildly, as they surely felt but could not yet see the enemy approaching the castle. He was breathing hard—the life of a human-turned-sheep had made him rather soft, and he hadn't been much harder to begin with—but still he pressed on and up the stone stairs to the laboratory.

The Dark Lord was little more than a barely breathing pile of sticks. He glared balefully at the black sheep as the sheep approached, and the mechanical metal disk Clementine called the Brack Butler waved its sharp, spindly appendages in a way that suggested the black sheep would get much more than a shearing if he came any closer.

The tower shook with a sudden blast of energy from outside. Dust rained down from the roof and walls.

The sheep really should have said something like, "My greatest apologies for the intrusion, my lord!" but instead he aimed a swift kick at the overprotective Butler, bleated, "Go on and get on!" and nudged his head under Lord Elithor's little wooden body until the Dark Lord was forced to either take hold or fight his way back onto the bed.

"Do you want to see Clementine again or not?" asked the sheep testily. He felt what remained of the Dark Lord's fingers grasp on to his coat. At least *that* would make his job easier.

"Hold on tight, my lord!" cried the sheep, and he bounded out of the tower with the Dark Lord of the Seven Sisters clinging to his back as the castle trembled around them.

Yes, the black sheep thought, he was *definitely* crazy.

* * *

Just as Alaric had done all those years ago, Darka searched for the perfect spot to break a girl's heart. She followed the black sheep's directions to the rocky slope at the foot of the western side of the Fifth Sister, where the trees grew up almost against the mountain's face. She noticed with unease the animals fleeing the forest. They paid her almost no notice in their race to get away from the Seven Sisters, and it unnerved her. Darka had gotten used to being the most dangerous thing in the woods.

The Whittle Witch was coming, and that meant Darka needed to complete her mission soon. She might even need the unicorn's horn to protect herself from the witch, if it came to that.

Better the devil you know, thought Darka, and wondered, not for the first time, how she'd gone from village farm girl who barely believed in magic to a unicorn huntress playing one evil sorcerer against another.

You know exactly how, Darka reminded herself. And then, since she had nothing to do but wait, she let the memories in.

* * *

Alaric had been distant for weeks. They'd had another false lead on the unicorn, and he blamed Darka for their wasted time.

"Maybe if *someone* double-checked their sources, instead of believing every piece of worthless gossip out of a barmaid's mouth because she *bats her pretty eyelashes*—" He'd stopped short and spat into their fire.

Darka sat back, stunned. He'd been the one to tell her to get close to the locals in the first place—to befriend them and listen to their stories.

Just like he had done, when he'd come sniffing around Darka's village.

She reminded him of that, and he didn't talk to her for nearly a day and a half.

He insisted they leave for the woods again soon. No explanations, no attempt to smooth things over with the contacts they'd been cultivating in the town. When she protested, he told her she was more than welcome to stay behind.

Without him.

Darka followed. He led them through the forest at a backbreaking pace, scaring off any game they might have hunted for food. By the time they finally set up camp—in a clearing that was far too exposed for Darka's tastes—she was burning with anger and confusion.

"What is wrong with you?" Darka asked Alaric. "Why are you acting like this?"

"Let's just get some rest," he snapped. They went to bed hungry. She heard him get up several times throughout the night, moving restlessly about their campsite.

And in the morning, with the sun shining cheerily down on them, Alaric broke her heart.

She awoke to find him diligently separating their

supplies into equal portions—two portions, she realized, for two separate journeys.

Alaric noticed her watching him.

"We both know this isn't working anymore," he said with a small, sad smile.

"What?"

The rest of his words were a blur—how it had been fun while it lasted but clearly, Darka wasn't cut out for his line of work. How it would be better for both of them if they went their separate ways—Alaric to his hunting and Darka back to her family.

As if they were not hundreds of miles away from her village. As if she could go back to her family now. As if their nearly two years together had not happened.

"What is *wrong*?" Darka asked him. "What happened to you?" And finally, when she could gain nothing satisfying from him in response: "*What did I do?*"

"Nothing, my love," said Alaric, taking Darka's face in his hands. "You played your part to perfection."

Darka stared at that small, sad smile—that condescending smile, she realized—and wondered if she'd been hunting the wrong monsters all along.

"My . . . part?" she sputtered. "What did you think I was doing, Alaric? Leaving my family and everything I've ever known behind, to . . . to travel across the world with you and *kill* with you, and . . . you think I'm just playing house with you? Playing adventurer? *I* haven't been *playing* at anything!" She shoved him hard in the chest, and he stumbled backward.

He righted himself, brushing the dirt off his pants with a short laugh, like he was pleasantly surprised at Darka's outburst.

"Ah, Darka, but you see . . . I *have* been playing—I've been playing a game, and a very long one." He ran a hand through his hair, looking almost—but not quite—embarrassed.

"What are you saying?" Darka asked. But Alaric was already shouldering his pack and turning away from her. She grabbed his shoulder and spun him around. "Why? Why are you leaving?"

"Because some monsters," he said, cupping her face again and running his thumb down her tear-streaked face, "just can't resist a young maiden's tears."

He left her there, confused and crying, and so very, very alone—or so she thought.

It was a matter of minutes before the unicorn found her.

* * *

The blue rose was lowered into the well with a rope. When Clementine and Sebastien pulled it up again—slowly and carefully, for they could not risk another drop touching anyone else—it had turned a wilted purplish black.

"Poison," Clementine said, her suspicions confirmed.

The few villagers gathered around took a step back with a gasp, as if they could become ill merely by hearing Clementine speak the word.

"Do you know of an antidote?" asked Kat Marie Grice, frowning at the shriveling flower.

Clementine shook her head. "Not by heart, no," she said. "I'd have to consult my father's grimoire, or the original recipe for the poison, and that's back at the castle . . ." She looked at the villagers eyeing her warily, some showing early signs of the disease. The truly sick—mostly the elderly and the very young—had been brought to the town hall. Clementine imagined more and more benches filling up with the people standing by her now, wheezing with swollen throats and bruise-colored skin.

Kat Marie started to respond, but a great tremor suddenly shook through the earth, sending them all struggling for balance. Clementine held up the old woman until it passed. The air buzzed with energy, cracking and fizzling with sounds that Clementine suspected only she (and perhaps the hedgewitch) could hear. A wave of dizziness washed over her. She clutched at the edge of the well until the world stopped spinning.

"The wards," Clementine gasped.

Sebastien rushed forward, but Clementine waved him off. It was finally happening. The Whittle Witch had arrived at last. Clementine should have known the poisoning would be a mere distraction. "She's attacking the castle . . . and my father! My father is still there!"

"You must go, my child," insisted Kat Marie Grice. She squeezed Clementine's hand. "You must go and retrieve the grimoire, before the Whittle Witch gets her hands on it." She lowered her voice. "Go, and save your father, if you can."

Clementine looked at the crowd's pinched, worried faces, and saw real fear in their eyes—but something else, too. For the first time, they were looking at her not *just* with fear or disdain, but with something that might have been a glimmer of hope. *She* was their only hope to retrieve the antidote—if there was one—and protect them from the Whittle Witch.

But what if she didn't make it back in time? What if the Whittle Witch caught her? Would it be better to stay here, to try and analyze the potion with the hedgewitches and see if they could come up with their own cure? To try and fortify the village—perhaps even cast their own spells of protection?

And yet if there was any chance—any chance at all—of saving her father and keeping the Gricken away from the Whittle Witch, Clementine knew it was her duty to take that chance.

"I'll come back," Clementine said, her breath hitching.

She hoped she was loud enough for the scared villagers to hear. "I'll come back. I promise."

Kat Marie nodded. "We know you will." She placed a quick kiss on Clementine's forehead. "Now quickly, child. Go!"

Clementine turned and scampered away, around and through the fastest paths she knew from years of skulking in their shadows. But when she finally broke out onto the main road, just at the edge of town, she heard running footsteps behind her.

"Wait!"

Clementine turned at the sound of the voice. It was Sebastien running behind her, sword in hand once more—and he wasn't alone. At least six of the Brack Knights—even Roderick and Gregor the Whiny!—trailed behind, hefting weapons ranging from their lake swords to an actual pitchfork.

Clementine stepped back. She'd envisioned encounters with angry mobs so many times—but she'd never pictured them being led by someone she had called a friend.

Clementine held up her hands in surrender, but she readied her fire spell—just in case. "Please," she said. "I'm just going to the castle to try and get my father's grimoire before the witch who's attacking does. It might have a cure for the sickness."

"We know *that*," whined Gregor. "So let's get going!"

Clementine lowered her hands. "What?"

"We're coming with you, of course," said Sebastien, planting his sword in the earth emphatically. Clementine had a feeling Darka would have taken him to task for that, but she was too puzzled to dwell on it. "As Knights of Castle Brack," Sebastien said, "it is our duty to protect you."

"You want to . . . *come with me*?" Clementine repeated, stunned.

"And we want to save our families, too," pointed out Roderick.

"You don't understand," Clementine said. "This witch . . . she's powerful. She's already broken through some of my father's wards—protective spells on the castle. She may have overrun it already. I'll need to sneak in through the mountains. It'll be terribly dangerous—"

"Which is exactly why you need someone who's handy with a sword," said Sebastien, unsticking his from the muddy ground with a *squelch*.

Clementine didn't understand. These boys didn't like her. They didn't trust her. They liked to play at being knights and the chance for a break from their everyday lives. She hadn't trusted them, either, and they had run at the first sign of trouble. And now they wanted to help her?

"But I haven't even saved your families!" Clementine said. They had no proof that she would return, other than her word. They had no proof that she could cure the sick, even if she did return.

"But you're trying," said Sebastien, "and we've got to try, too. That's . . . that's what friends do." A blush crept up his cheeks as he offered Clementine his hand. "Let's go."

That's what friends do.

Her heart racing and full, Clementine took it.

* * *

Clementine, Sebastien, and the Brack Knights crept through the craggy paths at the foot of the Fifth Sister, circling around to approach the castle from the east. The trees here, being farther from the larger forest, had not been exposed to the Whittle Witch's influence—at least not yet—and they offered no resistance as the group took cover under their branches.

"When we get there," Clementine said quietly to Sebastien, "I want the boys to wait in the mountains."

"But—" he protested.

"You will come with me," said Clementine. She paused and tucked a strand of hair behind her ear. It had helpfully turned a staid brown to blend in with the forest around them.

Sebastien thought it looked as lovely as a shining chestnut, but he also guessed now was probably not the time to share that particular thought. Also, he did not know if ladies appreciated being compared to food, shining or not.

Clementine cleared her throat, and Sebastien straightened. "That is, um, if you want to," she said. "After I find my father, we need to look for the Gricken."

"The Gricken?"

"You know the giant chicken that looks like it's made of book pages?"

Sebastien nodded.

"That's my family grimoire—our spellbook," said Clementine slowly, as if she were admitting some great secret. Perhaps she was. At any rate, the appearance of her earlier sunshine spell in egg form suddenly made a lot more sense.

"Huh," said Sebastien. "That's . . . different."

"The Gricken may not have all the answers—we'll need to check my father's library, too," said Clementine. "That'll be trickier . . ."

The trees ahead rustled, and without thinking, Sebastien swept Clementine behind him, his sword raised. A creature came bounding out of the forest, a giant black blur leaping straight at them.

"Get back!" cried Sebastien, swinging the sword. The creature let out a terrified bleat and dodged it just in time, losing its footing and rolling down the path.

"It-it's only me!" cried the creature in a raspy, quivering voice.

Sebastien nearly dropped his sword. It was only a

black sheep—but it was a black sheep that was clearly *talking.*

"Wait! Stop!" said Clementine. "He's a friend!"

"You can talk!" exclaimed Sebastien as the sheep got to his feet, mumbling about "overenthusiastic warmongers" and something called "toxic masculinity." The rest of the boys backed away, staring and whispering behind their hands.

"My apologies, but we've no time for the usual introduction to transfiguration today," said the sheep. "Clementine, you must come with me. I managed to get your father out of the castle—"

"Oh, thank you!" said Clementine, rushing forward to embrace the black sheep in a hug.

"But, Clementine . . ." The sheep hesitated. "He doesn't have much time left."

Clementine's breath hitched, but she nodded. If she wanted to say goodbye to her father—*or what's left of him*, thought Sebastien with a shudder—she'd need to do it now.

"Go," Sebastien found himself saying. He put a hand on Clementine's shoulder. "We'll keep on toward the castle"—he looked back to the rest of the knights, most of whom nodded—"and you can loop back and meet up with us there. Just tell us the way."

Roderick and some of the others looked like they might have wanted to protest, but they were silenced by a hard look from Sebastien. Dark Lord or not, Lord Elithor was still Clementine's father. Some of the knights had left behind sick fathers in the village, too, or mothers and sisters and brothers. They knew now what it might be like to never get a chance to say goodbye.

Clementine removed her arms from around the sheep's neck and turned her bone-crushing hug on Sebastien. He was rather surprised to find he did not burst into flames or turn into some sort of domesticated animal himself—you heard all sorts of rumors about the touch of Dark Lords. He was also surprised that it was a very good hug.

"Thank you," Clementine murmured into his shoulder.

Probably one of his top five hugs of all time, honestly.

Clementine hurriedly explained the best route for them to approach the castle, and before Sebastien knew it, she and the black sheep had disappeared through the trees. Sebastien and the Brack Knights pressed on—onward and upward toward the great shadow of Castle Brack.

CHAPTER 21

TIME TO SAY GOODBYE

or

The Power of Fragile Things

The black sheep led Clementine through the narrow and rocky paths between the Fourth and Fifth Sisters. They passed the lake, and Clementine couldn't help but think of the last happy afternoon she'd spent here, gently teasing the Lady of the Lake and helping her knights pick out swords. Today, the surface was as still as if it were covered in ice.

Clementine approached the shore. She knew she was far too exposed without the cover of the trees, but the Lady of the Lake deserved to know she might have a change in Evil Overlord to look forward to. The moment she crouched by the shoreline, a pale hand emerged from the water, followed by another, and then a dripping but handsome green-haired head. For once, the Lady of the Lake said nothing.

"The Whittle Witch attacks," Clementine said, though she knew Vivienne must be able to feel it as surely as Clementine could. She ran her fingers along the pebbles on the shoreline, too embarrassed to meet Vivienne's gaze. "The rule of the Morcerouses may come to an end."

"Do you seek my counsel, my lady?" Vivienne asked, resting her chin on her hands. Her ice-colored eyes looked deep into Clementine's.

Clementine nodded. "Yes, Lady," she said, chuckling slightly. It *did* sound rather silly for both of them to call the other the same thing.

"Protect the heart that has been given to you," advised Vivienne. "It is a fragile, powerful thing."

"I don't think I've ever heard that saying," said Clementine, puzzled.

The Lady smiled, reached out of the water, and brought her cool hands to Clementine's face. She planted a chilly kiss on Clementine's forehead. "Heed it, all the same," she said, and sank back down into the lake without another word.

The smooth surface of the water mirrored the unnatural stillness in the air. It sent a shiver down Clementine's spine. She hurried after the black sheep to find her father.

He lay on a bed of moss and leaves that the black sheep had undoubtedly made for him, nestled in a cluster of rocks, the great gray wall of the mountain close behind him. The black sheep shuffled away, muttering something about keeping a lookout. Clementine frowned. Although they were near the top of a steep slope, this wasn't the most strategic hiding spot. There was nowhere to run, with the mountain on one side and thick forest on the others.

But then, she supposed, her father was nearly done running.

Clementine knelt beside him and pressed her ear to his tiny wooden chest. She couldn't look into his eyes—not when they were no longer his, but painted on like a doll's. She felt only the faintest, slowest of heartbeats. She breathed in the smell of his robes. She was thankful that even now he still smelled like her father—like licorice and smoke and herbs and the slight but sharp traces of whatever chemicals he'd been using in his laboratory.

She wanted to say so many things.

I'm so sorry, Daddy.

I should have gone after her myself.

Please don't go.

How could you have fallen for her tricks?

I should have stayed with you, forced you to let me help.

Please don't go.

I did my best. I know you did, too.

I should have done better.

You should have known better.

I promise I'll stop talking to the Lady in White and I'll burn my garden to ashes and I'll be the best Dark Lord in training there ever was, and I won't let you down. Just please . . .

Please don't go.

But nothing came out. All she could do was breathe in the scent of him, the very last part of him. All she could focus on was the heat behind her eyes as she squeezed them shut, her tears soaking into his shirt, because the world had shrunk to the size of that feeling.

Clementine did not notice the unicorn enter the clearing. She did not hear its gentle step, or see its shining white coat or spiraling, sharp horn. She did not know that it had been drawn to her pain and her loss, and the loss of the mountains at the Whittle Witch's attack.

It was not until Clementine had finally whispered, "Goodbye, Father," that she looked up, and the world widened again, just a little bit, and she saw the unicorn standing there. Watching her.

Clementine had never seen a creature so beautiful. Their first meetings, cautiously watching each other across the mountains, had not prepared her for seeing the unicorn face-to-face. It was not a large creature—bigger than a deer, but nowhere near the size of a full-grown horse or nightmare. Its horn was longer and rougher than she had expected, the pale spiral run through with twisting shades of brown. Speckled and even chipped in places, it was the only part of the unicorn that showed signs of age.

Clementine could not quite look directly into its dark eyes. When she did, it was like looking at the entire mountain range and everything that had ever happened on it, and at herself—all at once. It was too much. She blinked, and the too-much went away. But the unicorn kept watching.

She was glad that it was here, in a way, even though it was too late. Her father was surely beyond saving. And yet how cruel was it that the unicorn appeared now—now, when her father was nearly dead and the castle overrun? What use was the unicorn now?

But as Clementine watched the unicorn, and the unicorn watched her, she knew it was not a thing to be used. It was not a flower to be picked or a horse to be ridden, or even a fellow sorcerer to be bargained with. It was power and magic. It was older than the souls of the mountains. It simply *was.* And so she did not expect anything of it, even as she took comfort in its presence. She was glad there was someone—something—else here in the valley with her and her father and the black sheep.

The unicorn took a step forward.

It carefully picked its way between the trees. The branches themselves seemed to part around it, as if in deference. The unicorn slipped between and around the rock formations on the slope with the grace of a dancer, its hooves barely making a sound.

The moment the unicorn stopped, just a few feet from Clementine, a soft *thrum* cut through the stillness. It was almost too quiet for Clementine to hear, and much too fast for her to even realize she'd heard it, until it was too late.

The unicorn reared back as the arrow sped through the air, but the creature wasn't fast enough. The arrow pierced the front of its left shoulder. The unicorn cried out, and the mountains shook, and the birds in the air shrieked, and the beasts of the forest roared, and the even the fish in the streams opened their mouths in silent screams, though they did not know why. But they all felt it.

Clementine was too shocked to scream with them. But Darka Wesk-Starzec, stepping out of her hiding place in the shadows, did not looked shocked at all.

She looked disappointed.

Shining silver blood leaked from the unicorn's wound, covering its white coat in a muddy dark gray stain. It reared again, and Darka raised her bow for a second shot.

"Darka, stop!" cried Clementine, jumping to her feet. Her legs shook beneath her.

"Stay back, Clementine," warned Darka. She lowered her arm, but only for a moment, slowly circling the bucking, whinnying unicorn. "You don't know what these monsters are capable of."

"B-best do as she says," suggested the black sheep weakly, cowering behind one of the rocks. He turned his head away from Clementine.

So that was why the black sheep had rescued her father and brought her here, to this particular spot. Not out of the goodness of his heart. Not so she could say goodbye before she lost everything, before she risked life and limb to try and save the mountain from the Whittle Witch.

Clementine was not the savior of the mountain. She was just the bait.

And she'd walked straight into the trap.

The unicorn tried to stumble away, but disoriented with pain, it merely backed itself up against the mountainside. Darka stalked its every step.

"Darka, please—don't do this," begged Clementine, her hands up in surrender. "The unicorn is . . . it's the lifeblood of the mountains. If you kill something so innocent—"

"Innocent?" Darka barked out a laugh. "Even if that were true—what is it to you? I thought you, of all people, Clementine—you and your father"—she nodded toward him, still lying upon the rocks—"would understand."

"My father told me to never, ever hurt a unicorn," said Clementine.

Darka's eyes briefly darted in her direction.

"The unicorn is . . . different," Clementine insisted, though she knew the words sounded weak. "It hasn't done anything wrong."

"And your townspeople have?" Darka asked, her lips twisting further into a smirk. "The villagers—the ones your father makes a living terrorizing—they *deserve* his punishments, do they?"

"N-no," Clementine said, her throat tightening as she thought of Sebastien and the rest of the knights. How could she *not* think of them? How could she have gone all of these years thinking her life—and her father's life—was just part of how the world worked? That it was occasionally regrettable, but definitely unchangeable: Dark Lords wrought evil. In the absence of a Good Witch or a hero—and every effort was made to stamp out *those*—the people had evil wrought upon them. And it wasn't so very bad for Lord Elithor's subjects, after all. There were Dark Lords *much* more irritable and given to gore. The villagers in the Seven Sisters Valley were lucky to live under her father's light touch.

This was what Clementine had told herself ever since she was young enough to understand what being a Dark Lord meant. But now, she knew that she had never understood it. Not really. Because now, as she watched the unicorn bleed, and thought of Sebastien and the knights, and *their* fathers and mothers, as well as her own—and even of Darka, and the brief moments they'd shared—she couldn't pretend this was how things should be. She couldn't pretend any longer.

The unicorn's front legs buckled. Clementine rushed toward it, but Darka turned, sweeping her bow to point at Clementine.

"Not a step closer," said Darka, her voice uneven. Her hands shook so much she had to keep letting go of the bowstring. "Isn't it your *job* to destroy everything and everyone, *especially* the innocent?" She tossed her head, shaking sweaty strands of hair from her eyes. "What kind of Dark Lord are you?"

Clementine's heart shuddered against her ribs. "That's just it," she said. "I . . . I'm not. I don't think the villagers deserve to be hurt. I don't think anyone does. I don't want to terrorize people, or kill them—or kill anything at all. Especially not the unicorn." Clementine hiccupped through her tears. She hadn't even realized she'd started crying. "Just like you said before, at the gatehouse. I'm not a true Dark Lord at all. " Clementine took a step closer to the unicorn. "And I don't ever want to be."

There was little time for Clementine's declaration to register. A voice suddenly echoed across the mountains—impossibly loud and soft, low and high, all at once—making everyone in the clearing jump.

"Castle Brack is mine," said the voice, sending chills down Clementine's spine.

The Whittle Witch had taken the Fourth Sister. She had taken Clementine's home.

"I would say I expected more from the Dark Lord Elithor Morcerous," said the Whittle Witch. "But I'd be lying."

Clementine clapped her hands over her ears, trying to keep out the magically enhanced sound. Darka pointed her bow this way and that, searching for the source of the voice.

"Now, *Clementine* Morcerous," the Witch mused. "From what I've heard, *you* sound much more promising. Why don't you come out and play?" The Whittle Witch cackled, her laugh echoing like crackling sparklers in the air. A remote part of Clementine acknowledged that it was a very decent cackle.

But Clementine barely heard the Whittle Witch's taunts, because at that precise moment, Clementine looked into the eyes of the unicorn—the wounded, sweating, panicked unicorn, who had evidently used Clementine's impassioned speech as an opportunity to remember that it was, in fact, the most dangerous thing on the mountain.

The unicorn pawed the ground, its eyes afire. It bent its magnificent head, and before Clementine could cry out, charged straight at Darka. The huntress saw the movement just in time. She released her arrow, and Clementine watched it fly, as deadly as a diving hawk, toward the unicorn's heart.

Clementine did not stop to wonder exactly whom she was trying to save. She simply knew that she could not let either tragedy come to pass.

She dove in between them.

It was impossible to say which struck her heart first—the arrow or the horn—and in the end, it did not matter. Either way, Clementine Morcerous was dead.

* * *

The Whittle Witch decided that she did not like Castle Brack. It was much too dark, and much too angular, and she could tell that everything in it—from the books on the library shelves that flung themselves at her face, to the chains in the dungeon that rattled threateningly when she walked by, to those black, shiny suits of armor that stood much too still with their freshly polished weapons—did not like her, either.

It would be better to start fresh, she thought, as she circled the castle on her broomstick. Better to build her new home with a clean slate. She took a deep breath of the clear mountain air, flying higher and higher, until she reached that special place where the snow never melted, even in summer. The Lady in White, the locals called it. There would be more snow even higher, above the clouds.

Nothing was cleaner than a fresh snow.

Not even Elithor Morcerous's wards, at the height of their strength, could have risen this high into the mountains. She was honestly surprised no one had thought to attack the castle from *above* before. But such complacency was what you got with hundreds of years of Dark Lords in power, she supposed.

There was nothing and no one to stop her from calling the winds to her aid, finding the spots of weak snow under the glittering eggshell surface, and pushing them to their breaking point. The sound of crushing, crashing snow rumbled in the air like thunder, and the wave of white cascaded down the mountainside, smothering everything in its wake. It was headed straight for Castle Brack and, if she was lucky, the village beyond.

The Lady in White crumbled under the weight of the avalanche. The Whittle Witch watched her disintegrate, from the top of her puffy head to her placid, stupid face, all the way down to her shining white petticoats. She was now a tool of destruction against the very land she was supposed to protect.

The Witch flew as close to the fracturing snow as she dared, skimming the frothing waves with her toes and laughing into its roar. She would need the unicorn, and soon. She could feel its power strongly here, and hoped the snow would be enough to flush it out. But for the moment, though she had lived for hundreds of years, she had never felt so alive.

CHAPTER 22

THE LADY IN WHITE

or, As She Would Prefer to Be Called, the Unicorn

Clementine awoke in her garden. It was bathed in moonlight, every flower in full bloom. Even the ivy shone under the moon's impossibly bright caress.

But the moonlight was not the only impossibly bright thing in the garden. The Lady in White stood across from Clementine, so tall she took up most of the far wall. It was almost frightening, seeing her this close. She was not as snowy white as she looked from down in the valley. Her skirts and her skin were streaked with gray and brown, speckled with bits of dirt and rocks and a few twigs. Clementine loved her even more this way. Though her eyes were made of ice, they looked warmly upon Clementine.

"Hello, Clementine," said the Lady in White. Her frosty lips never moved. It was as if her melodic voice simply appeared in Clementine's mind. And Clementine knew, though she could not have said how, that it was not *exactly* the Lady in White speaking to her. The voice she heard in her head belonged to the unicorn.

"Have I . . . died?" asked Clementine. She did not feel particularly sad about it—it was hard to feel sad about anything, standing next to the Lady in White in her favorite place in the world—but she did feel a little scared. She had spent so much time thinking—or not thinking—about her father dying that she had not given much thought to it happening to anyone else, least of all herself.

"Mostly," said the unicorn serenely.

"Oh," said Clementine. She supposed getting rammed through the heart with a spiral horn would not do much for one's health, but she gasped as she remembered Darka's arrow. "Have *you* died?" Clementine rushed to the Lady in White's feet, but stopped just short of her frothy, snowy skirts.

The unicorn chuckled. "Far from it, my dear." The Lady cupped Clementine's cheek. Her hand was pleasantly cool, and smelled like fresh snow and pine, with a hint of animal musk. "Thanks to you."

Clementine blushed, and even though she knew she was probably dreaming, her hair blushed red to match.

"Do you realize what your sacrifice has done, Clementine?"

Clementine shook her head. The Lady took Clementine's small hand in her giant one, and together, they strolled through the garden.

"Many, many years ago, when the first Dark Lord Morcerous came to the Seven Sisters," said the unicorn, "the Dark Lord coveted my power . . . Coveted it, and feared it. And so he devised a clever way—cleverer than any wizard before or since—to trap that power and to tie me to these mountains. With an evil spell, he separated the true source of my power—of most creatures' power, really—from my body."

"But . . ." Clementine thought of everything she knew about unicorns. "Your horn . . . ?"

The Lady shook her head. "Not my horn, dear." She placed an icy palm to her chest. "My heart."

Clementine gasped.

"He locked my heart away, high up in a frozen prison, where no one could ever find it," said the Lady, her voice turning harder than Clementine had yet heard it.

"The Lady in White," Clementine breathed.

The unicorn nodded. "And even if they did find it, no one but a Morcerous could ever break the curse," the unicorn continued. "And only then, by doing something no Dark Lord Morcerous would ever, ever do."

Clementine stopped in her tracks. "What's that?" she asked softly, though she thought she already knew the answer.

"Give up their own heart," said the unicorn, "in exchange for mine."

Clementine brought her hand to her chest, and the Lady placed her cool fingers on top of Clementine's. Clementine felt the Lady's icy touch, saw her breath steam in the air around them, heard the crunch of the Lady's snowy skirts against the ground. It was hard to believe that her life was over, when she could still sense all of these things. They walked on.

"Not many would sacrifice themselves for a creature they barely know," said the unicorn after a long pause, "or a friend who had betrayed them."

Clementine looked down, her eyes suddenly smarting. She hoped Darka and the black sheep, and her Brack Knights, were all right. She supposed they'd have to get on without her now.

"In exchange for your selflessness," continued the unicorn, "I will do something I have not done in a very, very long time: I will grant you one favor. I will grant anything you wish, as long as it is within my power." The Lady let go of Clementine's hand and peered over her perfect nose, right into Clementine's eyes. "Choose it well."

"Anything?" asked Clementine softly. The Lady nodded.

Clementine wished she knew how many times she would be forced to choose between the life she was supposed to want and the life she knew was right—or at least right for her. How many times she would have to shut the door on her heart and leave her father behind, even when she had the chance to save him, because she knew, deep down, that the world was better off without a Dark Lord ruling the Seven Sisters at all.

It probably wasn't even a choice. Her father would be gone by now, and she was certain even a unicorn's magic could not bring back the dead. That was surely one of the Three Rules of Evildoing for a reason. But it still felt like a choice, and it still broke Clementine's heart, even as she knew it was the right thing to do.

And another choice—a real choice—did tempt her, glimmering like a dark jewel just out of reach: she could ask the unicorn to kill the Whittle Witch. Clementine could do it, and the Whittle Witch would never darken the doorstep of Castle Brack ever again.

But Clementine remembered the words of Kat Marie Grice:

I warned Darka not to be consumed by revenge. But it seems I should have extended that same warning to you.

If Clementine used the power of the unicorn to avenge her father and her friends—if she used this creature that brought comfort and healing and magic wherever it roamed to *take* a life instead of giving it—then she would be no better than the worst of the Dark Lords.

Clementine took a deep breath, her decision made. The people of the Seven Sisters had a long struggle ahead of them, if they wanted to defeat the Whittle Witch. Giving them a fighting chance was the least she could do.

"Please, if you can . . . heal the villagers," said Clementine. "It's not too late for them. Please heal them. Heal everyone you can."

The Lady in White bowed her great glimmering head, and moonlight exploded through the garden, enveloping them both in its cold, bright embrace.

* * *

The unicorn had disappeared. That much Darka Wesk-Starzec knew.

It had simply blinked out of existence, leaving no trace of its presence behind—no trace, of course, except the tiny bleeding body it had gored straight through the heart. Darka knew she should have leapt up, grabbed a weapon—any weapon—and prepared for the worst. The beast could have been anywhere. It could have been preparing to charge again. It could have been preparing to turn the whole mountain to dust.

But all Darka could do was clutch at the girl in her arms, desperately trying to stop Clementine's bleeding. And even though she knew that it was useless, that Clementine was dead—had been dead, from the moment she stepped in between Darka and the unicorn—she could not let go.

"What have I done?" Darka whispered. She stroked Clementine's hair. It was a pale pinkish orange, which would have been as pretty as a sunset if it hadn't been streaked with blood. "What have I done?" she asked again.

Dimly, she was aware of a dull *whump,* a roaring in the distance, growing louder and louder, and the black sheep's wet nose nudging her and bleating to *Run, run now!* But there was nothing in the world that could make her look away from the destruction she had wrought.

What had she done?

It made no difference whether it was her arrow or the unicorn's horn that had dealt the killing bow. The fact remained that she had used Clementine—used a *child*—exactly as she had been used. She was able to admit it now. She knew that Alaric had wooed her, lied to her, accepted her love, and cruelly broken her heart—all to make her into the perfect trap for his unicorn.

Some monsters just can't resist a young maiden's tears.

She'd wanted to kill him, and then the unicorn did it first.

He'd been right. And Darka had been obsessed with

avenging him—obsessed with their love that had never been truly real—turning her into more of a monster than he'd ever been. She had manipulated a child, used a girl's grief over her dying father to bait her own trap. And just as Alaric had failed, so had she—but the price of Darka's failure was even higher.

A child was dead. Clementine was dead. And Darka had killed her.

"I have to congratulate you," said a voice, finally cutting through the fog in Darka's mind. "You've done my job for me."

A woman in worn robes and adorned with heavy wooden charms hovered over the clearing, riding on a broomstick. Her gray-streaked hair blew wildly about her face in the wind. She had a strangely ageless look to her: her skin was pulled taut across her high cheekbones, but crow's-feet spread out from her eyes in deep furrows, and the skin around her neck hung in drooping rings, like the inside of some ancient tree. Her dark eyes were alight with amusement.

"A surviving heir really would have made things much more difficult," said the woman, and Darka recognized her voice as the one that had echoed over the mountains moments before. The Whittle Witch inclined her head with a smirk. "Thank you." She touched down on the ground, gracefully dismounting her broomstick.

"Don't you dare touch her," Darka growled, clutching Clementine's body closer.

The witch snorted. "Like I said, huntress. I don't think there's much I can do to her that hasn't already been done." The witch's eyes darted above and behind Darka. "But as a thank-you, I'll give you a word of advice—I'd get off this mountain if I were you."

Darka turned around and saw the reason for the witch's warning. Through the trees, she could just glimpse the avalanche tearing down the Fourth Sister—and the disturbance seemed to have spread to this mountain, as well. Darka felt the ground tremble beneath her, and smelled snow and dirt in the air.

Squinting up at the Fourth Sister, Darka thought she must be seeing things that weren't there. Perhaps her guilt had consumed her mind already. But as she looked at the churning mass of snow, she couldn't help but see the outlines of white figures leaping through the icy waves—white figures that looked suspiciously like horses.

Like unicorns.

The mountains, it seemed, were fighting back.

Darka Wesk-Starzec did not have the darkest heart in the forest for nothing. She gently laid down Clementine's body, smoothing the girl's hair away from her face, and placed a kiss on her forehead.

The roaring grew louder, and the ground shook so

much it became hard to stand. Darka locked eyes with the black sheep, quivering just out of sight in the trees. They had both done this. They would both have to do their part in making it right.

"Suit yourself," said the Whittle Witch with a shrug, preparing to mount her broomstick. But the black sheep rushed out of the woods, straight into the witch's knees, and knocked the broomstick out of her hand. Darka dove forward, grabbed the broomstick, and smashed it as hard as she could against the nearest cluster of rocks. It splintered down the middle with a great *crack*.

"No one is getting off this mountain," said Darka. She tossed the broken ends as far down the slope as she could.

"What have you done?" shrieked the Whittle Witch. She advanced on Darka—whether to curse the huntress or defend herself from the onslaught of snow, Darka did not know. She supposed it didn't really matter.

The Whittle Witch's eyes widened with panic as she, too, noticed the pounding hooves and blazing white horns of the creatures charging down the mountain.

"Indeed," said Darka, and the avalanche exploded around them.

* * *

A funny thing happened as Darka Wesk-Starzec was supposed to be getting crushed to death: nothing. As the snow crashed over and around her, it transformed into a harmless pale fog. She could still see the unicorns—hundreds of white horses galloping past, their forms indistinct, blending in and out of the fog and into one another. But the unicorns did not touch her, and the few that did come close merely brushed against her like lengths of silk. The mist roiled in great clouds but did no harm—at least not to Darka and the black sheep.

The Whittle Witch was not so lucky. Though it was difficult to see through the clouds of white, Darka did catch one last glimpse of the witch, standing stock-still, as if paralyzed by fear. Darka watched as three of the ephemeral unicorns charged the witch at once. As their horns ran through her, the witch exploded into a shower of dust, which was quickly swept up in the coming wave and ground into the earth under the hooves of the stampeding unicorns.

Darka could only imagine how dark one's heart had to be to *disintegrate* at the touch of a unicorn.

The avalanche swept past them as quickly as it had appeared, leaving Darka and the sheep blinking and shivering in the mist. The moisture on Darka's face tingled, mixing with the tears she hadn't realized she'd shed. Her scar nearly hummed with the magic in the air, making the muscles in her lips twitch. Darka sank to her knees, hugging her arms to her chest. She felt hollowed out, as if every bitter feeling, every ounce of rage she'd carried in her heart and her gut since Alaric's death had been scooped out of her, leaving nothing but empty air in its place.

A moan from a few feet away let Darka know that she was not the only one who had been transformed, in one way or another, from the avalanche's touch. The Dark Lord Elithor Morcerous lay draped over the rocks where the black sheep had placed him like a gangly black spider, limbs splayed every which way. But he was most definitely not a spider—and not a wooden puppet, either. He was, without a doubt, a man—a man unquestionably healed and whole. His greasy black hair fell into his face as he began to stir awake.

A small blossom of hope bloomed in Darka's chest, bright and painful in the new hollowness there. She crawled on shaky hands and knees over to Clementine.

"Please, please, please, please, please," Darka muttered, fluttering her hands on either side of the girl's still, pale face. It was not lost on her that she was now pleading with the very same creature she'd tried to kill.

Darka jumped back—at her touch, Clementine's hair began to fade from its sunset shades to a frosty white, nearly as white as it had been when Darka first shot her in the forest. Darka bit back a sob at the reminder. She stared in wonder as a dark gray-brown streak threaded itself through the white, all the way from Clementine's temple to the ends of her hair.

And then, quite impossibly, the girl's chest began to rise and fall, and Clementine Morcerous slowly opened her eyes.

CHAPTER 23

A TRULY ADMIRABLE CHICKEN

or

The Black Sheep Gets Shorn

They sat on top of the gate in the outermost wall separating the (formerly) silent farm from the outskirts of the village, because it was the only part currently sticking out of the snow. It was one of the few recognizable structures on the entirety of the Morcerous lands.

The Fourth Sister had been utterly transformed. The unicorn-enhanced avalanche had gone tearing down the mountain and utterly demolished Castle Brack. Clementine and her father didn't even dare to try and pick through the ruins—at least not yet—because great chunks of stone continued to fall down the mountainside under the weight of the snow.

"There goes the tearoom," commented Lord Elithor with a sigh.

Clementine, for one, was a lot sadder about the library. She imagined the black sheep was, as well.

It seemed at least part of the avalanche *had* been real—enough to destroy the castle and smother most of the farm in over fifteen feet of snow. It was packed hard enough to almost forget there was an entirely different landscape beneath it—and Clementine thought that had rather been the idea. The unicorn had saved them, but she had also made her displeasure with the Dark Lord's regime known.

Nightmares and chickens (both fire-breathing and mundane) milled about the gate near them, curiously nosing through the snow. The fire-breathing chickens seemed disappointed to see their powers curtailed in the presence of so much wet, and clucked nervously. Clementine wondered how they had escaped the avalanche, and felt a brief pang of regret for the Brack Butler, and even for the snakes, nasty as they were.

Clementine heard a sniff and a shuddering breath from the other side of Lord Elithor, and sighed. Darka had not stopped crying since Clementine had awoken in the clearing, and now sat as far away from Clementine and her father as she could get on their perch, which was not very far.

Lord Elithor kept looking at her with his lip curled, and had at one moment on their walk to the castle pointedly leaned over to Clementine and said, "Must we suffer the presence of this continuously mewling woman?" Clementine had said yes, they did, and that had been that.

Clementine thought he was being rather harsh with Darka, considering his own whining. "What are we going to do?" asked Lord Elithor—and not for the first time, either. He had said little else since the avalanche, and seemed curiously diminished since his transformation—like a fearsome black cat suddenly faced with the indignity of a bath, turned into a smaller and damper version of himself.

Although perhaps it was just that Clementine could no longer feel as afraid of him as she once had. Clementine squinted into the sunlight glinting off the snow. Just as the mountain had been swept clean, so, she felt, had she. Watching the castle crumble, the weight she'd carried for so long—her fear of her father, and his expectations, and their family legacy—crumbled off her shoulders, too.

"For starters," Clementine said, "we're all going to have some uncomfortable conversations—whether you want to or not." Her father needed to explain how he'd gotten involved with the Whittle Witch. Darka needed to explain why she'd been hunting the unicorn. And Clementine needed to explain why she wasn't at all sad that their home was now buried under fifteen feet of snow. If this was to be a fresh start, she thought, there would be no more Not Talking About Anything. Or at least, there would be a lot more Talking About Most Things.

Lord Elithor grunted—a surprisingly undignified sound, coming from him—but didn't have time to say more, because they were no longer alone. A crowd was walking up from the village, struggling to tramp through the top layer of softer snow.

"Oh, for the sake of all that is evil," groaned Lord Elithor as he and Clementine turned to watch the villagers approach.

It took a while, because of the snow, and both sides clearly had loads to say to the other, which made the wait a bit awkward. They could only stare at one another until they came within shouting distance.

At the head of the crowd were Mayor Turnacliff, Henrietta (who looked hale and hearty, as far as Clementine could see), and Sebastien, who rode above the rest on the back of Clementine's nightmare—though you could barely call it a nightmare anymore, after spending so much time around Sebastien. Soon it would be merely an intimidating horse. Amazingly, the Gricken was perched precariously on the nightmare's neck.

Clementine was the first to hop down from the gate.

"Sebastien!" she called, waving frantically. He waved back and sped ahead of the crowd.

Clementine called, "I'm very glad you're not dead!"

He laughed and stopped the horse right in front of her.

"It looks like I can say the same," he said, his eyes wide as he took in Clementine's bloodstained dress and silvery-white hair.

"Oh, I'm fine," said Clementine, sweeping a dark gray lock of hair behind her ear with a blush. "It wasn't as bad as it looks. However did you get away from the avalanche?"

"We didn't," said Sebastien with a shrug as he dismounted the nightmare. "When you didn't show, I got the boys to set the animals free—we didn't want that witch getting her hands on them, did we? And by the time we heard the rumbling, well, there wasn't much point in running. But it just kind of fizzled over us—the villagers, too, sounds like—more like fog than anything else. And I could've sworn I saw . . ." He cupped his hands around the back of his head, which Clementine now recognized as his primary posture for Not Looking Bothered when he really was a bit bothered.

But his troubled expression soon vanished, his face splitting into a grin. "Well, never mind. Whatever you did, it worked! You saved us, Clementine."

Clementine's newly healed heart fluttered in her chest. "You helped," she allowed.

"*And* I saved your chicken," Sebastien pointed out.

"Lord Elithor!" The village mayor—a tall, barrel-chested man with a beard so meticulously curled it would have made even the most fastidious Dark Lord Morcerous look plain—had finally reached them, huffing and puffing. "As mayor of this town, I simply *demand* an explanation for . . . for . . ." He had only just seemed to notice the utter destruction of Castle Brack. "Oh," he said. And then, "Well, for everything! All of it!"

Mayor Turnacliff proceeded to go on a long rant about all of the abuses Lord Elithor had subjected the townspeople to—because there's nothing like kicking a man when he's just been de-puppeted, and lost his home and livelihood.

As the mayor's chin wobbled against his collar, and his face turned redder and splotchier, Clementine noticed the black sheep trying to obscure himself from view by burrowing into a snow mound. This was curious, as she highly doubted that a love of snow was one of his magical transfigured-sheep traits, like the ability to climb stairs. The black sheep *hated* being cold and wet.

"And now, you and your *spawn* have gone and poisoned half the village!" finished the mayor, with an extra glare just for Clementine.

"Have we?" asked Lord Elithor, with an appreciative eyebrow raise. He lowered his voice to speak to Clementine. "My dear, they certainly don't *look* very poisoned. Perhaps it's slow-acting? Or they've left the terminally ill behind in the village?"

"But Lord Elithor and Clementine *didn't* poison the well," piped up a small voice—it was Little Ian, standing with the rest of the former Brack Knights in the crowd.

"Ian's right," said Sebastien to the mayor. "And you know that as well as we do. The poison was the work of a sorceress called the Whittle Witch. Clementine didn't poison us—she saved us. All the sick are well again, aren't they?" There were a few reluctant nods from the crowd. "You lot should be *thanking* her." Sebastien stood firmly next to Clementine, his arms folded.

Darka, who was still crying, let out a particularly loud sob, which everyone politely ignored.

Mayor Turnacliff sputtered. "*Thank* her? *Thank* her? The daughter of the man who has kidnapped our children, baked our pets into pies . . ."

Now that's just a lie, Clementine thought.

"Turned our potato crop into stones, taxed us for wearing specific shades of black . . ." The mayor sounded ready to get on a roll again, and Lord Elithor's temper was simmering hotter and hotter with every comment—Clementine could tell, because his lips were pressing into a thin, flat line and the edges of his robes had started to smoke. She was sure this would most definitely *not* turn out well, when Henrietta Turnacliff stepped forward.

"My father may not be willing to thank you," Henrietta half shouted over the mayor, whose diatribe petered out in his surprise. "But *I* will." She looked at Clementine with her perfect curls and rosy cheeks and her chin held high, and did not look the least bit afraid. "On behalf of all of us—thank you for saving us from the Whittle Witch's machinations."

"Which we only had to be saved *from*," muttered the mayor, "because of *their* machinations against each other." He jerked a thumb toward Lord Elithor. "Wizards. Honestly . . ."

But Clementine hardly noticed the mayor's comments. As she looked into Henrietta's eyes, she saw something familiar there. Her visit to the hedgewitches' camp came unbidden into her mind:

"Please, I need something that will help me locate my brother," Clementine heard Henrietta tell the witch. "He's been missing for . . ."

But the turquoise-haired witch put her hand on Henrietta's shoulder and turned her to face the other way, and their conversation faded from Clementine's ears.

A chorus of baahs *arose from the sheep pen, and Clementine looked over to see the black sheep pawing the ground and scampering behind the witches' sheep.*

Clementine blinked. It appeared she wasn't the only one in the Seven Sisters looking to distance herself from certain family ties. Though, really, getting oneself turned into a sheep was a bit extreme.

"It was my pleasure," said Clementine to Henrietta, raising her voice so the crowd could hear. "From this day forward, you have my word as the future Dark Lord of the Seven Sisters: you have nothing to fear from me. And—"

"SQUAWK!" At that moment, the Gricken hopped down from the nightmare's back, squawked once more, and laid a perfect yellow egg at Clementine's feet.

It was as yellow as Henrietta's perfect blond curls. Clementine smiled.

"You are a very admirable chicken," Clementine said, and placed a kiss upon the Gricken's head. She straightened up and held out the egg to the confused-looking villagers. "And as a show of my good faith," she called out to them, "I will right another wrong that has been done to you. Sir Sebastien, would you please wrangle the black sheep that is unsuccessfully hiding in that patch of snow?"

The black sheep tried to make a break for it, but between the snow and the efforts of Sebastien, the nightmare, and a very aggressive Gricken, he didn't get very far.

"I told you I'd keep my promise," Clementine said to him, and cracked the egg over his head.

The words of the short incantation that filled her mind tasted like warm milk and losing baby teeth, and dirt and sorrow and ice cream, and even (though she didn't know it yet) a first kiss, as they passed her lips. As the spell oozed over the black sheep's head, his wool dissolved into a swirling rainbow mist, and then, from the tips of his toes to the top of his head, it reformed—into the shape of a blond, curly-haired, gangly young teenager.

"David!" cried Henrietta.

"Dave!" cried Mayor Turnacliff, because he had given the boy that nickname, and by the Seven Sisters, he was going to make it stick.

They both rushed forward to embrace their formerly missing brother and son. Sebastien led the crowd in celebratory applause, which distracted everyone just long enough for Dave Turnacliff to borrow someone's cloak to put on.

Clementine admired her knight's growing sense of tact.

Dave looked happy enough to see his sister, but when confronted with his father listing all the things they had to catch up on, his voice went oddly high and sheepy again, and he cried, "But I still don't want to be mayor!"

"I wouldn't worry, if I were you," Clementine told him. She thought of Henrietta fearlessly trekking to the hedgewitches' camp on the villagers' behalf, even when she was ill herself, and of how she had so boldly spoken to Clementine. "I think there's someone else in the

Turnacliff family more suited to the job, anyway." She patted him on the shoulder.

As the villagers chatted among themselves, and Clementine thanked each of her knights, and Lord Elithor smoldered alone in the corner until he melted the snow around him into a little puddle, Clementine noticed one figure drifting away from the crowd: Darka Wesk-Starzec.

The hedgewitches had reappeared at the edge of the forest, Kat Marie Grice at their head. They kept their distance from the villagers—now that the crisis was over, it seemed that some old divisions were determined to resurface—but when Clementine nodded to Kat Marie, the old hedgewitch nodded back.

Darka stopped just short of the witches, shivering in the snow. A few of them regarded her with narrowed eyes and crossed arms—she'd been working with Clementine, after all, and now it was certain at least a few of them knew her true identity.

But after a moment, Kat Marie opened her arms, beckoned Darka forward, and closed the last few steps between them. Darka fell into the old woman's arms, her shoulders racked with fresh sobs.

Clementine wanted to call after Darka. She wanted to tell her to . . . what, come home? Their home was destroyed. Darka had used her. Darka had shot her (twice). And yet now, when Clementine even thought of "home," she thought of Darka Wesk-Starzec and their days in the gatehouse quarters. And she wondered if, just maybe, Darka felt that way, too.

But Darka did not look back as the hedgewitches led her away, back to *their* home in the woods, and if it stung Clementine, just a little bit, she tried not to show it. Her father was cured. Her people were healthy. Her friends were safe.

And at the end of the day, she had a far more pressing question to answer:

Now what?

CHAPTER 24

TO JUST BE OR NOT TO JUST BE

or

Beyond the Mountains

Eventually, the crowd drifted off, leaving Lord Elithor and Clementine alone with their avalanche. Clementine was starting to feel the snow's chill, now that the excitement of the day was beginning to wane. She hopped back up onto the gate and sat, hugging her knees to her chest. A few moments later, her father clambered up after her.

It was just past summer, after all. Some of the snow was starting to melt already. They watched a great glob of it come sliding out of what had once been the castle's front door.

Lord Elithor finally broke the silence. "I heard your . . . impassioned declaration, back there in the clearing."

Clementine froze. She hadn't thought her father had been conscious for most of the last few days.

"Oh, yes, I heard everything," he said bitterly, shaking his head. "How you don't want to terrorize anyone, or kill anyone, or hurt anyone at all! How you don't even want to *be* the Dark Lord! Honestly, Clementine. Is this how I raised you? To be so ungrateful for the sacrifices your ancestors have made—that *I've* made—and to go gallivanting around, growing flowers and befriending peasants and healing the sick, without a care in the world for the legacy that is ours to protect?"

"That's not fair, Father," said Clementine. "That's not fair at all. You *know* I worked so hard—harder than any Morcerous has had to in quite a while, I'd guess—to keep the farm going while you were ill. I did care, more than anything."

"'Did,' I see." Lord Elithor pursed his lips. "So what could possibly have changed, Clementine? What could possibly have persuaded you to abandon"—he gestured to the white wasteland around them—"all of this?" He waved his hands, as if to indicate that Clementine should ignore the present state of their surroundings. "Was it those new friends of yours? And how did that work out for you, hmm?" he asked, his voice smug. "Your brave new knights—who bravely ran away at the first sign of trouble—or your unicorn huntress, who shot you through the heart?" Elithor's voice trembled, ever so slightly.

Clementine sighed. It was true that in some ways, much of what Lord Elithor had warned her about the people outside their castle walls had come to pass. Clementine had been disappointed. She had been betrayed. She had seen the people she'd grown to care about at their worst—in their pettiest, darkest, angriest, and least courageous moments. This was all true.

But she'd also seen them at their best. They had comforted her, and laughed with her, and worked with her side by side. She had seen them risk their lives to help her and the people they loved. And it was better, somehow, to have made those friendships, even if she'd gotten hurt. She could hardly remember the girl she had been a few weeks ago, with only her flowers and the Lady in White for company. She could not imagine going back to such a life—a life without real friendships, friendships that she had *chosen* to make. Now, she knew, she could make more.

And yet she did not think she could explain this to her father—at least, not today. And so she simply settled for, "Darka didn't do that on purpose."

Lord Elithor scoffed.

"And I *cared* because I . . . I love you, Father," said Clementine. "Even though we don't agree on many, many things. And I loved our home. I wanted to save it, and save you. But not so I could become Dark Lord someday."

"Oh?" sniffed Lord Elithor. "And what *will* you do? Where will you go? Do you intend to become a Good Witch, and leave your poor father, the villain, to rot in his ruined castle?"

Clementine resisted the urge to roll her eyes. No one could say Dark Lords didn't have a flair for the dramatic.

"Father," she said. "I think it's time *you* were honest with me, as well. Because let's face it. You're just . . . not much of a villain."

"*Excuse* me?" said the Dark Lord, his shadow growing as tall as a giant behind him. Clementine sighed.

"Turning people purple, Father? Really?"

The Whittle Witch's potion had been much more potent than Lord Elithor's had ever been—and Clementine knew her father wasn't a complete fool. No, there was a reason the Dark Lord Elithor confined his Dastardly Deeds to unfortunate transfigurations and mild curses and magical-artifact-market manipulation: his heart had never been in it, either.

And as it turned out, Lord Elithor did not have much of a rebuttal for that. He merely huffed. They watched some snow slosh out of the castle's broken windows.

"I don't know if I'll become a Good Witch," Clementine said. She thought of the way the sunlight magic had hummed in her veins, out in the mountain caves. She wanted to explore more light magic, but she didn't feel ready to commit to *any* strictly defined role at the moment. "Right now, I . . . I just want to do what most people do. I just want to *be*."

Lord Elithor threw up his hands. "And while you are busy *being*, my dear daughter, what will I be doing to actually put food on the table, hmm? Have you thought about this in all of your grand plans?"

Clementine had no grand plans to speak of, but at that moment, as she watched the last rays of the setting sun glint across the mountains, she knew what they had to do.

"I think what we both need, Father, is a fresh start," she said. "It's time you showed me what's beyond the mountains."

* * *

The woods really were a rather pleasant place, Clementine thought, when they weren't trying to kill you. As she walked through the sunlit paths, she regretted that she hadn't been able to spend more time in them when she was growing up.

Of course, her previous relationship with the inhabitants had a great deal to do with that absence.

As it was, the wards around the hedgewitches' camp wobbled and thrummed as she approached, announcing her arrival to anyone nearby. But as they didn't make blood pour out of her eyes or barbecue her like a kebab, Clementine took it as a sign that she was welcome to enter.

She found Darka sitting outside Kat Marie's tent, sipping a cup of tea, with a light blanket around her shoulders and looking about as done-in as Clementine had felt the last time *she'd* been in the coven's camp. She turned even paler when she saw Clementine.

"Clementine," Darka said softly. It seemed to take every ounce of her courage to finally meet Clementine's eyes. "I'm so sorry. I never meant for you to get hurt."

And Darka told Clementine everything. How she was from far away, on the other side of the mountains, where magic was much less prevalent and magical artifacts and beasts were hunted and traded by an adventurous and viciously competitive few. How Darka had been only eighteen when a stranger had come to town—a young, handsome stranger who'd promised her magic and excitement and adventure, who'd taught her how to shoot and fight and track animals in the wild. How she'd fallen in love with that stranger—and how he'd used her as bait, just as Darka had used Clementine. How Darka had refused to accept that he had tricked her and became consumed by her grief, swearing revenge on all unicorns.

How Darka thought she could never feel love

again—until she met Clementine, and trained with the Brack Knights, and spent her days surrounded by the beauty of the Seven Sisters. And then, how hard it was to give up on her revenge, when it had been driving her forward for so long.

"But I was wrong," Darka finished, her eyes brimming with tears.

Clementine wondered how any of them had any tears left after the last few days.

"I was so, so wrong," Darka said. "And if you hadn't—if the unicorn hadn't saved you . . ."

"Darka," Clementine said, putting a hand on the young woman's shoulder. "I forgive you."

"But—"

"No 'buts.' I forgive you for lying about hunting the unicorn," she said. "I even forgive you for manipulating me. I only ask for one favor in return."

Darka nodded. "Anything."

"Keep that bow of yours well away when I'm around," said Clementine, nudging Darka with her shoulder.

Darka let out a weak chuckle. "I think I can do that," she said, wiping her eyes with the blanket.

After a few moments of silence, Clementine cleared her throat. "My father and I are leaving," she said quietly. "He's going to show me what's beyond the mountains. And I . . . I was wondering if you might want to come with us." She picked at a stray thread poking out of her boot in the silence that followed.

"Oh, Clementine," said Darka with a sigh, "I . . . I wish I could. But you have to understand. The other side of the mountains wouldn't be an adventure, or a new start—not for me. Right now, it's still . . . a reminder. Of painful memories I'd rather forget."

Clementine's shoulders slumped, and Darka tentatively put her arm around them. Clementine leaned into her embrace.

"I understand," Clementine said, though the lump in her throat begged to differ. But Darka was right. *This* life, here in the hedgewitches' camp, was Darka's fresh start. It wouldn't be fair to make her face her past—not if she wasn't ready.

"I'm going to stay here," said Darka, "and train with the witches. I've . . . got a lot to learn. And I think I could find a place here, at least for a little while."

Across the camp, Shirin stopped in her tracks as she caught sight of Darka. She tucked a lock of her red-feathered hair behind her ear and gave a decidedly shy and un-Shirin-like little wave before walking on.

Clementine smiled. She didn't think Darka would have much trouble finding a place to belong here at all.

* * *

" 'A traveling magician,' " Lord Elithor complained for the hundredth time. "Whoever heard of such a thing?" But he hoisted his pack on his shoulders all the same. It made his usually billowing cloak bunch up around the armpits. Clementine bit her lip to keep herself from giggling.

"Plenty of people, according to Darka," said Clementine.

They really were going to have to work on her father's people skills if they hoped to make any sort of living in these new lands. She slung her own satchel over her shoulder and mounted her broomstick. Her father had *not* been pleased about that development, but really, why get tired and muddy trekking through the mountain paths when she could comfortably fly the whole way? She'd conceded to merely hovering by his side for most of the trip. Compromise was another thing they would have to work on.

Clementine turned for one last look at the valley—at the ruins of the place that had been her home since she was born—only to see a man on horseback come galloping around the corner at full tilt.

"Clementine, wait!"

Clementine raised her hands, and the Gricken hopped to her side, ready to supply her with a defensive attack, but the rider was no man—it was Sebastien, who had somehow managed to unearth an old Brack Knight's suit of armor from the castle ruins—or he'd stolen it back when he'd been training with Darka, more likely. He rode the nightmare, which at this point really did just look like a mildly alarming black horse in need of a good feeding. The armor did not fit him well, and it made great clanking and scraping noises with every step of the horse. Lord Elithor's hair stood on end at the sound.

"Sebastien," said Clementine. "What are you doing here?"

Sebastien sat up tall on the nightmare. "Coming with you, of course! Word in the village is you're going beyond the mountains. Which you really should have told me, you know, since I'm your most trusted Brack Knight and everything. I felt pretty dumb, being as surprised as everyone else."

"I'm sorry," said Clementine. She hadn't meant to make him feel left out. But . . . "Wait, what? What do you mean, come with?"

"It is my sworn duty as a knight to protect you," insisted Sebastien, removing his helmet and bowing slightly in the saddle.

Clementine felt her cheeks go hot. She had *not* planned on any other additions to their traveling party. "Can't you . . . Don't the villagers need protecting?"

Sebastien looked a bit torn at that but perked up almost instantly. "Nah, the other knights can take care of that," he said. "Plus, something tells me there's going to be a lot less to protect them from, since, uh, your dad's not going to be around."

"'*Dad*,'" muttered Elithor weakly. "I've just been called a 'dad.'"

But Sebastien only had eyes for Clementine. "Where you go, I go, my lady."

"Oh, Seven Sisters," groaned Lord Elithor.

"Well . . . I . . ." said Clementine. It was suddenly taking quite a bit of effort to stay on her broomstick. "I suppose having someone who can swing an ax around might be handy . . ."

"Yes!" Sebastien pumped his fist in the air in victory. The plates of his armor shifted and got stuck as he made the motion, and he had to bang his arm against his side a few times to be able to bend his elbow again.

"Sebastien, do your parents even know about this?" asked Clementine, crossing her arms. "Or am I going to have to add 'kidnapping' to my list of Dastardly Deeds?"

"If we don't get a move on soon, I plan on adding 'murder' to mine," grumbled Lord Elithor. He tramped on ahead through the muddy snow.

Clementine turned to Sebastien, half expecting him to be riding away from her as fast as he could—and ready to hastily explain that her father didn't *really* mean he'd murder them—but Sebastien showed no signs of bolting.

Instead, he merely flicked the nightmare's reins and followed behind Lord Elithor, grinning at Clementine all the while.

With a little push off her toes, Clementine flew after them, and their journey beyond the mountains began.

* * *

Dear Council of Least Esteemed Evil Overlords,

It is my pleasure to inform you that since your last letter, I, Clementine Morcerous, have assumed the full duties of the Dark Lordship of the Seven Sisters Mountains. In the last few weeks, I have completed no fewer than three Dastardly Deeds:

1. A magically enhanced weather phenomenon
2. A stampede
3. An unfortunate transfiguration
4. A (possible) kidnapping

As you might imagine, completing all of these Dastardly Deeds in such a short amount of time has taken its toll on my "work-life balance," as some might say. As such, my father and I will be taking a well-deserved extended vacation.

Lest the Council be tempted—and what kind of Evil Overlords would you be if you weren't?—to try and replace me as Dark Lord of the Seven Sisters, or to capture Castle Brack while my father and I are away, I warn you that this would be most unwise.

The unicorn of the mountains is a friend of mine, and she does not take kindly to strangers staking claims on her domain.

Wishing you a positively dreadful day,

The Dark Lord Clementine

ACKNOWLEDGMENTS

It is extremely rare, at least in my experience, that an idea for an entire story stems from a single encounter. And yet somehow, several years ago, as I sat with my old high school friends on our former English teacher's floor, coaxing her baby daughter to mimic the sounds of her toy farm animals, inspiration struck—and it struck hard. I couldn't be more thankful to Alice, Chelsea, CarolAnn, and of course, the original owner of "the silent farm"—little Clementine. A special thanks to Alice and her lovely husband, Chris, for humoring me as I spun out *The Dark Lord Clementine* all the way from amusing anecdote to story idea to full-fledged novel. Clementine, you are extremely fortunate to have such rock-star parents. This gives you very little excuse to ever transform into a Dark Lord in the future.

Many thanks also to:

Brooke Mills, nicknamer of the original Dark Lord, baby Leah Fallyn.

My partner, David, for charging through the living room with a broom handle and pretending to be a unicorn for the sake of my art. You are, as some grandmotherly types might say, a keeper.

Harvard John and Alex Trivilino, for helping me whip the beginning of this book into good-enough shape to get it sold on proposal—and alerting me about all of my plot vacations.

My agent, Victoria Marini, for believing in this story when it was nothing but a zany idea and a prologue, even though she hates prologues.

Krestyna Lypen, Elise Howard, and the team at Algonquin Young Readers. This is our third date to the dance, and I'm very thankful you still want to take my stories out for a spin.

Jessica & Sean Abbott, Nancy & Raj Tandon, Carolyn & Lisa Rosinsky, Harvard John, Brooke Mills, and everyone else who contributed technical expertise for everything from unicorn-related injuries to castle defense. Any mistakes are due entirely to my bumbling incompetence. (Or maybe witches. I could just blame it on witches.)

David Crowther, the host of the *History of England* podcast, for letting me name a sheep after him. David, I can only hope I'm near the top of your list of strangest listener emails.